# Delhi

*Delhi OMG!* traces the journey of Dinesh, a middle-class offspring, as he meanders through life and the city of *Dilli* in his struggle for survival.

The journey takes him through the many signature spots in the city, exposing the underbelly and presenting a side which is rarely seen. The loss of innocence riddled with myriad splashes of contrasting, funny and often contradictory shades, this tale attempts to expose the superficiality that lies beneath, in a way that is shocking, real, hard-hitting and humorous.

Consumed as Delhiites are in their world of make-believe and maximising their returns, with all of them trying to be what they are not, Dinesh discovers that the city allows them to revel in the belief of having actually succeeded.

But have they, really?

Welcome to Delhi … as we think we know it!

**VINOD NAIR** was born in 1967 in New Delhi and graduated in B.Com from Delhi University. He went on to complete his study in International Management from the Chartered Management Institute (UK). Having worked for over two decades which have seen him travel to most places around the world, he is now heading the Human Resources function in a US multinational company based out of Gurgaon. *Delhi OMG!* is born out of his experiences, incidents, and events that helped him appreciate and depreciate the essence of survival in the city worth dying for. Vinod stays in DLF (Gurgaon) with his wife and seven-year-old daughter Carissa. This is his first book on the intriguing yet fascinating city of Delhi.

# Delhi OMG!

**VINOD NAIR**

Om Books International

Reprinted in 2013 by

**OM**

Om Books International

Corporate & Editorial Office
A-12, Sector 64, Noida 201 301
Uttar Pradesh, India
Phone: +91 120 477 4100
Email: editorial@ombooks.com
Website: www.ombooksinternational.com

Sales Office
4379/4B, Prakash House, Ansari Road
Darya Ganj, New Delhi 110 002, India
Phone: +91 11 2326 3363, 2326 5303
Fax: +91 11 2327 8091
Email: sales@ombooks.com
Website: www.ombooks.com

ISBN: 978-93-80070-68-1

10 9 8 7 6 5 4 3

Printed in India

*To my daughter Carissa*
*for making life worth living in a city to die for...*

*Last thing I remember, I was running for the door*
*I had to find the passage back to the place I was before*
*"Relax," said the nightman, "We are programmed to receive.*
*You can check out any time you like,*
*but you can never leave!"*

— Hotel California, Eagles

# Prologue

The body lay still, face down and motionless. Was it alive or was it dead? It was hard to tell from a distance. Everybody wished that it would still be alive but feared the worst. As they moved closer to the body, cautiously and suspiciously, it stirred a bit but almost instantaneously became still.

The body belonged to each one of us and was perhaps a part of each that had chosen to delink itself from the rest. It represented an existence that had been nurtured and raised, exploited and allowed to exploit, lived with and lived without, provided joy and infused sorrow, all in one sweeping motion. The life form had served its time but there remained some remnants of life for it to carry on. In all the time that it had survived, it had lived to the full. This was the life of Dinesh in the city.

Dinesh started his journey of life in this city. Born and raised here, it was a roller-coaster ride. From the humble beginnings in Netaji Nagar with the *babu*s to the uppercrest airs of Vasant Vihar and Jor Bagh, from the aspiring wannabes who stay in Vasant Enclave to the community that congregates at the Delhi Gymkhana Club and feels posh over subsidised drinks and peanuts, from having great friends to becoming dangerous liaisons, from free sex in college to a night of indulgence that you pay for under the garb of an escort service, Dinesh had seen it all but had yet not seen enough as the city relentlessly surprised him with its contradictions.

From the sleazy yet enticing world of Palika Bazaar to the kebabs at Khan Chacha, from the delightful *chaat* at Shah Jahan Road to the dining experience at the Aman's, from the chicken tikkas at Al Kauser by the roadside to the roadside *dhaba*s at the New Delhi Railway Station, the contrasting contradictions is what makes Delhi so endearing. Nothing is what it seems. There is always something more to see and assess.

Dinesh's journey takes him to Vandana and, infused with a certain sense of purpose and life, he questions his own self and bearings, his own approach to the city and its ways. Dinesh's journey to discover a sense of balance is fraught with ups and downs at every step. People take away enormously from this city and he wonders how the city extracts its share from them. The share of collateral. As time goes by and he works out his competition and common restraint among his clan, he figures that no one gains and no one is a winner. This city will give you everything you desire and deserve, but will also expect its share of return. Consumed with the shallow belief that a resident address or a fancy car is one's passport to acceptability, the hollowness of each individual eats into him. And the city allows that to happen, creating an illusion that it is being consumed.

The body stirred to life, it was alive. The city and Dinesh had agreed to coexist on their own terms, and each term was an illusion.

Welcome to the 'New' Delhi!

# Part I

Part I

# Government Babus and
# Public Schools

Those were 'the Wren & Martin days'. Dinesh would trudge along the path from the government Type IV accommodation provided to his father in Netaji Nagar under his exalted status as a government official, to his bus stop about 500 metres away. On the way, other students of the same school would join in. All of them would wend their way—some grudgingly, some permanently frowning and others cheerfully— to the bus stop which seemed farther than it was because of the heavy backpacks everyone, including Dinesh, had to bear like their crosses.

Bus no. F5 would arrive at 6:30 a.m. sharp and in seconds, the cross-bearers would be on their way to the Mount St Mary's School at Delhi Cantt. At times when the bus failed to arrive by 6:30 a.m., they wished it wouldn't turn up at all so they could avail of a 'bonus' holiday without having parents sizing them up suspiciously. If a conscientious parent didn't then pack them into a car to still drop them to school, their day would be constructive: endless rounds of cricket on the rectangular green patch dividing the two rows of houses in Netaji Nagar. A boundary shot smashing through a car's windscreen or dismantling a windowpane would automatically signal the end of the match. No questions asked. Each one would then waddle back home with whatever belonged to them: a bat, a badly bruised ball, two and a half wickets stuck together with fevicol and one batting pad.

Fabian D'Silva and Fritz D'Silva were two brothers who also joined Dinesh on his way to the bus stop. Fabian, the elder of the two, was a football enthusiast and a good soul. His brother, however, assumed a more cheerful and frivolous disposition. They used to stay in a single room in the Type II classified government quarters. It was easy to understand what Type II meant: two rooms—a living room and one bedroom with a bathroom, and a toilet referred to as a 'latrine' by the locals. Their father worked at the Taj Hotel at Mansingh Road which was the fancier one, but stayed as a tenant in one of the rooms of Type II accommodation allotted to government officials only. Ideally, government servants occupy government flats, but then there are so many innovative and creative ways of making money in this city.

Netaji Nagar is home to the city's babus, ranging from peons to Joint Directors who stay in Type II to Type V houses built during the Raj and allocated by the government depending on grade, seniority and sycophancy. A Type II typically stands for a two-room unit whereas a Type V denotes a five-room unit. Even today, these buildings do not stand out as eyesores. Not necessarily architectural marvels, these houses were as relevant and basic as it could get. They lacked the pomp and show of the swimming pool and park facing bungalows of West Delhi deceptively called 'Apni Kutiya' ('Our Humble Cottage') but served the purpose well. The smaller houses were assured of their sense of identity whereas the monstrous bungalows prided themselves in being referred to as humble cottages. Each one was trying to be what it was not. Single-storeyed houses, each one is like a typical town house, with a large rooftop common to both, the government servants a.k.a. tenants on the ground floor and the first floor—an ideal place to laze about on a sunny day in winter. Dinesh used to enjoy flying kites during July and especially on 15th August.

*"Bo kaate… Vo gayee guddi teri…" (There it goes, I have cut your kite.)*

These much coveted units (free of cost government residential units) are always an issue as they are limited in number. More people chasing fewer units. In true *Dilli* fashion, everybody wants a house immediately. The Joint Director has a Type V house that is large and spacious, with even a fireplace in the living room. The ground floor has a lawn as well.

Peons, drivers or assistants occupy the Type II houses. An added source of income for an underpaid government 'servant' is not a bad idea. So, it is not uncommon for these two-room units to be sublet while the allottee and his family live cheek-to-jowl in a single room. The single room also includes the use of a bathroom, toilet and the kitchen. It almost ends up like a call centre unit with predetermined shift timings for its use.

Dinesh often wondered how a family could give away the extra room to a stranger who also shares their toilet and bathroom, hopefully independently. And no matter what the rank of the official is, he or she would still be referred to as a 'government servant'. So much for the days of the Raj being over.

Fabian and Fritz used to stay with their parents in one of the rooms of a Type II government house. Each time Dinesh passed their house, he would knock on the lone window in their room and they would exchange a few words after which he would change and come out for a game of either football or cricket. Of course all this happened only after a serious day at school or on a weekend.

The three friends and almost neighbours used to sit together in the school bus and eagerly wait for the bus that would bring in the cute schoolgirls from Loreto Convent. Since Mount St Mary's school was an all-boys school, they used to look forward to these moments as manna from heaven. Only a narrow road separated Loreto Convent, an all-girls school from Mount St Mary's, and a church which, located right in the middle of these schools served as a moral compass for the more adventurous in both schools.

Since the bus services used to be common on some routes for both schools, they used to, as did their other schoolmates, look forward to the three girls who would share the bus on the way to their school and back.

"You think she will come today?" Dinesh would ask Fabian every day.

"Undoubtedly!" was always the reply.

They would then wait expecting that one walk past them in the bus and that one look of acknowledgement. Of course, most of the time neither happened but the players remained resilient.

Dinesh was hoping to make some exchange that would sow the seeds of lasting friendship. But that was not to be. And since Loreto Convent is only up to Grade 10 and Mount St Mary up to Grade 12, if he had pinned his hopes on someone for ten years without much success, he had to embark on yet another exercise in futility, the futility of hope, in the last two years at school.

Dinesh's school did experiment with the thought of allowing the girls from Loreto Convent to move to his school post Grade 10. It was a revolutionary idea because of what the school had to experience in its aftermath. All hell broke loose. What do you expect from students deprived of any interaction with the opposite sex for ten critical and formative years of their schooling lives? To then be thrown into the vortex of temptation and be suddenly exposed to this burst of the female form in all shapes and sizes. Pieces of innovative graffiti appeared magically on bathroom walls, linkages were established, curiosity stoked in the most bizarre fashion until it reached a point where the entire revolutionary idea was discontinued within just two years.

Dinesh never looked back on his schooldays with the slightest sense of nostalgia. He hated it as he was clearly not 'with it' or 'with the times'. He had all the trappings of a 'South Indian' or a 'Madraasi' and was often the butt of taunts, that is, when he was not squarely bullied. So he chose to remain with Tavish and Pratip, his select group of friends with whom he hung out all the time. A good student, he never believed in bunking classes or doing what most boys around him used to do. To him such things were not 'right' and it was not long before he was typecast as a 'boring' person to be with.

He was considered a *guru* in English. His interest in the language stemmed from his infatuation for his English teacher, as is a common occurrence during the schooldays of many. When she used to praise him for something he had done, he used to feel proud and wanted. This led him to memorise <u>Richard II</u> back-to-back and he wasted no time in rattling out quotes from the Shakespearean classics at the drop of a hat.

> *You urged me as a judge but wish you had urged me as a father.*
> *Things sweet to taste prove in digestion sour.*

It did impress her, but matters did not move any further. Before long it was obvious that whatever he was imagining in his bouts of infatuation would never have translated into reality, notwithstanding *Richard II* or Shakespeare. Even they could not have helped.

One of the events that everyone used to look forward to was the 'Social' which allowed the Class 10 batch of the school to interact with the Class 10 batch of an all-girls school, which in this case was the St Thomas school. With an aborted attempt to impress the girls at Loreto Convent coupled with a nascent attempt to charm his English teacher, Dinesh was just hell-bent to make a moment of this, a moment to remember. Dinesh was paired with a girl called Sunaina. An awkward teenager interacting one-on-one with a girl was not just designed for success especially since such an interaction had not happened for the past sixteen years of his school life.

He approached her with a degree of trepidation. She looked up amidst the deafening din of *Frankie goes to Hollywood* as he yelled, "Would you like to take a walk?"

There were at least a million other ways to start a conversation. He could and should have asked for so many things under the sun. Even a mention of the weather would have sounded more interesting. She leaned forward and asked him to repeat what he said.

With his elbows touching her breasts, he shouted out over the music, "Would you like to take a walk with me?" To his surprise, she agreed.

Neither of them spoke as they made their way through the long corridors of the school and whatever they did speak about was surely pathetic in content. As they approached a poorly lit section of the corridor, she looked at Dinesh with a masked sense of fear and anxiety and said, "Maybe we should head back now." He agreed. Both of them felt so awkward and uncomfortable. The confines of the auditorium replete with over a hundred students and the loud music to give them company seemed infinitely more comforting.

The story told to his friends the next day was different. Short of making love, they had done everything else and 'she made the first move'. All his friends had similar versions of their conquests the night before and if all of it had to be believed, there was a mass orgy on that evening, in the splendoured auditorium of the Mount St Mary's school.

Tavish and Pratip were the two inseparables in Dinesh's life at school. Tied together by an invisible bond, the three struck an association from Class 8 and thereon. They were referred to as the 'Three Musketeers' in school both by their classmates and by the teachers. They were from diverse backgrounds both culturally and socially and for that reason, perhaps, found solace in each other's company. Tavish and Pratip used to stay in Janak Puri in the SFS (Self-Financing Scheme) houses whereas Dinesh was well ensconced in his government quarters. Those were the days when quarters used to mean either a tenement or one-fourth of something. The quarter, as it is termed now, will invariably lead you to a liquor vend.

The three would spend time at each other's house on weekends and watch movies at Chanakya. It was followed by a 'Big Boy' burger at Nirula's with the ₹25 that they got as pocket money for a month. Those were the days of carefree abandon, of bunking classes and hiring a VCR for the night. There were so many of these small shops which used to rent out VCRs and VCPs for ₹100 or so for the night with three VHS movies free. Dinesh and his two buddies would stay up all night with endless bouts of coffee to watch these movies, carefully selected through consensus. The selection would invariably include one pornographic movie to satiate the carnal desires of boys who had been subjected to the inhuman experience of spending twelve years in an all-boys school. Those were the days they used to masturbate at all odd hours of the day over a scantily clad woman that showed up on a magazine poster, when even Debonair was nothing short of Playboy. Those were also the days when they used to watch cops and robbers on TV and end in school, hiding behind the trees, behind boulders and throwing stones as a substitute for bullets.

This last aggression stimulation role-play was one foolish act that was to stay with Dinesh for the rest of his life. On one afternoon during the lunch break, the cops were taking on the thieves in school. Dinesh was the leader of the gang. They were hiding behind a row of pillars next to the school auditorium and pelting stones at the cops who were another set of boys from his own class. The excitement was growing with each passing minute and each pelted stone. As Dinesh emerged from the pillar to pelt another stone at the 'cop', he felt dizzy with pain and fell to the ground. A stone pelted by the opposing team struck him between his eye and nose. Everything around him went into a daze and his last memory was of being escorted with a broken nose and a swollen eye to the first-aid room in his school with blood splattered all over his navy-blue school shirt. He was administered first-aid and sent home. His father was informed and Dinesh was taken immediately to the Rajendra Prasad Institute of Ophthalmic Sciences at the All India Institute of Medical Sciences. The doctors tested his eye and gave injections to reduce the pressure. This went on for some days and with regular doses of Pilocar eye drops, his left eye made a full recovery, or so he thought.

Life went on as normal but after many years, a cataract started forming in his left eye. He was taken to the All India Institute of Medical Sciences once again where the doctor stated that nothing further could be done except that he would have to wait for the cataract to mature.

"Mature?" Dinesh wondered thinking that he may have walked into a fertility clinic by mistake.

"Yes, mature," Dr Bhatia continued. "Till such time the cataract covers the entire black section of your eye." Dinesh nodded, pretending to understand.

Since it did not bother Dinesh too much and left with no choice, he let it go and decided to wait for the cataract to mature. This incident, however, helped him mature faster than the cataract. Post that day he vowed never to play with sticks and stones any more, any time, anywhere.

How these stories seemed so distant yet so close at the same time. The present has its seeds in the past and try as he might, he just couldn't shake it off. The transition from the days of the socials to now were in diametric contrast to each other but one thing remained the same. Dinesh was miserable then and he was miserable now!

School made its way to college and the stage came when Dinesh had to decide what he wanted to do with his life. The 'Three Musketeers', who had been together for so many years, detached themselves in the pursuit of their individual dreams. Tavish's pursuit drove him to the USA and Pratip went to Mumbai, leaving Dinesh alone in Delhi. Just doing a job was not enough to fill Dinesh's day that was full of loneliness. So he walked his way into a job with Rolta India Ltd. and did two other things in parallel. First, he enrolled himself with Alliance Francaise de Delhi to learn the French language coupled with the covert intent of developing a relationship with the fairer sex. The guys were boring with their predictable line of conversation which almost always centred on cricket and sex. He was lonely and felt more comfortable opening up to a woman than a guy, in

11

ways more than one. Second, he enrolled himself for evening classes for an MBA course in Human Resources. With a job for income, French language for relationship-building and a potential MBA in the horizon which would further augment his income and his relationship building potential, things looked set and he seemed to have worked it all out.

The French language classes in the early morning hours at South Extension, followed by his job in Greater Kailash II and his MBA classes at Pushp Vihar began to take their toll on him. Since he was reliant on public transport, the stinking crowd within the bus ensured that he turned up for work every day looking dishevelled in wrinkled clothes. His black Oxford shoes would have turned a different shade of grey by the thousand stampings they had received during the bus travel. This was not a style statement either.

Soon enough, he invested in a bike with the down payment paid through months of hard savings and through the generous loan given to him at a personal level by his boss at Rolta India Ltd. Atul Dev Tayal was a wonderful person to work for and somewhere Dinesh thought that he liked him too. It was a personal loan and Dinesh remained grateful to him for that gesture. Somehow, he did not want to ask his parents for any money. He wanted to achieve it all by himself, without having to rely on the safety net of home and food that his parents provided. The fact that he was staying with his parents helped him save more and the bike came sooner than he expected.

The Kawasaki Bajaj was his pride. With a down payment of ₹8,000 and an equated monthly instalment of ₹400, it fitted in well with his salary of ₹1,500 a month. He knew that he had to keep going. He was prepared to catch up with time and eventually overtake it.

Dinesh repaid the loan before time and Atul smiled. Somewhere deep down Dinesh thought that Atul was well aware that this would happen. Leaving Rolta India for another opportunity was painful but Dinesh was a man in a hurry and Atul recognised that.

His parents returned to Kerala after his father's retirement from the government services, and Dinesh was left by his lonesome self in the Type IV government flat. He had the rent-free house to himself for three months, the time allowed to keep till it would be reallocated.

His friends made the most of his vacant house while he was away at work. It felt strange to Dinesh that while he was staying with his parents he craved to live alone by himself and resented their interfering ways. Now that he had been afforded the opportunity to be alone by himself, the freedom had ceased to matter and seemed rather irksome.

During this period of independence, he was also introduced to a girl through some common friends from college and from his work-life. He was working with an American firm specialising in desktop publishing, a job that he had moved to post his days at Rolta India. He soon started spending time with her. She was a mischievous and a full-of-life Bengali girl. She was dusky, average-heighted and used to work in an advertising agency. Dinesh found a friend in her. A friend he could chat for hours with. She was intelligent and he could see that a certain intimacy was developing. His last recollection of a conversation with the opposite sex was with Sunaina during his schooldays that had barely lasted minutes and ended with the cacophony of the school band. This was more flesh-and-blood.

Since this was his first brush with the opposite sex in an intimate context, it developed into something sexual soon

13

without much effort from both quarters. Both were equally virile and raring to go. They made love many times and the Type IV accommodation in Netaji Nagar suited the purpose. Each time they made love, Dinesh could see the increasing sense of expectancy in her eyes. That some day Dinesh would say that he loves her and the relationship would transcend mere physicality. However hard Dinesh tried, he could not bring himself to doing it; provide an end point to the relationship that would have made her happy. It was not long before she realised the futility of the relationship and drifted away and apart. He did not stop her, he had no right to.

By now, he had spent a significant amount of time in Netaji Nagar, the home of the babus. Right down from hopping on to his school bus when he was a kid to the stage of living alone, studying and working his rear off to making love to a woman he was not in love with. The transitory phases were too bizarre in contrast to settle under one roof. The myriad images were far too many to accommodate in the Type IV government quarters and something had to be done.

Dinesh moved out in two months.

# East of Lord Shiva's Abode

After much back and forth, not alluding to more sessions of passion, Dinesh managed to secure a *barsaati* for himself in East of Kailash. This was his first step into the world of pomposity. East of Kailash, one of the more affluent areas, though not completely posh, in South Delhi offered a stark contrast to the otherwise mediocre existence that he used to lead in Netaji Nagar. Things were simpler, less layered and cheaper in Netaji Nagar but there was a different zing to this place. Everything seemed larger. The plot size, the size of the houses, the driveways, the cars and even the people. The people too seemed larger in size, girth and larger in the size of their egos.

A *barsaati* is a unique term used to classify a dwelling atop a house. It is a terrace top that typically has a single or a couple of rooms with a wide open area punctuated with water tanks of all shapes and sizes. This could easily be mistaken as a testing ground for the real survivors or tenants who dare to take on the forces of nature. In the winter, these are the coldest areas in the house since these are mainly open from all sides and in the summer, the open areas get so baked under the vicious summer sun that it's impossible to set foot in any of them. During the monsoon, the rains keep you in and if it rains hard, you have the arduous task of keeping the water from flowing into the room. This was indeed a shock to Dinesh as he was accustomed to living in a Type IV house with a large lawn all to himself. Reality had to set in but Dinesh wasn't sure if the changeover had to be so drastic for him to understand.

The *barsaati* had one room with an attached bathroom and a kitchen. He was single and since he used to spend a great amount of time at work, all he needed was a place where he could retire for the night.

This *barsaati*, however, proved lucky for him as he managed to get a job with one of the reputed software majors as an HR Analyst. The money was good and although the job meant long hours, he did not mind at all. After all he had no one waiting for him back home.

Loneliness was his biggest enemy here. Not left with many friends, a feeling of emptiness used to engulf him each night. Having led a sheltered, cocooned life with his parents for over twenty years, with a safety net that he was oblivious to at that point in time, the real world was beginning to hit him. Things that he used to take for granted were uncertain now: like a good meal, medical attention, even sewing a missing button was a chore. When he had them in abundance they did not matter, and when they were lost in oblivion he was left craving for them.

The doorbell rang and Dinesh opened it without a thought. The cook walked in and within a few minutes, had conjured up a dish which looked like rice and potatoes. Dinesh was not fussy any more as this was harsh reality that he had to accept. He remembered the time he wasted so much of good food since at times he did not like the colour and now, even at its brownish best, a potato dish without salt with an excess of *garam masala* was most palatable. Life had changed in a flash and taught him the hardest lessons rather soon.

His friends would occasionally hang out with him but frankly Dinesh knew deep inside that he was not an interesting person to hang out with. There was always a sense of disconnect that he used to have with them. He used to think often that they were forcing their friendship on him because it helped them get access to a *barsaati* which could possibly be used for a one-night stand. Maybe because they also thought that this illusion of friendship would allow them to use his mobike for whatever little need they had. Neither of these happened.

Delhi held little in store for him despite all his expectations from this great city. It robbed him of many things that he yearned for. True, honest relationships, the company of selfless people or even the prospect of coming home to a well cooked meal. Even the memories of his mother as she used to hug him every time he used to come home after a hard day's work seemed like distant dreams. Although he got his freedom without what seemed like constant interference, yet it had come with a heavy price tag. The price was loneliness.

Although Delhi gave him freedom, it also gave him the unwanted company of solitude without even affording him the opportunity to choose an alternative. Dinesh had, by now, begun to expect little from the city and it gave him very little in return as well. With a perfect match of expectations and returns, the balance worked out. The assets matched the liabilities and the other way around.

*Amisha...*

Into this world of lonely existence entered a woman with whom Dinesh got closer than he should have. Loneliness or the sheer need to have a sounding board, the friendship that started off as a chance meeting at work one day developed a life of its own as time went by and destroyed everything in its wake: his friends, his senses and his own feeling of comfort. What was innocuous at one point in time developed complications with muted expectations that grew so much in volume that it assumed deafening proportions.

She was a classic (read tall, slim and *gori*) Punjabi girl. Her streak of independence and her sense of confidence appealed to Dinesh because it bridged a major delta in his personality.

His *barsaati* was a convenient rendezvous for both of them. She used to stay in Kidwai Nagar and regular meetings at work and over lunch ensured the birth of yet another friendship. He had little to do and her company provided him with a perfect escape from his ever growing sense of loneliness. He liked the idea of being her friend, although he did not think that he fulfilled any of her expectations of being a friend.

Working in the same office was convenient and complicated at the same time. Convenient because that meant they could meet every day and complicated because it set tongues wagging. He was a gawking executive nurturing dreams of becoming a corporate honcho and it wasn't long before his long hours on the phone with her at the other end led to the obvious discomfort to many in the office and added to the delight of the schemers and plotters who wanted to see him fail desperately.

It was his first major job and he was young enough to allow it to go to his head. He could see that the old-timers who had been well ensconced in their role resented him as an invader on their well manicured turf. He did not know what he did not know and soon fell prey to the devious designs of his jealous colleagues who were provided with the much sought after fodder by none other than himself. Clearly he had no one else to blame.

Amisha was blissfully unaware of the goings-on and the fact that she got to spend time with him was enough and all that mattered to her. Over a period of time, they got closer. After his experience with the Bengali woman at Netaji Nagar, there was an inbuilt mechanism of self-control that he had developed. His family had searched the countryside and finally zeroed down on a woman from Mumbai. Dinesh had remained non-committal and chose to adopt silence as his only weapon to stall the pace of his parent's enthusiasm. To the credit of his conscience, he did mention this to Amisha and she acknowledged the fact. His parents had provided him with a conscience metre which he could tap into any time. He felt cornered into a relationship that he wilfully moved into but dreaded going the distance. Amisha did not mind and hoped against hope that the distance between him and his wife-to-be in Mumbai coupled with the distance between him and his parents in Kerala would fizzle out any spark of hope. Amisha hoped that with the passage of time and with the advantage of proximity, she would eventually win Dinesh over. Whatever the reasoning was, he could never bring himself to commit to even a basic degree of physicality of even as much as kissing her. He just liked her company and they would talk for hours, sometimes without any meaning. Also they would go for long drives around Hanuman mandir on Baba Kharak Singh Marg where she would take time to apply henna with his name hidden within the intricate patterns on her palm.

"Can you find your name in here?" she asked offering her palm before him as they sat on the cement slabs outside the Hanuman mandir. Dinesh held her hand and looked hard, "Ok, here is the 'D', there is an 'E' here... I give up!" She smiled like a schoolgirl and got up.

"Let's go!" she said. "Did you know that tomorrow is *Karva Chauth?*"

19

"So, what about it?" Dinesh replied as he pulled the helmet over his head.

"Will we be meeting tomorrow?" she asked without offering a response to his question.

The following day was a Sunday and Dinesh had other plans. "No, *yaar*! I have to finish some household stuff and have some relatives over for lunch. Wish we could meet but.."

"That's ok!" she said not allowing him to complete. "I just wanted to know."

As his bike reached her house, she got down and looked at him through the visor. "Take off your helmet," she said.

Dinesh obliged. She looked at him, smiled, turned and made her way into her house.

Distances make the heart grow fonder but that did not happen in this case. The distance grew wider and the paths forked out, both with the company that he worked at and with Amisha. It wasn't long before he decided to resign from the services of the company. It was the right thing to do, for her sake and for his. He had many other job offers awaiting him and with an MBA under his belt, the decision was so much easier to make.

He could see that she was falling in love with him and although he enjoyed the attention and care, he just could not bring himself to accepting it. God knew what he was looking for and God only knew whether he would ever have the sense to recognise it, even if it ever came before him stark naked. Dinesh was gnawed on the insides with the guilt feeling of having let her down, of having led her up the garden path knowingly or unknowingly, of having betrayed her never expressed love for him.

That was never the intent or design but was a result of inadvertent actions, of the state that he was in and of the phase that he was going through. He could sense that it affected her more than it possibly affected him but the pain was equally bitter and stinging. There was collateral damage too. With her, he parted ways with some of his friends who were closer to her and shared her sentiment that he was wrong in doing what he did.

"Maybe so," thought Dinesh.

"We want you to write an advertising slogan for a company that produces coal. It need not be too long… hmm… just a catch line. It should address the fact that coal is not all about pollution, mafia, cartels, politics, and corruption. It should convey a positive feel about the coal trade. You have five minutes to think of something," said the creative head of the advertising agency Dinesh was interviewing with.

The move to advertising happened by chance. The agency's location was close to his house and the money was good. He was too lazy to pursue too many jobs and although there were offers waiting for him, he decided to interview and try his luck here.

"Ok, sure," he replied.

He was back after a quick visit to the coffee vending machine. "Are you ready?" the interviewer asked.

"Yes," Dinesh replied and extended the sheet he had in his hand on which he had written down the slogan for a company engaged in the coal business.

"This is sheer brilliance!" the creative head exclaimed, looking visibly delighted.

"Please wait! I'll be back." He disappeared and from within the glass walls Dinesh could see that he was showing the piece of paper to a woman seated in another cubicle. She smiled and nodded her head in acknowledgement of to what he was saying.

He returned some minutes later with a smile on his face, "I like what you have done. When can you join?"

"As simple as that," thought Dinesh. "As soon as you would like."

He returned with an offer letter in his hand. In excitement, he left behind the sheet of paper on which he had written the slogan.

### Not Everything About Coal Is Black

The advertising firm had its fair share of glamour—beautiful women, willing women, smart execs, parties and so forth… It provided the perfect filler to the significant portions of his lonesomeness. The city was finally willing to offer him the tools to combat his state of mind.

The days there were great. He had a neat workstation which he shared with another egoist copywriter named Hitesh, who lived life king-size and always seemed to have the self-impression of being a cross between Brad Pitt and George Clooney—actually not even a cross, that he was Brad Pitt. He was some years younger to Dinesh but shared the same interests he had… women, alcohol and video games. He was married to a woman named Maya and they had a settled life of their own. It seemed too good to be true as Dinesh knew well enough.

One thing about Delhi is that nothing is what it seems and there is no sense of settlement.

As part of his work, he had to meet people from the advertising world and from the print media: editors, reporters, journos, etc. During one such meeting he met a strikingly attractive journalist called Nisha and the chain of events that unfolded following that meeting was to change the course and direction of his life in a different way.

"I am going to G.B. Road tomorrow. Want to come along?" she asked while they were having a cup of coffee at Barista.

The invite alone shocked Dinesh. "Why do you want to go to G.B. Road? Doesn't your job pay you well enough?" he joked.

Nisha wasn't amused, "I am doing a story on sex workers, especially the child sex workers. I have been trying to get this meeting organised for the longest time and finally have been asked to come and meet one madam in a *kotha*. I do not want to go alone so it would be great if you could come with me."

"Sure," replied Dinesh. Her attractive company could have taken him anywhere but he did not tell her that. "I can only offer you my physical presence. I hardly know anything about the place except that…"

"It's a whorehouse," said Nisha completing what he wanted to say but could not have brought himself to say in front of her. His middle-class values did not permit him to mouth expletives in front of a woman, nor smoke in front of elders and so forth. With time, this city would ensure that he detached himself from much of the value systems that he held so close to his heart for so long.

"Yes, it's only your physical presence that I am looking for," she said sending his thoughts through to another dimension. She smiled almost as if she read his mind and Dinesh felt almost naked.

"C'mon, let's go, you naughty bastard! I will fill you in on the history and details on the way so you are educated about this place and do not think of this place as merely a whore joint and nothing else."

Along with being so beautiful she was also intelligent and knew much about the place where they were headed. Dinesh concluded in his mind that it was important for her to research on a subject to ensure the continuity of her current profession.

"The history of G.B. Road," started Nisha, "can be dated back to the Mughal era. It is said that there were total five red-light areas or *kotha*s in Delhi then. The nightlife of Mughal patrons enabled the flourishing of the livelihoods of sex workers in these areas. Then came the British Raj, when a British collector consolidated all the five *kotha*s to one area and christened it on his own name, Garstin Bastion Road or simply G.B. Road. The name was officially changed to Swami Shradhanand Marg in 1965."

She then held out an Eicher Delhi map and pointed out to the link roads and where they were headed. On the map G.B. Road did seem well connected. The New Delhi Railway Station was a ten-minute walk. Banks like Dena and HDFC were down the lane and usually utilised by customers who ran out of money in the pursuit of their carnal desires within the *kotha*s. There are off-season discounts here. Pretty much a corporate hospitality industry. The only thing missing was the frequent flier miles or perhaps those too existed within its dark folds.

"What's this story you are doing?" Dinesh asked trying to seem interested in her assignment but distracted by the perfume that she had worn.

"Oh, it's about child prostitution. You know, it's more rampant and wide-spread than we think or know."

"Are you saying that all of G.B. Road is replete with *kotha*s indulging in prostitution of minors? That's illegal, isn't it?" he said obviously sounding naive.

Nisha smiled, "All of G.B. Road isn't that. It's more widespread than it seems but its epicentre is G.B. Road. On the eastern fringe of the capital, New Seemapuri is a typical location where child prostitution flourishes. It has around 4,750 *jhuggi*es. The approximate population of the area is 28,000. In this slum colony, *jhuggi* dwellers are migrants from Uttar Pradesh, Madhya Pradesh, Bihar, West Bengal and neighbouring countries like Bangladesh. Women *dalaal*s, mostly original inhabitants of Bangladesh later settled in India after their marriage, go scouting for minor girls deeper into the impoverished villages of the bordering districts of Bangladesh such as Satkhira, Jessore, Jhinadah, Meherpur, Rajshahi, Nawabgang and Joypurhat."

"And..?" Dinesh asked suddenly beginning to get interested in the story.

"A women *dalaal* scouts for minor girls with certain characteristics. Acting a *ghatak* (female matchmaker) as a cover up, she negotiates with the parents of a minor girl and settles a sham marriage with a male *dalaal*. Then she informs the male *dalaal* in India. Pretending to be a legitimate bridegroom, he ties a nuptial knot with the minor girl. The so-called bridegroom is able to induce the poor parents to give their minor daughter for this fake marriage by paying them ₹15,000 to ₹20,000."

"Ouch!" he exclaimed both at the fact that was being revealed to him and at his sheer ignorance. Nisha was rattling off these facts without too much of a sense of emotion and Dinesh realised, soon enough, that it was the nature of her profession. For her these were all statistics and a story that she needed to bring to a close.

"We have reached!" she exclaimed with a sense of relief. "Driver, please stop next to that bearded man standing near the Maruti." The car obediently braked to a stop alongside the man as his face broke into a smile.

"*Aayee*, madam!" exclaimed the bearded man as he waved the car to a stop opposite what seemed to be a row of unending hardware shops. Nisha recognised him and got out of the car to shake hands with him. "Hello, Prakash. How are you?" she said. Then introduced Dinesh as a friend. It was now Dinesh's turn to break into a smile.

"We cannot go into the *kotha*s because we need to take permission and that is rarely given," said Prakash. "The pimps do not want too much of publicity especially since it ruins their *dhanda*, but I have managed to have one speak to us. It cost a bit but he can tell you how this whole racket of prostitution of minors is conducted and managed. Do not ask him his name."

Nisha nodded, and so did Dinesh not knowing why.

They met a skinny man, who was incidentally also bearded, inside a hardware shop. He looked at both of them and then looked back at Prakash. Prakash nodded and the anonymous bearded man seemed more comforted.

"*Namaste,*" Nisha said.

"*Salaam valeikum,*" he replied. "Prakash *sahib* told me about what you were looking for. Where do you want me to start from?" He continued to walk into the store with Nisha, Dinesh and the bearded escort following him till they entered a smaller room ensconced within a large hardware shop.

Nisha scrambled for her writing pad and pen and lost no time in rattling off her brief covering everything from the organisational structure at G.B. Road, the clientele, the popular category of prostitutes to the bigger story of child prostitutes.

"There exists a three-tier system at G.B. Road," began the bearded informant occasionally looking around to ensure that he was not being seen by his brethren and risk possible expulsion or even murder. "In the first tier come the *malkeen*s. Initially when they came into this area as minor girls, the *malkeen*s themselves originally operated as sex workers. Some of them, who had demonstrated sufficient enterprise, could save enough money and finally became *malkeen*s. About one in 200 becomes a brothel owner," he paused for a sip of water. "In the second rung are the madams. A madam is one who cannot afford a *kotha* but has saved some money. She hires a place and keeps a few minor girls who earn for her along with her. Eventually she does not prostitute herself but becomes a manager."

"Which tier do the prostitutes generally belong to?" interrupted Nisha.

"I am coming to that," the bearded man said, appearing a trifle miffed at being stopped in his flow. Nisha returned to her notes. "The sex workers comprise the third tier at G.B. Road. Here, as many as 60 per cent of the sex workers are minor girls. The rest are adults. Eventually, when they can no longer earn their living as prostitutes, some of them take up petty jobs as housemaids in the nearby residential colonies like Dilshad Garden and Anand Vihar, while others work as babysitters or cooks for the working prostitutes. And when they cannot keep even these jobs due to physical inability or old age, most are simply forced to move to the pavements where they are reduced to rag picking and begging. Some of these women, however, manage to keep in contact with their families in their native places. Later in life many of them end up earning their livelihoods by acting as procurers of minor girls whom they encourage and trap into prostitution."

"A woman doing this to another woman?" Dinesh thought. "How could they?" The need to survive at any cost drives people to do anything.

"*Dalaal*s are a significant link in the prostitution business. They help both in transporting minor girls and selling them to the *kotha malkeen*s and call girls. However, sometimes they also act as pimps when they supply minor girls to politicians, officials, and businessmen."

"How does the prostitution among minors work so seamlessly?" asked Nisha. "The law can prove if the girl is a minor or not."

"It is not that easy," responded our bearded friend. "The police extort money from traffickers, prostitutes and *kotha malkeen*s and is even involved in trafficking. After a minor girl is brought into a brothel, the *kotha malkeen* calls on the local sub-inspector or assistant sub-inspector and constable and requests them to make a new entry for a newly bought minor girl for which she pays ₹10,000 to the police. Some minor girls have to first satisfy the sexual urges of these sub-inspectors, *havaldar*s and constables."

Dinesh winced.

"*Sab ki* setting *hoti hai*. The farce follows set stages: a trumped-up case is registered against these minor girls falsely alleging that they were trying to solicit clients in a public place. The minor girls are then arrested and kept in the lock-up while the police prepare a challan wherein their age is entered as 21. This entry is apparently sufficient to transform overnight these minor girls into adults for all subsequent court proceedings. After this, these minor girls are produced before a magistrate and released on bail. The police thus violate all norms as well as exploit all legal rules and regulations with impunity to help perpetuate child prostitution within the *kotha*s. The *kotha malkeen* then gets an agreement signed by the newly bought girl on backdated court stamp paper stating her willingness to work for the *malkeen* as a domestic servant. Simultaneously, by a false promissory note, the girl states she has taken a loan of ₹40,000 from the *malkeen*. By this the minor girl enters into servitude under the *malkeen*. A frequent modus operandi for returning a child to prostitution is that someone from the *kotha* turns up masquerading as the minor girl's mother, aunt or grandma. They convince the magistrate of the genuineness of their relationship with the girl with the police's assistance. And the remand home is then forced to release the girl into the hands of those pretending to be her relatives."

"It is the land of no return…" Dinesh exclaimed.

There was a pause as the bearded man continued, "The minor girls are supplied along the Delhi-Uttar Pradesh border to the truck drivers. Minor girls from this slum colony have been sold in Arab countries also. The preference is for the North-East area, especially the Nepali girls. Nepalese minor girls in G.B. Road *kotha*s are predominantly from Kathmandu, Birgang, Biratnagar and Nepalgunj. The demand for Nepalese girls by the *kotha malkeen*s is high since clients prefer fair-skinned girls. These girls are sold in different brothels in India for up to Nepali ₹60,000."

There was a knock on the door and the bearded man peeped through the gaps in the wooden boards before opening it. A young girl, not any older than seven to eight years stood in front of them. *"Abba, maaji bula rahin hai,"* she said in her childlike voice.

"I am just coming," he replied and turned towards his audience as she continued to wait for him.

*"Ab is bachchi ko hi dekh lo.* She is seven years old and has already landed up here," he said exhibiting an emotion of sadness perhaps for the first time during the entire session. "She was sold to one of the madams here at *kothi* no. 65 by a *ghatak* and every time I look at her I begin to hate myself and my work."

"Is she..." Nisha paused.

"Not yet, but is being readied for the profession," said our bearded informant almost anticipating the question. "She is under the tutelage of one of the madams. Once she is ready, she will either be sold or put up for the night. The madam will take good care of her as she will get a lot of money from the first night."

Repulsed by the content of the conversation, Dinesh looked at Prakash and gripped Nisha's arm signalling that it was time to go. The little girl continued to look at them. She had striking blue eyes and jet-black hair. She seemed tall for her age and smiled a very innocent smile as Dinesh stared at her. Dressed in a floral pink frock, Dinesh noticed that she was wearing slippers of different sizes and different colours. At a fashion show, these may end up as a fashion statement but out here it merely represented the gradation of poverty and helplessness. The location influences the meaning of the exhibition.

Prakash looked at Nisha and asked, "Are you done? Shall we leave?" His voice betrayed traces of impatience mixed with fear.

"Yes," replied Nisha as she put her diary back into the satchel that she was carrying. She seemed surprisingly detached but Dinesh was uncomfortable. "Is there no way she's rescued or given a better life?" he asked.

The bearded man looked at him in horror, "Shhhhh! Don't ever dare say that here." For the first time he looked scared. "She is guarded like a hawk and you can imagine why. You will be killed for even saying so. Everybody is mixed up in this racket and there is no way out. I think you had better leave before they start sending out others to look for me and find you here as well." He looked worried and eager to leave.

Nisha and Dinesh quickly got up but Dinesh could not take his eyes away from the girl standing at the door. He reached out into his front pocket and pulled out a chocolate bar and handed it over to her. She reached out and grabbed it with a gleeful look in her eyes. Prakash, Nisha and the bearded escort were leaving by the door and Dinesh started to follow them.

"What's your name?" Dinesh asked her as he followed the rest of the gang.

"Va-n-d-na!" she replied before she scampered off towards *kothi* no. 65. She was gone in a flash but her bright blue eyes and the jet-black hair were to remain etched in Dinesh's mind for years to come.

Nisha did not talk about that evening after that day even as she filed her report to great appreciation. For her this was just another story, another statistic. Dinesh wondered if the city had contributed to that. It numbs you of your sensitivities and robs you of your emotions with each passing day and the stark realities, such as the one experienced, only add to the pace of the desensitising process.

As time went on, Dinesh got more involved with his work and Nisha. They started seeing each other more regularly and although he resented her insensitive approach towards life, yet he found those same qualities essential to survive in the city.

Hitesh sensed the goings-on and smiled each time Dinesh sat beside him near his workstation. Hitesh had just secured an out-of-turn promotion and Dinesh wondered how he had managed to pull that through. "Was there something that he was missing or was he just too naive to notice," he wondered.

"Are you screwing her?" he asked.

"What do you mean by screwing?" Dinesh queried in return. "Screwing who?"

"Are you making out with Nisha or not?" Hitesh continued. "It's ok if you are because she can take you places. She is well-connected."

"What do you mean well-connected?"

"*Arre, chutiya hai kya.* She knows people who know people," Hitesh replied in an excited tone. "That is the way to move up the ladder, man. Hard work and all that is alright but you have to be selfish to some extent. Use people to move up in life. That's how it works in this city. Nisha is one of the great windows you have. She can get you introduced to right people."

"I have never thought of Nisha that way," Dinesh replied. "She is a good friend and I get along well with her."

"That's alright, Dinesh but you are not fooling me. Tell me, haven't you filed a positive report about her competency and resourcefulness and put in your recommendation for the PR firm she co-owns?"

"Yes, so what?" Dinesh replied beginning to lose his patience. "The firm thoroughly deserves it. They have done a good job."

"Well, you also know that based on your recommendation, she has bagged a key account through us as a recommended outsourced PR firm."

"I fail to see the connection."

"My friend," Hitesh continued with a smirk on his face. "If you have not been using her, then it is obviously the other way around. You have signed on the recommendation document and her purpose is achieved. She was with you for a purpose ... now she does not need you. So stop pursuing her." So saying he turned back to face his computer.

Dinesh recoiled in shock and did not say a word. It was all beginning to add up. The way she would get up to answer a mobile call in the middle of a dinner, get ready and leave with a quick kiss showed the detachment that she had to the moment Dinesh had begun to treasure. She had also started to avoid his calls shortly after she had bagged this big PR deal through him. It all comes around in this city. What had happened to Amisha is what was happening to him in turn. The city ensured that it delivers justice. Curiously, Dinesh did not find too much of a distinction between the women at G.B. Road and women like Nisha. For the former as well as the latter category, it's a question of survival. The survival stories for one category adorn the walls of the many *kotha*s in G.B. Road and are therefore much despised and frowned on but still much in demand. The other category finds mention at Page 3 events and is therefore looked upon as socially acceptable. It's how perspective distortion can determine the acceptability or the rejection of what happens across all stratas. The location of the event was the ultimate barometer of acceptability just as an address in South Delhi.

It was well past 8 p.m. and Dinesh was winding up and leaving the office. It had been a crazy day. He was still reeling under the impact of a lost love. He tried calling up Nisha but got an automated message in Tamil. He figured that she was travelling and somewhere in South India. She did not bother to call back either and he could see the eventual death of this still-nascent relationship.

Hitesh was not around and Dinesh assumed that he had left for the day. As he got up to leave, his gaze accidentally fell on the IP phone allocated to Hitesh. Hitesh had forgotten to log off. It had Nisha's name as one of the missed callers.

It stunned Dinesh. Not sure of what was happening, he walked up to Hitesh's workstation and scrolled the missed callers' list. It had Nisha's name on at least four occasions. Why would Nisha want to call up Hitesh so fervently while avoiding his calls? The answers eluded him.

His mind weary, he decided that he has had enough for the day. It was nearing 8:30 p.m. now and it was time to head home. The day's events had left him numb. As he was about to turn back, a thought passed his mind. He approached Hitesh's workstation again and selected the 'received calls' icon on the phone. The listing showed Nisha's name on six occasions. A series of thoughts were beginning to come together to form a picture that had until now remained blurred. "Son of a bitch…," muttered Dinesh under his breath.

"*Sahab*, don't you want to go home?"

Dinesh turned around with a start. It was the security guard tasked with the daily responsibility of switching off the lights after all had left. He was smiling his toothless smile. Dinesh hoped that he had not been seen fiddling with Hitesh's phone but at this point even that did not matter. "Five minutes."

"Ok, *sahab*," the guard responded.

He switched off the lights around his cubicle and walked through the long stretch of many workstations punctuated by cabins meant for senior personnel of the company.

The picture was getting clearer but Dinesh needed to be sure. As he neared the end of the corridor, it occured to him that he should get some sandwiches from the cafeteria as it was too late to go home and cook. His cook would have come and left by now. He took the steps up and passed the third floor on to the fourth. The cafeteria was at the far end and he could see just one attendant and his undernourished assistant packing their goods to retire for the night under the solitary band of light that lit up the snacks area. There was no one in the office though Dinesh was not sure if there was anyone else on the executive floor above.

He waved to the attendant as he made his way through the corridor and the attendant waved back in despair almost simultaneously switching off his mobile. His assistant quickly stifled his lecherous laugh at what was being shown to him on the mobile.

"Anything left to eat?" asked Dinesh.

"Just some vegetarian sandwiches, sir. The chicken is all sold out!" said the attendant with boredom and disinterest writ large on his face.

"Ok, just give me two sandwiches and a juice pack."

Dinesh collected the sandwiches and the pack and headed back towards the exit. He turned back and could see the attendant and his assistant exiting from the service lift while still engrossed in some movie clip that was being shown on one of their mobiles.

As he approached the main lift area, he thought he heard a familiar voice behind the closed doors of one of the huddle rooms. He stopped and listened and with whatever he could hear, his heart started beating faster.

"Nisha, it does not matter if he is calling you. The work is done and there is nothing that he can do to change that." It was Hitesh's voice.

There was a pause as the voice at the other end said something. Dinesh looked around. There was no one but he feared the security guard who would appear any minute.

"He has his signatures on the approval note just like I told you. Your PR firm is now officially empanelled. You do not need him any more. I spoke with him today and he considers you a good friend. The deal is signed, I have got my promotion, you have got your contract and all that remains is the 10 per cent you owe me for setting all this up."

Dinesh closed his eyes and looked skywards. The picture seemed less pixilated now.

"Of course, I love you baby. I had to have him as the fall guy so that the deal does not trace back to me. It is all done now and you just relax. When are you back?"

There was another pause. Dinesh turned around and thought he heard some noises. He quickly retraced his steps and walked through the exit gates wishing the guard goodnight on his way out. He was in a daze and he felt miserable to be used to such an extent. He drank the juice and handed over the sandwiches to an urchin on his way to the parking lot. He had suddenly lost his appetite.

As he mounted his bike, the only sane thing he had mounted in many months, the pixilated images assumed crystal clarity and his face involuntarily broke into a smile. Hitesh was using Nisha to further his ends and get the 10 per cent that would make him richer by at least a couple of lacs. Nisha, in turn, was using him to further her career which would make her richer by at least a couple of million rupees. And Hitesh was using Dinesh as a fall guy just in case anything were to go wrong with the deal and it came up for audit. It would never be traced back to Hitesh as it had Dinesh's signature on the recommendation note.

Dinesh knew that he had been had, and a pity that it was not even enjoyable.

He started his bike and was, soon enough, on his way home. If he had left an hour later, he would have been able to see Hitesh leave with his boss in her car towards her house.

The usage relay maintained its continuum.

# A Melting Refugee Pot

After some years had gone by, Dinesh moved to Malviya Nagar, the abode of the refugees from Pakistan who had migrated here in the early 50s post the partition of India. This was a different world and the uniqueness that each transition infused into his life was amazing. From the middle class opulence of the Type IV flats in Netaji Nagar to the well heeled, *Krack* lotioned gentry at East of Kailash that stared up at him in his *barsaati* tenement, he had managed to make a seamless transition to a refugee colony. Houses jostling with each other for space and each house an architectural nightmare. 100 square yard plots boasting of three and even four bedroom houses while each room followed the other. The first room being the living room followed by the bedroom followed by another bedroom and eventually culminating with the toilet. All in one perfect sequence and seeming almost like train bogies. Dinesh had his reasons to move into a place like this. Firstly, it was far larger than the *barsaati* that had been his home for over a year. Secondly, and more importantly, it was relatively inexpensive. Thirdly, the South Delhi tag that is so important from a social acceptability standpoint. It is so essential to be a part of South Delhi even if it is by extension. Like most relationships, where a poorer cousin attaches himself to a wealthier one, where success is relative since it brings in so many relatives, many aspirational localities prefer to be known by their richer neighbour. Masjid Moth becomes Greater Kailash IV, Vasant Enclave and Vasant Kunj are referred to as places 'next to' Vasant Vihar, Nathupur is DLF and so forth. The localities will be far removed from the original but when you cannot afford an original Hussain, you have to make do with prints signed by the artist. So even if the limited edition series says 25/5,000, it is still a limited edition. Dinesh often wondered on how exclusive a limited edition of 5,000 copies could possibly be. The original was definitely more acceptable than substitutes for the same. A reprint, however, could well be a part of a calendar nailed to a distempered wall in one of the train bogies in Malviya Nagar.

*"Kaam kahaan karte ho?"* the Bihari landlord asked.

"Software company *hai!*"

"Indian?" he asked quickly.

*"Nahin*, American," Dinesh replied.

His eyes lit up. It was amazing to notice that the colonial instincts had not diminished with time in spite of all these years of independence. Dinesh knew that he had one thing that would work to his great advantage, His roots! His ultimate trump card in dealing with professional landlords.

*"Rehne wale kahaan ke ho?"* he continued.

"Kerala," Dinesh replied.

His eyes resembled a million bright torches in a dark sky. He was elated but clearly did not want to give away any trace of emotion lest he loses his advantage. A Keralite boy or rather a Malayalam boy, to most Punjabis, working in a good firm is what most 'professional' landlords would aspire to get either for their daughters or for their houses. In both cases, it ensures that it will be well looked after. By extension, Indians have their comfort communities as well.

Like God, racism in India is ominipresent. Most of the TO-LET ads that come in the classified section of your favourite newspaper scream racism. A South Indian is preferred for a house to be given away on rent. The stereotype of a South Indian being a submissive, conservative, scared to default Indian who will always pay the rent on time, never get into any argument, will vacate the house whenever required (even if it is the middle of the night) and will pay for anything that is asked for. Thankfully the LTTE chief (Prabhakaran) and Veerappan are not classified as originating from the South! These obvious traces of racism spill beyond TO-LET classifieds to find mention even in the matrimonial sections of all newspapers.

The matrimonial section screams the need for a *gori* bride in almost every advert. The bridegroom could be of any colour as long as the potential bride is "*gori* and slim-trim". Dinesh recalled the *gori* fixation that Hitesh had and also remembered being told that he would have preferred a *gori* wife but got stuck with Maya.

"If given a choice I would have preferred a *gori* wife," He had said.

"Is that because you are from Bihar?" Dinesh queried, trying hard not to sound sarcastic.

"I am destined for much more," said Hitesh evading his direct question. Dinesh did not probe any further.

The black-white divide is visible across other mediums as well. Most of the visual advertisements before or during a regular television programme will feature a servant or a help typically of dark complexion almost implying that the colour dark is to be equated with the servant class. None of the specifications apply to the male sex. Once you have battled your way through the monochromatic filtering, there is the sex bias that you need to overcome. The male can be of any colour and can engage in any trade but the female has to be *gori* and of course 'slim-trim'. Brazenly, there are more advertisements promoting fairness creams than there are advertisements which prohibit the killing of a girl child—so common in states like Haryana, Punjab and Bihar—leading to the acute problem of a skewed sex ratio. What is even more shameful is that national capital territory of New Delhi has one of the lowest sex ratios among the Indian states.

The saga of discrimination and covert racism also continues in shops and restaurants alike. An expat or a *gora* is sure to get an entry to any club or bar which otherwise prohibits stags or single men. In a shop, a white man or woman is instantly referred to as a 'Sir' or a 'Madam' and somebody who is 'black' or 'brown' is ignored or is the object of snide, racist remarks. This is rampant in Delhi where everything that is fair *(gori)* and has a western accent is acceptable and our heads bow with respect and reverence or plain lust. Most of the shop owners in Vasant Vihar B-block market are pretty much expats themselves. Dinesh had noticed an accent too in a couple of them. They even offered to help the white customer carry the bags to the diplomat's CD on the number plate car parked outside whereas the 'poor' non-white Indian waited to be served. All that is required to overcome this is an evolved streak of exhibitionism and arrogance.

Relationships or the mere mention of them play a big role in conversational upmanship. *"Tu jaanta nahin hain ki mera baap kaun hai."* Well, obviously not. How the hell was one expected to know, anyway? However, this is a classic operating procedure with most people trying to get their way through the arrogance of their purported, mostly self-created, imaginary societal positions within their kith and kin.

"Kerala *mein kahan?*" the prospective landlord enquired.

"The whole of India is your fiefdom and you would invariably establish a connecting link if I were to tell you where in Kerala I was from," thought Dinesh. But controlled himself and replied, "Palghat."

"Oh, such a beautiful place! I had gone there on a holiday many years ago and would love to go there again." Dinesh could see that he was beginning to enjoy the conversation as he gazed around the room.

The house was typically what you would expect from a Malviya Nagar colony. A straight row nestled within a 60 square yard plot. The more well-off lot can afford to buy two 100 square yard plots next to each other and therefore have a 200 square yard plot. There is only a front and a back view since the house is sandwiched from both sides by other buildings, each one more unauthorised than the other. Extensions are made and floors added in rampant disregard of the bylaws. At some stage the houses get within such close proximity that the neighbours remain neighbours no more. They become a part of your household.

Adjoining Malviya Nagar is Khirki Extension which sets new standards in non-compliance. Dinesh would have found a more economical rental alternative there but he had chosen Malviya Nagar instead. With practically no sewage in place, the rains play havoc as the so-called roads get flooded and mix up with garbage and litter all round providing the illusion of a swimming pool to many of the street urchins who dance and frolic with gay abandon amid these polluted waters. The cow dung dropped by many cows and bulls that roam around mix with these waters and the urchins play on blissfully unaware, ignorant or just plain reconciled to the fact that they can never get the real thing. The dream of clean water is but an impossible dream.

The house where Dinesh sat was a true representation of the classic 'old-refugee-money-finds-new-modern-environment' scenario. He sat on a settee (an improvised sofa without the backrest) and opposite him were two one-seater sofas. At right angle to the sofa was a bed or a *diwan* (which is a bed but called a *diwan*) where his potential landlord sat. One side of the wall flushed with a cheap bookshelf-cum-cabinet. So here he sat on a *settee* that is not a sofa but works as one and stared at a *diwan* that is not a bed but acts as one. Each item has to have multiple uses or it is simply not worth it. All items need to offer you the value for money and this leads to creativity that is hard to beat. You can have a sofa-cum-bed (a sofa that doubles up as a bed), and a box-bed (which is a bed but has a large cavity—almost like a horizontal almirah that is used to store anything from an alphabet book you used to read thirty years ago to a cloth bag that you think will come in useful thirty years from now). Anything that can stretch the maximum out of the minimum.

The cabinet facing Dinesh was replete with godforsaken items. Items that you would necessarily confine to a garbage bin but these were at display in full public view. Plastic flowers adorning over a million deities, flickering bulbs outlining the area where the statues and pictures of the gods and goddesses lay, old VHS tapes of *Ramayana* and *Mahabharata* and the James Bond collection, etc. From the corner of his eye, Dinesh thought, he sensed the curtain move a wee bit and someone trying to squeeze a view from within the many folds but he ignored it.

"There is a problem," it was the landlord again. "I have already committed to give the second floor to another person."

"Then why did he subject me to all this interrogation," Dinesh thought.

"I will need to check with him and if he shows his disinterest then I can consider you," the landlord turned to spit out the *paan* he was chewing into the ashtray that had assumed a colour different from its original shade.

Dinesh got up, thanked him and left the room. He was a trifle annoyed at having wasted in having his antecedents verified with the full knowledge that another person had already been spoken and committed to. It was well past 7 p.m. and as he was about to straddle his Kawasaki Bajaj which would take him back to his royal *barsaati* that he thought he heard somebody call out his name. He looked up and it was the landlord gesturing him to return.

"Possible change of heart?" he thought, not knowing what to expect.

Dinesh steadied his bike and went up the stairs for the second time. This time the room was populated with more people than he thought were present in the first place. Two girls, who looked like they were in their early teens, and an elderly woman, who would be the landlord's wife.

"I have spoken to the other guy and have told him that I was keen to give the house on rent to you," the landlord said. "You seem to be a nice boy. You can come in by 1 March and the rent will be ₹3,000 a month plus electricity and other charges as actual."

Dinesh was elated, although not sure of a man who opens and closes deals so swiftly. "Can we look at ₹2,500 as the rent since I have just started working?"

He looked at his wife and his daughters. Dinesh thought he saw one of the daughters give a slight shake to indicate a yes.

"Ok, ₹2,750 a month with a revision in 6 months."

"These Bihari landlords drive a hard bargain, but it seemed alright given the circumstances," Dinesh thought.

"You will also have to give a deposit of three months rental as security which will be refunded to you at the time of vacation. This will be an interest free deposit," he said with a wry smile.

Dinesh thought of negotiating it down to two months deposit but decided against it. He did not want him to change his mind again. He agreed and left the place, relieved that he had finally managed to seal a long vexing issue.

As he straddled his bike for the second time that evening, he instinctively looked up to get an idea of the façade. He couldn't see much in the dark. As he revved up his bike, shifted to the first gear and moved, he thought he saw the elder daughter wave to him from the corner of his eye.

"Maybe I am imagining things," thought Dinesh. After all, it had been a very long night.

In rolled the 'tempo traveller' with his 'bare necessities'. A box-bed (of course), a portable black and white TV, a table, a chair, a worn out carpet and a small cupboard. These were his possessions either bequeathed to him or handed over to him by someone or the other. None of these were actually purchased by Dinesh as his priorities lay elsewhere, but this was all set to rise dramatically in ways he did not think possible.

*"Abe bhonsadike... peeche le,"* shouted one of the labourers as he gesticulated animatedly to the tempo driver who was reversing the tempo towards the gate of the house. The driver did his job, got down and walked his way to a place under a tree. He took out a *beedi* from his front shirt pocket, lit it and was, soon enough, puffing at it in total bliss. A classic example of specialisation and division of labour. A driver will never help the labourers in moving furniture or hauling it up with

the aid of a *rassa* or rope as it is simply not his job. It is not in his job description. He is paid to drive and he is a driver. It does not behove him to be doing *mazdoori*. He will watch as the three or four labourers grunt and groan while hauling up the bed and cupboard, ten times their weight, atop two floors but will not flinch a muscle.

The labourers, mostly from Bihar, don't specialise in this, but do it anyway since it is the easiest option of work to start with as a migratory tribe. As two labourers tied the rope across the four sides of the bed box, two others, already up on the second floor tried to haul it up. Dinesh rushed up to the second floor to ensure that he would give a helping hand to the two who were struggling in their efforts to haul up the weighty bed box. As he reached up, he heard a loud bang below and looked down. The door of the box bed had opened and the contents had sprayed on to the road. To economise on the cost of an additional tempo, Dinesh had dumped most of the things into the bed box so that all his belongings collectively occupied lesser volume. Yes Sir, maximum for minimum...

Unfortunately, this had rendered the bed box unstable in its flight upwards and the door had swung open spilling all the contents out on to the road below.

The labourers were grinning from ear to ear as the 'Playboy' centrefolds spilt out and lay bare on the road. These were carefully preserved over the years but now open for all to see. *"Ye bade logon ki aish hai, behenchod,"* muttered one as he stared at Pamela Anderson and her outstanding assets. For him, it could well have been Ramkali, the local village belle whom he had long lusted for. *"Itne bade hai,"* he remarked with an air of being deprived of the best the world had to offer.

Dinesh shouted out from above, partly embarrassed and partly concerned at the attention all this had generated. He did not want his landlord to think of him as Hugh Hefner. The labourers sensed his annoyance and quickly collated the spoils and packed it into the bed box once again. They were still grinning from ear to ear.

An hour passed and all his belongings were in place now, badly bruised with scratches and dents from all the rubs on the railings in their painful journey up two floors.

Dinesh paid the labourers and as expected, they asked for an additional ₹50. *"Itna upar charhaya hai aur mehnat bhi dugni lagi hai sahib."* Dinesh, half tempted to tell them that even he did not earn so much as they did, paid them nevertheless. He was just too tired to argue and haggle. He even gave them one of the Playboy centrefolds so they could satiate themselves on their way back without much effort.

*"Bas itna hi samaan hai,"* queried the landlord who was watching all this from his first floor. Thankfully, he had missed the Playboy centrefold episode.

"Not really! I have six more trucks waiting to enter the area but your fucking gully is just too small," Dinesh wished he said so, but refrained.

Any activity of such nature involves mass attention and sometimes Dinesh wondered as to how people in Delhi and India in general can complain of lack of attention. Somebody slips on the road and a huge crowd gathers around like flies drawn to a carcass. No one will offer a helping hand. Just watching and satiating their voyeuristic instincts. Any accident involving vehicles on the road and a million bystanders crowd around the injured victim. A dozen motorists who stop in the middle of the road to peer and enquire, inevitably asking:

*"Kya hua?"*

"Nothing, *yaar*. There has been an accident."

"Nobody dead?"

"*Nahin yaar*, just managed to escape. Lucky *hai saala.*"

An exchange of smiles and the motorist is on his way. Somebody being beaten up on the road or a woman being teased is all a voyeur's delight. An army of people would be watching, commenting, sympathising, offering their own perspective on the incident but not offering a helping hand. This city and its people do that all the time, expecting the most by giving the least, the minimum.

"Yes, uncle. That's all I have!" Dinesh replied. He returned indoors to arrange the belongings in their right place.

Barely had he finished moving the bed, placing it right, adjusting the cupboard and fine-tuning the TV set that the doorbell rang. "Who can that be?" Dinesh needed to be left alone. He walked up to the door and after a few fumbles with the new door latch turned it open.

It was the landlord's daughter. The elder one who he thought he had seen waving to him a bit earlier. She was holding a metal tray in her hand with a cup of tea and some biscuits.

"*Mamma ne bheja hai,*" she said most shyly.

"Thank you," he said as he accepted it and smiled. She smiled back and ran back downstairs leaving him more puzzled than ever before.

As he set about living his life in the new surroundings, many aspects of his life came to the fore. How life is but a compromise and how most opportunities can be exploited in every which way possible. Right down from one room in a two-room government flat let out on rent in Netaji Nagar, a woman who enters a sexual relationship to allow for love to follow, a protected seven-year-old awaiting her entry into prostitution at the right price, a colleague who makes you a fall guy in a deal right up to a landlord projecting an impression of doing you a favour in offering a discounted rent when all that he is demanding is the market rate. There are no shades of grey here, just the truth as one sees it and that is all that matters.

Dinesh took his time to survey the area and came across an interesting fact around a section of the M-block market. There were rows of small shops, more like kiosks that were initially allotted to the migrants from Kashmir. It worked well for some time and rapidly went on to resemble a miniature version of Ghaffar Market. However, very soon, the potential of what could be achieved sunk in with the allotees and sure enough, in true characteristic style of all things Delhi, the Kashmiri migrants sold off their kiosks for a sum of ₹5 lacs to the local retailers in the area and vamoosed with the spoils. Nothing was quite heard of them after that and Dinesh presumed that they had, in all probability, set up shop elsewhere, with the sole purpose of maximising their gains with whatever was available in the minimum.

Malviya Nagar was the place that Dinesh brought his wife to, for the first time after marriage. Quite a transition in his mind as his wife was born and raised in Mumbai. She had graduated in Architecture from the Sir J.J. College of Architecture. He had been given to understand that only a marginal percentage of students pass from this very prestigious school and the number of applications received every year totals over thousands for less than 100 seats. This was pretty much the case with a majority of the more reputed schools around in Delhi as well. Most of the schools make a parent wish that that they did not have a kid in the first place. You begin to wish that you had more money that you were born to parents who were extremely well connected and knew people who know people. When he married her, Dinesh belonged to none of these essential categories. She was so much a *Mumbaikar*, Dinesh often had trouble aligning his Delhi conditioned mindset with hers.

One day Dinesh was walking down to the market and instinctively got drawn to the *golgappa-wallah* to taste an inventive concoction, *golgappa*. It's called by many names: *puchka* in Kolkata, *pani puri* in Mumbai but it is the one thing that Delhiites swear by. The *golgappa* supplements with other inventive creations such as *papdi chaat, ragra patis* etc, usually under one stall but always in demand any time of the year. It is a builder of the identity of Delhi just as *vada paav* or *pav bhaji* would be to a *Mumbaikar*. Dinesh had sampled these creations from all parts of the country but nothing came close to the Delhi *golgappa*.

As the man dipped his fingers into the spicy water and served him his first *golgappa*, his wife winced and looked away, "How can you eat this stuff?" she asked under her breath.

Dinesh ignored her as there was no way he could convince someone that a hollow bubble made of either wheat flour or *suji* stuffed with pieces of potato and *chana* and then dipped into a spicy water concoction with bare fingers could taste good, be hygienic and not give you a delhi-belly the next day.

"We have," Dinesh thought as he opened his mouth wide to house a large stuffed bubble, "moved on from the days when the water used to prepare the spicy concoction was chilled with commercial ice that was transported in an open hand drawn rickshaw which was sometimes covered with a tattered, filthy piece of Hessian. This would have been moved through the ground to its final resting place replete with all the muck and dirt. We have moved on from the times that the *golgappa* was pierced with a dirty fingernail that may have been in unwanted orifice only minutes earlier. We now use only perfect ice that is extremely hygienic, the water is Bisleri and not something that came out of an illegal bore well or from a regular water supply pipe that had been broken open to fill tankers (often rusted). These would then be sold for a hefty price to commercial and residential establishments alike. The fingers are no longer in contact with the tasty bubble but covered with a thin plastic glove and held in place with a rubber band. In all these changes, one thing had remained the same, the taste!

"Give me some of that water," mumbled a lady who had just finished swallowing five *golgappa*s. She was referring to the spicy water concoction that all those who consume *golgappa*s have to have. It is an absolute must and more importantly, free of charge. It is something to wash down your throat.

*"Thoda saunth bhi daal do,"* she continued as the man poured her a small glass of the concoction. The *saunth* is basically a sweet and sour concoction that gets poured into the *golgappa* and forms part of the stuffing along with the potatoes and gram.

*"Bachche ko ek paapdi dedo zara,"* the woman was at it again. "Please dip it in the *saunth* too."

*"Thode chane aur aloo de dena,"* cried out another after completing her quota.

*"Ek khali golgappa milega kya?"*

This continued and will continue through the day. Invariably, the consumer will ensure that he has ended up consuming more of the *golgappa*s that he hasn't paid for than what he is going to pay for. This will be in the form of the ingredients that go into the making of the complete *golgappa—paani dena, saunth daal do, chane dena aloo ke saath, bachche ko ek paapdi dena* etc. This is a city that thrives on anything that is free and it manifests itself at all times of the day. The huge lines outside temples during the distribution of *poori-halwa* served in large dried leaves bears testimony to the fact that the folks pay their obeisance first to the food that is free and then to God from whom they seek blessings. There will be endless lines of rich and poor alike and at the end of the ritual, the road will be littered with leaves strewn around post consumption of the *prasad*. These leaves will be licked clean by stray dogs and the leaves would be munched upon by the cattle that roam the roads of Delhi, merrily and totally oblivious to the million people and vehicles that surround them.

The vehicles slow down or literally come to a standstill thereby causing a traffic jam but it does not matter. Be it any major religious festival or the fulfilment of a wish for which the concerned person has promised to repay in this fashion, the roads get littered with all forms of paper plates, leaf plates or styrofoam cups, thrown away by the consumers after a free meal. It's tradition and nobody seems to object. After all, anything in the name of religion is always right and dare not be questioned. This consumption and the need to eat and drink for free betray the intrinsic nature of a Delhiite wanting to maximise the gains but never wanting to pay a price for it.

*"Thoda paani pila do ... saunth bhi daal dena,"* Dinesh muttered as the *golgappa* vendor graciously obliged with a smile.

His wife now led the way to the vegetable vendor not wishing to recount the experience that she had been through, that of having witnessed the horrific sight of *golgappa*s being consumed as a comfort food.

She examined the tomatoes closely and asked the vendor, *"Yeh* fresh *hi hai na?"*

Dinesh laughed out loud and said, "Do you really think that he is going to tell you that the tomatoes are stale and should not be bought?"

She did not answer but seemed to understand his point of view. The vegetable vendor replied, *"Ek dum* fresh *hai,* madam. *Subah hi mandi se aayein hain."*

"Isn't that always the case? Just arrived, indeed," Dinesh thought to himself. He bought the rest of the items not forgetting to ask for the chilies and coriander that is assumed to come free with the vegetable purchases. After having equipped themselves with the vegetables for the week, they made their way back home, only to be greeted at the door by the landlord.

"Coming back after buying vegetables, are you?" he said, staring unblinkingly at the turnip leaves sprouting from within the eco-green bag. He had a curious knack of stating the obvious. Dinesh smiled, now knowing how to respond.

"I had come to collect the rent," he continued.

Dinesh smiled again, not knowing how to respond.

"Can you give it to me now? I really do not want to come up again for this. These stairs are killing me."

Dinesh wanted to tell him that he should not have bothered to come up in the first place if he was eventually going to crib about it, but refrained lest it spark off another round of extended conversations which he was least in the mood to encourage. He handed over the vegetable bags to his wife and took out the house keys from his pocket. He opened the door and invited him in, as his wife went in with the bags.

"Ah! You have kept the house well," he mentioned as he plunked himself onto the sofa. Dinesh thought he heard the sofa groan.

His wife returned with the money and handed it over to Dinesh. He counted and handed them over to the landlord. He counted them again with his saliva laden fingers. Then he handed Dinesh a piece of paper.

Scrawled on the paper were some figures and a corresponding 'Rs' amount. It didn't take Dinesh long to figure out that the figures were ostensibly the number of electricity units that he had ostensibly used up over the month and the corresponding figure was the amount due. It seemed high but he did not want to protest or question the veracity of the bill in the first month. After all, he was a guy from Kerala and a certified *Madrasi*.

As time went on, Dinesh and his wife bought things and the household items grew in size and number. The agony of having to endure endless hours of power cuts was getting to him. The compartment style construction of the house ensured that there was no ventilation and the stifling heat coupled with the humidity only made it worse. They would spend endless hours, sometimes in the middle of the night, lying on the floor that was relatively cooler, fanning themselves and keeping the door open in order to catch even a whisper of a breeze.

As he lay on the floor one such night, Dinesh looked out at the lamp post that had a million cables and wires attached to it criss-crossing each other to a terminal atop the post. His apartment on the second floor was almost adjoining an electrical post. It didn't take much to figure out that the natural propensity to get that extra had moved people to secure illegal connections that were draining the already depleted and limited electricity supply available. Over 40 per cent of the electricity supply is lost in transmission and distribution. Theft of electricity by industrial units owned by powerful people posed a major problem. In New Delhi alone, about US $50,000 worth of electricity is lost every hour. Electricity can be produced but the country and more importantly the capital city of Delhi thrives in the knowledge that there is power shortage. It has almost assumed a legitimate status as most newspapers carry schedules of power cuts of differing duration across various localities. If all the power lost were to be retrieved by some divine intervention, the cables supplying the same would simply burn off as their poor quality would not be able to sustain the full capacity of the electricity load.

The government, each successive one, ensures that you are self reliant in every way. You have to produce your own power by way of generators, invertors or whatever power generating medium you can think of. You need to provide for your own water as the water supply provided by the government, which comes for an hour in the morning and half an hour in the evening, is not fit for human consumption. The chlorine content is so much and the water is so hard that the utensils used to boil this water quickly develop white scales that are almost impossible to remove. It wasn't long before Dinesh, driven by sheer fatigue, went to sleep with these thoughts. The next day he bought a generator.

The generator's purchase worked in more ways than one and helped in throwing light on many a thing that had remained hitherto unknown. During one such scheduled power cut at almost one in the morning, Dinesh walked up to the generator sleepy-eyed and dragged it to the balcony area. Trying hard to keep his eyes open, he checked the petrol valve and pulled the cord that in turn helped kick the engine to life. It huffed and puffed like a typical Punjabi aunty climbing up the stairs of her *kothi* in Tilak Nagar. The generator purred to life after initially belching out a thick cloudy mix of kerosene and petrol. The living room was illuminated and the ceiling fans started rotating.

Dinesh heaved a sigh of relief at the prospect of not having to yank the cord for a second time. He wasn't really feeling up to working out at one in the morning. As he turned to close the door behind him he thought he noticed some light on the first floor balcony of the house. Out of sheer curiosity, he leaned over his balcony and peered down. He noticed that the light was coming through one of the rooms on the first floor. The portion of the first floor balcony was being lit up in turn with its luminescence.

Struck with an even greater sense of curiosity and having quite lost his sleep, he walked down the side stairs in order to get to the bottom of this. He peered from behind the walls and was surprised to see that the first room on the first floor was lit up, well and proper.

It did not take him long to realise that he was being had, yet again. The landlord did not have a generator nor did he have an inverter, yet his area was being lit up. Dinesh ran up and switched off his generator and the lights on the first floor went out.

"Son of a bitch," he said under his breath.

The convoluted wiring to the house had ensured that a part of the house occupied by the landlord on the first floor was being supplied electricity through the second floor terminals. This meant that Dinesh was paying for a part of their electricity consumption in addition to his own. A fact revealed by the generator and the very reliable power cuts in Delhi. At least the power cut had ensured that he saw things in their true light. He tried to wake his wife and relate the incident but she did not stir in her sleep.

Dinesh was tired of being had again and again. The simplicity and his trusting ways coupled with his calm demeanour had only worked to his disadvantage in this city. A city which would provide all opportunities, but would also ensure that it extracted its pound of flesh as collateral. Maximum for the minimum, always!

The house was to be his abode for over five years. The properly documented lease agreement of the first year magically disappeared in the subsequent years as faith and trust replaced the commercial aspects. Never mind the fact that they continued to pay for the additional electricity for the first floor. The rent used to arrive on time; they were amiable, friendly and mixed very well with the landlord's two daughters. His wife got along very well with the youngest daughter—a relationship that defied personality types, spanned many years and became so deep that it endures to this day.

## Tarika...

The elder daughter was a firebrand and actually the second eldest in a family of three daughters. The eldest was married off to a doctor who was always under a misconception that he was the world's best. The middle one, as later events revealed was a lesbian, actually a bisexual after a string of multiple flirtations with guys who messed her up, and something that got successively complicated as time went by.

Tarika, the youngest one, lived life king-size and had her priorities set right from the start. She was not particularly attractive, was much on the heavier side, had a delightful complexion, almost pinkish, and was far fairer than her Bihari contemporaries. She fit completely well into the *gori* circle. She, as Dinesh discovered later, was always quick to anger, wanted to drive her destiny forward the way she wanted and had scant regard for her father who considered her a liability.

Once she had set her focus on something, she would do anything and everything to achieve that and there would be no compromise. No compromise at all. She had her heart set on going to the US at any cost and would stop at nothing to achieve that.

"US *jaane ke liye to mein ek bikhari se bhi shaadi karloon*," she had once told Dinesh. In his wife Tarika found a soul mate, somebody she could confide in and although she was a role model and a source of great inspiration to her, she did know that eventually Tarika would do her own thing on her own terms.

"What is it with this US fixation that most girls seem to have and most guys so brazenly flaunt?" Dinesh would think often. He had seen and met guys with an accent that could make an American blush and although they had never been to the US even in their dreams, their tongues had travelled the distance. One trip to the United Airline office for a tourist trip to the US and pop came the accent. When Dinesh was completing his French at the Alliance Francais de Delhi in South Extension, he would invariably stumble upon so many guys with an accent that was cultivated with a great degree of hard work and effort. It was so easy for so many of them to get the American accent whilst learning French. The only thing that gave it away was when they would decide to punctuate what they were saying with a *behenchod*.

"That movie was really cool and hip, *behenchod*."

Tarika was also a girl who had got so little from her own world. The Bihari community is such. The three daughters were all products of an attempt to have at least one boy, a fact that the landlord so openly spoke about in front of his daughters. Dinesh had a theory on this (perhaps his own version of Freakonomics). Any family having a girl child will always have a second child. Any family having a first boy child need not necessarily have a second. Most families having three children will, in all probability, have the first two children of the female gender. The quest for the male child is more complex and sought after than the quest for the Holy Grail, but considered just as holy.

Bihar is a place that has been voted in most opinion polls as the most under-developed and lawless place in the country.

Fodder scams, violence, floods, lynchings were all part of the deal. There were hopes that were associated with each new term but each time the hopes quickly vanished into oblivion. The more things change, the more they remain the same.

Tarika resented her restrained lifestyle and was a self-crowned bounty hunter, in search of a guy who would be her passport to the US. Dinesh wondered if that would work, and if at all it did, he hadn't seen it yet. He thought Tarika just got deeper and deeper in her denial of truth. She was clinging on to some peer-speak nonsense that had no basis in reality. But no amount of suggestions or pointing out facts will ever sway her opinion. It was frightening to see a human being reduced to spouting cowardice. Her incapacity for critical thinking was reflected in the story she narrated about a guy she befriended and the scars, or the lack of them, she inflicted on herself out of their certain 'fun' trip to Jaipur.

"I was in love with that *kutta*," she would say.

She was eventually married to a bartender from New York. She did not care who he was. For her, it meant going to the US and eventually getting a citizenship. It was not long before she had two children from him, a boy and a girl, until one fine day she divorced him citing physical abuse as the primary reason. Before all this happened, she ensured that she had secured herself a green card. Q.E.D. She achieved what she had set out to, never mind the price she had to pay in return. Everything in life comes with a price tag, after all.

Dinesh was not sure whether it was a price one would consider paying to be in the US. To him, settling down in Austria, Spain or Ireland held infinitely more charm and appeal than the US. One of his friends from school had moved shortly after an aborted entrepreneurial attempt and had settled himself in the US. He prided himself as an American and took greater pride in his children having all the upbringings of an average American. Before leaving for the dream nation, he had stayed in Janakpuri for over twenty five years.

Everyone had, either consciously or subconsciously, always thought it right to take away from the city of Delhi and never considered it their own to belong to it. The more things change, the more they remain the same.

"*Aaiye*, sir. How are you?" exclaimed Mr Kapoor, Dinesh's chartered accountant.

Mr Kapoor was introduced to Dinesh through a common friend as the person who could manage filing all his tax returns. Dinesh did not want to engage with the Income Tax department and needed somebody who was street smart and could help him manage his finances. Although not a chartered accountant, Mr Kapoor had an excellent knowledge of the Income Tax Act and knew his way around the corridors of the Income Tax office. He was a lawyer by profession and the income tax activity was something that fitted in well into his overall scheme of things, a natural diversification of his flourishing legal practice.

"I am well, sir," Dinesh replied. "How are you?" he asked.

"*Arre*, what can possibly happen to me. I am very well myself! God has been kind and everything is going great."

Dinesh had to hand it to the man. Rarely had he ever seen him in a sombre or a depressed mood. Always jovial and full of life, he was armed with a veritable army of anecdotes from the legal arena as well as those drawn from his personal experiences by way of Income Tax department. He was always a pleasure to be with. Short and fat, he reminded Dinesh of Danny DeVito but there the similarity ended.

"Here is the Form 16 you wanted," Dinesh said as he handed over the certificate that had been issued to him by his company. The certificate confirmed that the tax had been deducted by the employer from his salary and deposited with the Income Tax department.

"Ok, this is fine!" he said as he examined the same. "You seem to be doing well in life." He was obviously basing his comment on the salary figure that the certificate showed. Try as he might, that was something that Dinesh could not hide from him. "God has been kind," Dinesh said almost repeating what he had told him.

He smiled and continued, "Ok, where is my cheque?"

Dinesh pulled out his cheque book. "Here is your cheque," he said. Before he could write the amount, Mr Kapoor quickly interjected, "Make it ₹3,000."

"That is too much," Dinesh said protestingly.

"*Arre* Dinesh, you must understand. The charges have gone up. Have you seen how the prices have increased? Besides you have also had an increment in your salary. That justifies an increase in my fees too. After all, I have not ever asked for an increase over the past three years." Dinesh could have argued and continued protesting but it is hard to do that with someone who has direct access to your salary and your savings plan. He gave in and handed over a cheque of ₹3,000. "Thank you, *yaar*. Here, have some tea," he said as the side door opened and a woman walked in. "She is my wife." Dinesh looked at her and almost saw a personification of sadness, dejection and depression, almost a study in contrast to this jovial character that he called his C.A. She smiled a bit as she kept the tea on the table and he could see that the effort was really forced. Mr Kapoor was obviously not much in love as they hardly exchanged glances and he continued to read through his Income Tax returns file. Dinesh thanked her and she walked back through the door she had come in from.

"Is she alright?" he asked hesitatingly, not wanting to intrude into anything personal.

*"Haan haan,* she is like this only," Mr Kapoor replied.

Mr. Kapoor looked absolutely disenchanted with her and Dinesh wondered how this father of three could actually have a wife like that and yet maintain such a full of beans and non-chalant demeanour all the time. *"Acchha* Kapoor *sahib,* I will take your leave," Dinesh said as he hurriedly finished the tea. "I need to take my wife out for shopping."

"Ok, *baad mein milte hain!"* he said as he shook his hand, smiled a warm smile and returned to his heap of papers marked 'DDA Returns'.

Something had switched Dinesh off and made him uncomfortable over the past few minutes. As he got down the stairs and walked toward his bike, he could decipher the puzzling incident that had left him uncomfortable. He drove off with the figure placing a cup of tea in front of him still deeply etched in his mind.

Over the next many months, he continued to meet Mrs Kapoor over brief periods as he used to come to drop in his tax related documents for Mr Kapoor. One day, he got late and arrived around 6 p.m. and found out that Mr Kapoor was not at home. She greeted him at the door and asked if he would like to come in. It seemed fitting to accept the invite.

*"Nahin,* aunty," he said, "I just wanted to handover these papers."

"That's ok *beta,* won't you have a cup of tea at least until Kapoor *sahab* returns. He should be here shortly."

He did not want to disappoint her with a refusal so he agreed. He sat down on a red velvety sofa as she made her way into the kitchen. He picked up a magazine and lazily browsed through it. Some minutes later she returned with a tray that contained one cup of tea and some biscuits.

"Thank you!" Dinesh said as he helped himself to the cup of tea. She did not say a word nor did she acknowledge as she sat in front of him. "Are you ok, aunty?" he asked.

She looked at him and seemed hesitant to speak, as if she was battling an acute sense of depression.

"How can I be ok when it does not matter to Mr Kapoor whether I am dead or alive? He was supposed to be back by 4 p.m. and has still not returned. He does not return my calls. He must be with that..." she paused and Dinesh looked up at her not knowing what to ask "...with that woman in Kalkaji."

"What woman?" Dinesh asked almost instantly biting his tongue since he did not want to get into this.

"He is seeing another woman in Kalkaji and I know about it. He does not care. He wants to get rid of me so he can settle with her. He has even bought a house for her and they both meet in that house."

"Why are you telling me this, aunty?" Dinesh asked feeling increasingly uncomfortable both with what was being said and with the visible degeneration in her physical comfort levels as she shifted and squirmed in her seat.

"I have no one to talk to, *beta*. My daughters do not care for me and I have no one," she was almost on the verge of shedding tears. "It would not be long before the sluice gates opened wide," thought Dinesh.

He finished the tea and thanked her again. "Take care of yourself, aunty," he said as he headed for the door. She did not respond.

Dinesh continued walking towards his car (a new second-hand acquisition) and looked back one last time as she closed the door behind him. Head bowed, a picture of utter dejection and despair. Apparently, the woman had everything. A husband, three children, several properties around Delhi, and a good bank balance considering that her husband had a flourishing legal and finance practice. However, like most things in this city, it was all superficial. What lies beneath can leave one aghast. The veneer can fool many, perhaps all, but it comes apart with time.

Dinesh drove back to his house but his mind was still with the woman who had chosen to open her trauma to a stranger. Two days later, he came to know that Mrs Kapoor had committed suicide. She burnt herself in the kitchen by pouring kerosene over herself and that was the last time one saw of her. There was no one in the house then and Mr Kapoor was upstairs in his home-office area. He apparently did not hear anything and when he finally did, it was too late. Death by burning is such a common occurrence in the city nowadays that such news items do not evoke much attention any more. Be it suicide, killing for dowry, the most common 'accident' happens in the kitchen.

There is a more sinister patriarchal logic to the burning of wives for their dowries. A new study, the first of its kind, provides appalling proof of what many in India already acknowledge — that many of the unusually large number of kitchen burning accidents affecting young married women are in fact dowry-related murders, or forced suicides, acts of unimaginable violence against wives who can't meet their husbands' or in-laws' demands for yet more money. The study suggests that in spite of India's strict anti-dowry laws and long-running campaigns by women's groups, incidents like these are on the rise across India. Worse still, the guilty nearly always go unpunished either because police and forensic pathologists fail to investigate the cases, or because rampant corruption scuttles them later.

63

It seemed strange to Dinesh that in traditional Indian homes, young women learn to cook when they are around 13, which is when most accidents would be expected to occur. In the West, most burns victims are children and the elderly and in India, in stark contrast, only 4 per cent of the deaths were among girls younger than 15. The number jumps to 16 per cent for women aged 16 to 20—the age at which most women marry—and to 28 per cent for those aged 21 to 25. The most damning statistic is that every one of the married women was burned in her in-laws' home.

"Please accept my condolences," Dinesh said as Mr Kapoor looked up at him with a blank look in his eyes. He seemed sad as he sat surrounded by a group of relatives and other neighbours from the area. Dinesh and his wife were at his house to pay their condolences. He acknowledged and said, "We cannot prevent what is fated to be."

Dinesh looked at the picture of the woman on the floor with a garland around her picture frame and a lamp lit in front of her. Strangely, she looked much more at peace.

A year later (the minimum time prescribed by law before one can remarry in the event of death under unnatural causes), Mr Kapoor married the woman from Kalkaji.

Girish moved into a house just two houses away from where Dinesh used to stay in Malviya Nagar and both were delighted. To Dinesh, it meant a more robust, stronger and dependable support network. He visited them often on the first floor as the landlords used to stay on the ground floor. It was a house set in a 300 square yard plot built with two dwelling units on each floor. The floor on which Girish stayed did not have anyone staying in the adjoining dwelling and it almost always remained dark.

"How come no one stays here?" Dinesh enquired from Girish one day.

"Oh, that! The tenants to whom it was rented stopped paying rent one day and refused to move out."

Dinesh had a problem with people who refuse to acknowledge the wealth or position of anyone who has worked so hard to achieve it and wish to seize their prosperity the easy way, by simply walking in and refusing to move out.

"The landlord should just throw their stuff out of the house," Dinesh opined rather innocently.

"I believe the matter is in court and these guys," Girish said pointing to the invisible neighbours. "Have some clout, I am told."

Some days later, Dinesh saw a young man atop the first floor of his friend's house. He was visiting his friend and as he took the steps to the first floor, the boy made his way to the until now unoccupied house. "That's the invisible tenant," exclaimed Girish. "Come on, let's not stand here."

As Dinesh made his way to his house, an attractive woman stepped out into the balcony, glanced at him and walked her way to the balcony railing as if she was expecting someone. She looked attractive and most would have given her a second glimpse. But there was a sense of waste around her. Like a new car that has been through to many rallies or like a demo car in most car showrooms. Run down and beaten because of so many people having test-driven it. Same analogy. She had a figure to die for, was well groomed and was clad in a bright-coloured *salwar* suit that accentuated her curves to good effect. For the apparent youth that her body displayed the face seemed more aged, more used and more ravaged.

The guy followed her and looked at Dinesh as if he had looked at someone or something he should not have. Moments

65

later a stretch limousine drove itself to the road below and honked. The woman was expecting them. She rushed down the stairs and got into the car. The boy moved into the house, came out with a few beer bottles, locked the house and left in another car. All was done in less than five minutes.

A stretch limousine in Malviya Nagar is like expecting springs, fountains and swimming pools in the middle of the Sahara Desert. This was something out of the ordinary!

"Wow!" Dinesh said as the car struggled its way out of the narrow roads of the refugee colony.

"The limo or the woman," Girish enquired mischievously as he handed him a can of Heineken.

"Both. You do not normally find either in Malviya Nagar. She must be a call girl for sure," Dinesh said rather judgmentally.

"Seems like… different cars and different guys that keep dropping in and she keeps going out with them in a similar fashion. I cannot tell but who wants to know, anyway!"

Dinesh kept quiet, not knowing how to respond…

Shortly before noon one day, the woman Dinesh had seen on multiple occasions in Malviya Nagar was killed in a plush South Delhi farmhouse owned by Romesh Sharma, serving time in Tihar Jail on a host of charges, including his alleged links with underworld don Dawood Ibrahim.

"He who lives by the sword, dies by the sword," exclaimed Girish profoundly as they saw painters and carpenters going about their job of renovating the section of the house that was until now illegally occupied. The landlords, noticeably elated that the court had ruled in their favour, went about telling everyone what a whore Kunjum was. As Dinesh was walking out they wanted to tell him too and, "Let the dead rest in peace," came the response.

Delhi abounds with such cases and sensational exposes of similar nature keep springing up with alarming frequency. The *tandoor* murder case was one such.

"What about the Sushil Sharma case?" asked his friend. "That too is a similar example, much like the footballer, actor O.J. Simpson's case."

"You know what?" Dinesh said, "Fewer Indians have heard of O.J. Simpson but anyone who reads an Indian newspaper has heard of Sushil Sharma. The similarities are bizarre. Both O.J. and Sushil were jealous. Both used to abuse their wives is what the newspapers would have us believe. Both left the cities where the crimes were committed shortly after the victims were killed and both have lawyers who claim their clients were framed by the police."

"But there could be one difference," continued Dinesh. "As we are getting to see, it has become clear that many Americans want O.J. Simpson to be acquitted, but here, the demand is to hang Sushil Sharma. Police claim that Mr Sharma returned to his flat, checking to see if his wife had been in contact with her alleged lover. He pushed a button on the telephone which automatically redialled the last number called. When Mr Sharma discovered that the last call had been to the man's home, he allegedly went into a rage, shooting Sahni twice with his Armenius .32 calibre revolver. The chargesheet says that after wrapping the body in a plastic table-cloth and a bed sheet, Mr Sharma went to the Bagiya restaurant and with the help of a worker, stuffed the corpse into the *tandoori* oven. Police later found it charred beyond recognition. When he was arrested ten days later in southern India, with his head shaved, Mr Sharma said he had left Delhi on a pilgrimage."

"I have a problem seeing chicken being slaughtered in front of my eyes, so I wonder how." Dinesh let his thoughts trail.

"We live in a dangerous world today and the more we try to escape it, the more it chases you. There have been so many of these instances in which the woman embraced an individual who had deep-rooted political connections only to end in a graveyard either by death or simply by living a life after that that was no different from no life at all. Kunjum, Naina, and even Fiza, which is the most bizarre of all the cases."

"Oh yes! That was another one. *Pata nahin*, what the deal is," Dinesh said. "I think he is going through guilt pangs right now and wishes reunion with his lady love whom he feels he betrayed by abandoning her to her fate after using her to satisfy his lust. This is what post divorce syndrome is like, isn't it."

"Who the fuck cares," the friend said clearly revealing his boredom with the topic. "In India, a post divorce syndrome is rare. *Saala*, it takes ages to get a divorce first. The procedure for getting a contested divorce is cumbersome and lengthy and the legalities can take up to several years. By the time its over, the couple have already gotten over most syndromes. Three cheers to the judicial system."

"As our society becomes more liberal, more and more such cases will take place," Dinesh said still laughing over his Girish's last comment. "This situation is becoming more and more common among the rich class in big metros like Delhi and Mumbai, where leaving the first wife for the sake of a younger partner is becoming more common. People begin to find flaws in their existing partners, as they find they do not have much in common with them. This used to be a western concept. And now, its here too."

"Actually," the friend continued, "artists will find a lot more in common with artists, similarly with journalists and so on. Therefore couples working in one field find it easier to be attracted to each other. But this lasts as long as they are working together for once monogamy is discarded and promiscuity becomes the norm, the desire to experiment with new partners only grows."

"It is all over for you to see, *yaar*," Dinesh said. "Look at Tarika. She is willing to do anything and will stop at nothing to move to the US. It's not the married ones alone, it's also the young ones who are absolutely directionless."

"Forget it," his friend said as he began to get up. "Want to have some dinner or will you be having it at home?"

"I will leave," Dinesh said. "It's late and I have to catch some sleep, have to go to office tomorrow."

They hugged each other, took their last swigs of the beer and bid adieu. As he walked down the stairs, he thought, "Such complications!" The city allows all this to happen and stands as a mute spectator as we all go about destroying our lives. Murders, passion, lust, lapses of judgment leading to lives being thrown asunder, being thrown into the vortex of hopelessness from wherein extricating oneself is well nigh impossible till such time that you perish with it. It had been a dark and gory night.

# LIG, MIG, HIG and No 3G

*'Maula Mere Maula Mere…'* went the mobile ringtone as Dinesh rushed over to pick it up. The screen showed 'Anuj calling' and he quickly pressed the accept button.

"Want to go to Buzz tonight?" Anuj asked without wasting a minute on pleasantries. Anuj was a person he had befriended since his days at Rolta India Ltd. Dinesh enjoyed his company for the effect it had on him. The energy was contagious.

It was Friday night and Dinesh had just returned from work. "That would be great," he said immediately. Buzz was an immensely popular night club and he used to love the music and the ambience at that place.

An added benefit was that it was in Saket, just a stone's throw from Malviya Nagar. Saket brought back instant memories. The place which had its first multiplex called Anupam PVR which one rarely used to go to, as it rarely screened good films. But once it transformed itself into a multiplex, the revolutionary concept caught everybody's fancy and people thronged in droves. Over time, the place became a focal point around which many related ancillary units sprung up like mushrooms after the monsoon season. More pubs, more restaurants and more places centering in and enabling people to have a good time.

In Sanskrit, Saket means a place said to be close to heaven, thus a place where God lives, but the real Saket is far from it.

Saket was the ancient name of the city of Ayodhya, an important Hindu religious place, said to be the place of residence for Lord Rama. Saket was the name of the famous epic Hindi poetic work of Maithili Sharan Gupt, an account of the Ramayana through the eyes of Urmila, a lesser-known character. Beyond this the similarity ceased to exist in reality. The realty prices too had moved up in keeping with developing area. Dinesh wished he was living here as it would have been more socially acceptable.

"It's a good deal and you must consider it!" It was the real estate broker at the other end.

Dinesh was evaluating alternatives of buying a house and Saket was a good choice, more from an affordability standpoint. Since all the 'builder' houses commanded a huge payment in black or cash, it forced him to consider only those which had a sizeably larger white or cheque component.

"What kind of an accommodation is it?" he asked.

"DDA *ka hai*, sir, but why don't you have a look at it?" Dinesh wasn't sure whether to be happy or sad. To be happy at the prospect of potentially buying a house with a higher white component, or to be sad at the prospect of having to look at a DDA house. *"Ab yeh din bhi dekhne honge,"* he thought.

"What is the black/white ratio?" he asked almost dreading the response that he would be getting.

"It's a cheque deal, sir," said the broker most triumphantly. Finding an all white deal in Delhi is like finding a good-looking woman in Netaji Nagar. "The buyer wants everything above board." Dinesh could not believe what he was hearing but continued with the initial questioning.

"What is the square feet area?"

"Sir*jee*, super area will be approximately 1,400 square feet and the carpet area will be around 1,200 square feet."

"Oh god!" he said out aloud, but the broker had not finished. "You can always cover the extra open area like the balcony and the verandah and get an another 300 square feet. Everybody does that and it is so common that it isn't illegal any more." Safety in numbers! When too much of illegality happens, the government considers the easier choice of legalising it and priding itself with the thought of having resolved it. The unauthorised areas which boast of fancier apartments and *kothies* than the ones in legally approved areas authorise over time. Issue resolved and everybody is happy.

"Oh, but that would not be legal, would it?" he still asked betraying his pronounced sense of naivety.

"*Arre* sir*jee*, what are you talking about? You must be joking. The unauthorised structures here are more than the authorised ones," he laughed out loud almost as if he was proud of the fact. "Almost every DDA house here converts into a bigger place so do not worry at all."

"Ok, when can we have a look at it?"

"Tomorrow morning?"

"Ok, let's meet opposite Anupam multiplex tomorrow at 11 a.m." Dinesh said as he checked his watch.

"*Theek hai*, sir."

And the phone went dead.

"Look at that babe, isn't she hot?" said Anuj as they wound their way through the open area adjoining the Anupam multiplex on their way to Buzz. The open area was pockmarked with *paan-wallahs* and all kinds of street sellers selling pirated books and worn out Mills and Boons.

"She is cool," Dinesh said almost forgetting for a moment that he had his wife back home waiting for him.

For Anuj it did not matter. He was twice divorced and always looking around for a good lay. But he was a good soul. Almost like a package of contradictions, like the city of Delhi.

The Anupam complex has some of the finest and easily accessible food joints and night clubs. It has *dhaba*s and cheap eating joints and it also has great restaurants jostling with each other for the extra odd square feet. The *dhaba*s draw the larger crowd, though. The food is much tastier at less than half the cost. The onions too come free.

They walked into Buzz and although they had a no stag entry policy it did not apply to them as they were regulars there. The place was crammed as usual. It was smoky and people wrestled with each other for their drinks, a place to sit or just make eye contact with someone who took their fancy. The music was loud and they had to shout into each other's ear to help understand what they were trying to say. Much was lost in transit.

Anuj winked at the waiter and handed him a ₹50 note. The waiter gave an understanding nod and within a few minutes, they got seats in one corner of the place. They ordered their drinks and were soon tapping their feet to the music. The waiter placed a soup bowl in front of them and Dinesh asked him its utility. "Sir, this is an ashtray."

It confused Dinesh.

The waiter bent down and spoke closely in his ear. "Since we have a ban on smoking in public places including bars and pubs, we cannot put ashtrays on tables. We allow the people to smoke but do not want to display the ashtrays."

"That's strange," Dinesh said. "This place is so smoked and you think that not having an ashtray displayed publicly is going to help?"

"*Ab kya karein*, sir. This is what the authorities suggest. We take good care of them and they ensure that we do not get into any trouble. After all we both need each other to survive."

◈

He fumbled with the lock and after a few twists and turns got the lock open. The door opened and the broker waited for Dinesh to enter the flat.

The dusty place was cobweb-ridden. The walls had major cracks and almost one entire section had massive water seepage, evident through the plaster on the walls making it rusty brown in colour. Dinesh was not sure whether to go in but decided in the affirmative. Might as well make the most of the visit.

"Two bedrooms with attached bathrooms, sir and one study," the broker proclaimed proudly almost as if he was showing off a palace that was his own.

"A study in a DDA flat?" Dinesh asked with a great sense of disbelief. That sounded like a vegetarian restaurant in Tilak Nagar.

"Sir, it was an open balcony on the side which the owner converted into another room. Good work, isn't it?"

Dinesh did not answer and opened the bathroom door. The stench was unbearable as a few pigeons fluttered in panic as they tried to fly out of the partly broken toilet window.

There was a dead one lying on the floor and Dinesh chose to look past it.

"This house has been vacant for a year," said the broker trying to justify the sorry state of affairs. "The owners are out of the country and they do not plan to return. So they want to sell the flat. Ah, and can you come this side for a minute."

Dinesh walked in the direction he indicated and it led to a large open balcony. "You can cover this and you will have a spacious living room. Nobody will object."

"But," Dinesh protested, "this is a first floor house and if I were to extend the portion, wouldn't the people on the ground floor protest or raise an objection?"

"*Arre* sir, when you extend your portion and lay the floor, it almost becomes a roof of the house below. You see, a floor on the first floor is the ceiling on the ground floor. You can enter into an agreement with them. They also get an additional area without having to spend too much on it. Both of you can be happy."

Dinesh could not help but smile, not because he admired his creative genius but because of the innovative ways that figure out in the pursuit of wanting to beat the system. "There is a garage too with a servants' quarter on top of it," the broker continued without a pause. "I can give that on rent and earn an added income on it, right?" Dinesh asked trying to sound knowledgeable with the ways of the world through the half-hour crash course that he had been subjected to.

"Good idea, sir*jee*!" said the broker agreeing, "But there is a small problem with that."

"What?" Dinesh asked almost surprised as this was the first time the broker had evinced a sense of anxiety and concern.

"If you want to extend, draw additional power beyond your approved capacity besides getting a bore well installed, you do not want to have the authorities on your doorstep every day for one reason or the other, do you?"

"And so…" Dinesh continued to question.

"The garage and the room above that serve as a place for them to bring in a girl occasionally for an hour or two. It won't disturb you. They will just be using those rooms and will leave as quietly as they came. The garages and the servant quarters here serve that purpose. You can make that out yourself. The house with the fanciest extensions will have an alternative use for the garage and the servant quarter." the broker said and let out a laugh.

From a blatant violation of the law in extending your coverage area to the officials who turn a blind eye in return for using a part of your property for their self-gratification. It's all about maximising your position without wanting to tread the straight and narrow path, which to most now seems more exhausting and less beneficial. Maximum for minimum…

Dinesh told the broker that he will get back to him. It's been over ten years and Dinesh was confident that he would have realised by now, that a call was not going to come from a certain 'sir*jee*' whom he had shown the house to many years ago.

After an hour or so at Buzz, they decided to go to the *dhaba* called 'harichutney.com'. *"Aaiye,* sir. *Yahaan par sab kuch milega,"* said a waiter equivalent as he began to rattle off close to twenty of their most popular and commonly accepted dishes. "Please tell me what you would like to have?" he asked as he wiped the table with a dirty rag and made them feel comfortable to the best extent he knew and could.

Both Anuj and Dinesh looked at the menu in a laminated sheet. It had nearly everything. *"Chaar kadak roti* and *daal,"* Dinesh said as they began munching on the onions served with *pudina* chutney. This is just so standard an accompaniment at any *dhaba*. Onion juliennes served with *pudina* chutney, sometimes served with sliced tomatoes and radish too.

Dinesh looked around and could see the place jam-packed and more were waiting for their turn. This was competition too as each *dhaba* owner through their *chhotu*s tried to woo a potential customer with promises of a great meal and experience.

As the *roti*s arrived with the *daal*, Dinesh noticed some constables making their way into the kitchen of one the *dhabas*. He beckoned to the waiter and asked, *"Yeh andar kyon jaa rahen hai? Kuchch hua hai kya?"*

*"Yeh bahut behenchod log hai*, sir*jee. Saale bhadue…* they want to eat and then even want to pack food free to carry back with them to the police team waiting in the police van. If we do not cooperate then they will ensure that we shut shop and do not operate. We have no choice but to quietly agree to whatever they ask for." This was the power of the uniform and position! Free food, free sex, free power, everything for free. Maximum for minimum…

They finished their meal and paid a princely sum of ₹65 for a great experience. It was delicious. As they were walking away, Dinesh could see one constable carrying with him three plastic bags laden with food.

He bid adieu to his friend Anuj. They had had a great time and now that it was almost 12 a.m., it was time to call it a night or morning—neither of them was sure, nor did they care.

Dinesh walked to the parking lot and on the way passed a eunuch who was soliciting customers. "A blow job for ₹50," he was told by the parking attendant. He wanted to throw up at the thought. A couple of boys who must be freshly out of school were talking to one of the eunuchs. Soon, Dinesh knew, a deal would be struck.

As he paid the standard ₹20 to the parking attendant, he came closer and whispered in his ear, "Sir, when you exit the gate, make sure that you turn left. It's a longer road but it is what I would recommend considering that you are in high spirits."

His play on words was not lost on Dinesh. "Why is that?" he asked. "Sir*jee*, the traffic cops are out there on the road and they are challaning all who have had a drink too many. They have breathalysers and the fine is up to ₹5,000. Since you are a regular here, I thought that I should warn you."

"Is that why there are hardly any cars in the parking lot?" Dinesh asked.

"Yes, sir. Most people prefer to eat and drink out at these fancy malls and nobody wants to come here any more. There are no police check-posts outside the malls so people find it safer and more convenient to go there," he said ruefully.

Dinesh thanked him and drove off from the left side. As he passed the intersection, he could see at least four cars halted on the right side and the drivers put to the breathalyser test. Some failing, while some others paying the money.

"What a way to get rid of the high!" he thought.

As he passed about 50 metres, he saw the same boys getting into a Ford Fiesta with the eunuch seated in the back seat.

# Indian Expatriates

With the passage of time, life moved on and Dinesh flitted from one job to another till he bagged a big job in a diplomatic mission. To him this was path-breaking: first, it provided him with an insider view of the diplomatic life with all the myths that surround it and second, it gave him the much-needed work life balance.

This was his fourth job and with each movement he learned more and unlearnt far more. He learnt that true work experience is irreplaceable, never mind what they teach you at IIM. The one thing that held him in good stead was the MBA that he got while he was working in his first job at Rolta India Ltd. That was important as it helped him to define the framework of a corporate entity and therefore helped him to work around it. It did little else. What you see and absorb is infinitely more useful than what one learns in books. Especially in Delhi where things work at their own free will and most are a product of a compromise.

"*Namaskar*, sir*jee*," exclaimed the driver Qazid as Dinesh parked his bike which he had held as his first love in spite of having purchased a car outside the Mission.

"*Namaskar*," Dinesh said and smiled at him.

Qazid was quite a character. Corrupt and amoral to the core and largely despised by the other drivers assigned to the various diplomats and expats at the High Commission. Call it professional jealousy or a general dislike. He was a carpenter, a plumber, a generator expert, but officially, a driver. Hard working but very, very wrong.

It is not wrong to say that most High Commissions and diplomatic missions are largely run by the drivers and servants. With their knowledge of the streets and with an acute desire to keep matters of personal nature away from the official eye, most diplomats prefer to consider their drivers as their confidantes. The drivers run their lives. Every aspect that you need to convey to the concerned diplomat either needs to be routed through the driver or will be conferred with by the diplomat anyway. The dice is cast when the diplomat arrives in the country for the first time and is being driven to the house in Vasant Vihar, Shanti Niketan or West End (these are diplomatic colonies now with even the landlords assuming a demi-expat status).

Over time, these localities have assumed a quasi-diplomatic identity and the landlords revel in it. You do not just rent out a house to a diplomat, you ensure that the diplomat sponsors the refurbishment, renovation and any other addition and variation done to the house during their stay. A fancy driveway roof, for example, costing around ₹50,000 is left behind when the diplomat vacates the house at the end of his tenure. The landlord then gives it to another diplomat at a higher rent since the house now comes with a fancy covered driveway!

The driver is the first point of contact in an alien country and all the diplomat has as an Indian contact.

"Welcome to India, sir!"

"Hello," the diplomat will mumble rather suspiciously at first since he has been briefed not to trust an Indian, and never a Delhiite.

"Let me help with the bag, sir. Please, sir you sit in car. You want AC?" These are the preprogrammed words of greeting and are part of the standard working procedure.

And then the saga of eternal friendship and faith begins. If the diplomat is single, then the relationship becomes more intense and deep as that would mean protection of many secrets and convenient forgetfulness towards other significant details. With the *gora* fetish that runs rife among the Delhi folks and especially among the Delhi women, it is easy for a diplomat with the right colour to befriend a woman at a local pub or restaurant. One thing leads to another and the woman and each successive one in turn finds easy and unfettered access to his house. Sometimes the driver has to ferry the women back and forth in the 'CD' car, but all of this remains a secret. A service the driver ensures he is well compensated for, both in cash and in kind.

The servant's quarter is available to the driver and his wife. The driver's wife customarily becomes the house worker in the house. Between the driver and the house worker, they practically run the house and the diplomat's life. Over time, the house worker becomes a caretaker within the house while the driver manages the outside errands.

On many occasions the house worker gives in to the carnal desires of the diplomat while the driver is busy with a prostitute in the servant quarter. These servant quarters are quarters of vice where everything happens, and everything wrong.

A residence given to a diplomat is the ultimate dream for any of the professional landlords in Vasant Vihar or adjoining areas. Dinesh had the particular misfortune of dealing with one while negotiating for a house lease for one of his senior diplomats, a 'white' man. This is important as most of these landlords are hesitant to give it to a 'black' man or somebody from the Muslim community or the Arab world.

"Is your house available for rent?"

"Only for foreigners," said the voice at the other end. Dinesh wondered if any of the locals in a foreign land would ever say this when giving out a house for rent and even if they did, would they have said "no" to an Indian.

"Yes, he is a foreigner," he said having got used this note of introduction in any rental conversation with the professional landlords in the diplomatic colonies of New Delhi. "You see, I work for the South African High Commission and..."

"Is he black?" interrupted the would-be-landlord.

"No, he is not," Dinesh stated most impatiently.

"Are you sure?"

"Of course I am!" How can a person not be sure whether a person is a black or a white. These landlords knew how to stretch the limits.

"Ok, you can show him the house any time," came the reply. "Please let us know a couple of hours in advance. You know the terms and conditions don't you?" Dinesh wanted to tell him that it's too early a stage to be talking about it, but mumbled a feeble "Yes" and put the phone down.

It doesn't take long for the driver to get involved himself in the process. Having seen the frequency of the brokers coming in and out of Dinesh's office, they had invariably smelt an opportunity that they would never let go.

"Let's go," Dinesh said. "We have a house to inspect."

"This is through which broker?" asked the driver. Dinesh wanted to know why and how this makes a difference to him, of all the people. "How does it make a difference to you?"

"I know *saab*'s taste, sir*jee*. So I will be able to brief the broker better."

"Bullshit," Dinesh said to himself. All that he wanted to do was to establish a connection with the broker so he could negotiate the commission he could get from him. In return, he would assure the broker that he holds the key and that he would recommend the property positively to the diplomat, thereby clinching the deal. Almost all brokers agree and most of the time the diplomats also end up using those brokers who their most trusted drivers recommend.

Mr DuPlessis carefully surveyed the house and nodded his acceptance as the landlord and his wife looked at each other. The Guptas had convinced themselves of the colour and desperately wanted to close the deal. They seemed every bit of the typical landlord community. Devoid of any class or elegance and obviously money hungry to the extreme.

"We would like to have twenty four months' rent in advance in cash, to be adjusted every month. I am sure that will not be a problem," said Mr Gupta most presumptuously.

Dinesh did not blink. He had heard this before.

DuPlessis looked at Dinesh and he nodded to suggest that they could do this.

The landlords were resenting his presence with the diplomat. It was obvious. Left to their own, they would have had the hapless diplomat stripped to the bone with demands of all hues, shapes and sizes. "Should we discuss the details in private?" asked Mr Gupta motioning that Mr DuPlessis accompany them to the room inside.

"We should discuss what we have to in his presence," said Mr DuPlessis indicating that Dinesh should be present throughout the conversation.

As he was not going to get rid of Dinesh, Mr Gupta continued, "Ok, that's fine! If both the rental amount and duration are acceptable to you then I have a favour to ask of you."

The presence of Dinesh made him uncomfortable. He had no choice and he said, "Can I also have one of my briefcases kept in your part of the house once you move in?" he enquired as he looked at DuPlessis and Dinesh in turn.

It did not take Dinesh long to figure out on what was happening here. Since all houses rented by diplomats are out of bounds to local law enforcement agencies on account of diplomatic immunity status that they enjoyed, the rented house will never be subject to a search. An ideal haven for the landlord who wants to hide away all the documentation pertaining to their ill-gotten gains in this novel fashion. The briefcase would contain details of properties and income not declared to the tax authorities, *benami* papers, possibly foreign currency as well.

Dinesh took DuPlessis aside and told him that this was disagreeable as it circumvents the law of the land. It seemed ironic as it meant that we were being forced to enforce the law of the land through a foreigner rather than through the local citizen. Mr Gupta not only wanted the house rented out to a white at a fancy rent paid two years in advance, but also wanted the diplomat to be the custodian of all his confidential and illegal activities' proof.

DuPlessis agreed with him and refused the landlord, "I am afraid we cannot do that Mr Gupta."

The landlord was glowering at Dinesh, the architect of this refusal. Dinesh did not give a fuck as he had scant respect for people of this kind. "Ok, that's fine. It was just a request if you could consider. If it cannot be done then so be it."

"Thank you," replied Mr Duplessis. "We will get in touch with you for the paperwork and the finalisation of the lease agreement. We would like to close this at the earliest."

"Oh, we too, we too!" Mrs Gupta spoke for the first time.

As they were leaving, the landlord asked Dinesh for his mobile number. Although Dinesh was initially not sure, he decided to partake with it nevertheless since they would have to work on the lease agreement and they would require frequent interactions.

DuPlessis thanked him once they arrived back at the Mission. As he walked to his desk, his mobile rang. Dinesh picked his phone and could see that it was Mr Gupta calling.

"How are you Dinesh *sa'ab*?" It was Mr Gupta with a new found sense of camaraderie.

"I am good," Dinesh replied not wanting to prolong the conversation with an insect.

"*Arre yaar uss* diplomat *ko manao*. I will ensure that you are taken care of. Both of us can benefit. The foreigners can go and hang."

Here is a man least bothered about potentially corrupting a fellow Indian so that his corruption could flourish as well through a foreigner who wanted to be honest and follow the rules of the country he was in. Things were not beginning to make any sense!

"I told him that this would be illegal," Dinesh replied.

"*Arre chhor yaar*. Nothing is illegal. You try to explain to him that this is the way the rental system works in Delhi. It happens all over the place and I am not suggesting anything new. You have been in Delhi long enough and you should know. The tenant is expected to help the landlord."

"By keeping your suitcase in his house?" Dinesh asked growing somewhat weary of the conversation.

"Yes, that is common. And also by paying the rental amount in cash up front. These are standard practices."

"We are already doing you a big favour by paying you the rental amount in cash, Mr Gupta. You will, obviously, not be paying any amount in tax on that, will you?"

"That's none of your business," Mr Gupta snapped.

"Well, then let me tell you what my business is. It is my business to know and advise the diplomat what you propose to keep in the house that is being rented by the Mission and whether it, in any way, contravenes the law of the land. "Goodbye Mr Gupta," Dinesh said not bothering with the niceties any more.

"Ok, listen, don't get angry. Let's talk. We are okay without the arrangement as agreed. Let's sign when you are ready. Ok?"

"Ok, Mr Gupta, I will get the paperwork ready and we should be ready with the cash in three to four days time. We can then close out all formalities thereafter. Are you ok with that?"

"Ok, *theek hai*," he replied.

"Bye," Dinesh said, and he responded as well.

Sometimes, you can catch some additional comments as the phone is making its way to the cradle. It's usually by the person at the other end sharing a thought, a view with another in the room or just a form of expression. This is what happened in the case of Mr Gupta as well.

*"Saala behenchod!"*

The reference was obviously to Dinesh.

The city of Delhi functions on a 60:40 basis where 60 per cent denotes the black component of the deal and 40 per cent denotes the white component. A bit of bargaining and the black component may come down. The black component is dealt in cash and it is not unusual to see bags loaded with cash finding its way into houses at all odd hours of the day once the deal has been struck. Dinesh's experiences at the High Commission in Vasant Vihar flashed across his mind and he smiled knowingly.

Even white money sometimes converts to black. For example, more than 50 per cent of the value of property transacted in the real estate market in Mumbai is in black money. Since the transactions are in black they may not be secure. Legal receipts for payments cannot be given and people have to depend on faith. Since black income is spent in an unaccounted fashion it leads to further tax evasion. For example, black income used to buy expensive durable goods such as televisions and refrigerators might involve evasion of sales taxes.

The lease transaction went along fine and Mr Gupta came in with an additional security man so he could cart the money away without any fear. As he left, Dinesh couldn't help but imagine the money the country was deprived of by taxes. He had a job to do and felt constrained in having facilitated this robbery of the state.

Maximum for minimum…

"Hey, Dinesh!" It was DuPlessis. He had since moved into his new house. He was in a way relieved that the matter closed out sooner than he expected. Staying in a single room in a five-star hotel for over a month had begun to bother him. "We are having a party this Saturday night and would be great if you and your wife would join us."

"Sure, it'll be a delight," Dinesh replied.

"Great, see ya at eight then."

At the party, DuPlessis mentioned to Dinesh how Mr Gupta had asked if he could get some of the bottles of duty-free alcohol the diplomats get as part of their monthly quota. DuPlessis had, of course, refused but wanted his view. Dinesh told him that he had done right by refusing. As if all this wasn't enough, Mr Gupta now wanted to milk the tenant of the benefits he enjoys by virtue of being a diplomat. "Doesn't this man know when to stop?" Dinesh wondered.

The party was in the lawns and the gathering was full. It was a ground floor house with a roomy lawn. Mr Gupta and family occupied the first floor. Dinesh pitied DuPlessis for having to put up with such neighbours, but quickly remembered what they say about not being able to choose your parents and neighbours.

After loads of alcohol and great food, it was time for Dinesh to go. As he was walking out, he met Qazid at the gate with his ever smiling face. Dinesh greeted him and he greeted back in the traditional Muslim way of greeting, "*Salaam*, sir."

Dinesh got into the car and reversed it. As he was beginning to leave, he thought he saw Mr Gupta and his wife on the first floor, peering down at the happenings in the lawn below from behind the cover of their curtains.

Dinesh felt sick.

## Qazid...

Among the group of five drivers that were part of the office pool of drivers, Qazid was the most hard-working as well as most amoral. The other drivers despised him but yet were cordial to him since he was a useful man to have around. Qazid knew of every nook and corner of Vasant Vihar, Shanti Niketan and Westend and had a story to tell on each. One could tell that he was corrupt but then almost all the drivers, housekeepers, helps around the area have their own set of skeletons tucked away in their cupboards. Since the diplomats trust them so implicitly and the potential moneymaking opportunities are so immense, it's easy for them to be sucked into the vortex of corruption and deceit.

"Sir*jee, aap Rajasthan aao.* We will ensure that you have a wonderful time. You can hunt for deer there, even blackbucks," said Ramprakash, one of the senior drivers of the Mission who hailed from Rajasthan.

Dinesh was taken back. This was the time that Salman Khan, a Bollywood superstar had been arrested and booked under charges of hunting and killing a blackbuck in Rajasthan. The black buck is a sacred animal, protected and worshipped by the Bishnoi community.

Dinesh was instantly transported to the last time that he had visited this community in Rajasthan. The Thar Desert in India is full of ironies—one of them being the Bishnoi community of Rajasthan. Here peace is maintained with aggression and robust health rubs shoulders with regular famine, and penniless women flaunt heavy gold jewellery and wild animals leave the supposed security of the jungle to stroll around village huts and farmlands. The Bishnoi tribe of the western Indian state of Rajasthan has, over centuries, made a unique blend of ecological sense and religious sensibility their faith's cornerstone.

What surprises you as you approach a Bishnoi village is the sheer freedom with which a spotted deer, blue bulls, and black bucks race along the roadside or frolic in the open fields. "Animals are sacred," says Bana Ram of Guda. "Before he passed away, *Jambaji* told us that in his absence, the blackbuck should be revered as his manifestation. That belief continues. Hunting blackbucks for us is like killing our guru. One call of *Shikaar* and 500 villagers will assemble here this moment to teach the offenders a lesson. We'll kill our own children before we let these animals be killed."

Which is why the worst thing to happen to a hunter is being caught by the Bishnois. "Once, an Indian Air Force captain was caught hunting. We stripped him and forced him to lie down on the hot sand in the middle of summer. He'd never dream of hunting again," adds Bana Ram.

The killing of a blackbuck from a significance and impact standpoint to a Bishnoi can well be imagined!

"But is that not illegal?" Dinesh asked Ramprakash. "After all Salman Khan was arrested for that offence, wasn't he?"

"Arre no, sir! He was arrested because he is a big star and that makes news. We still kill black buck and deer and nobody says anything. It is all bullshit."

"So do you actually go hunting?"

"Of course, sir. We take our jeeps and hunt them. Later, in the night we have the barbeque. You should really visit us and you will enjoy every bit of it."

It is always a dicey proposition to accept an invite of this kind from a driver or their ilk. It is akin to 'Operation Honeytrap' that the FBI undertake to trap someone. If he were to make one trip, he could be rest assured that the tales of his misadventures thoroughly laced with all the spices in the country will spread far and wide. All the perfumes of Arabia will not then sweeten his little hand. It's amazing how the stories concocted through the figment of someone's sick mind can find its way into the system with such accuracy that you are left reeling under its impact.

Qazid had a drinking problem, well not really a problem from his perspective. He used to drink regularly, sometimes at the residence of any of the diplomats with the security guards who were his best buddies. Post that, he would take the CD vehicle and roam around in search of a girl who could satiate his carnal desires. He was also usually the first one to volunteer for any of the repair and maintenance jobs at the Mission as it meant that he could benefit financially through marked up bills or kickbacks.

His personal life was a mess. He used to get drunk and beat his wife. At times he even used to report drunk to work. Dinesh knew that he was living on a short fuse and it wouldn't be long before it exploded on his face. It was something waiting to happen, and it did sooner rather than later.

One day all hell broke loose and Qazid was fired from his job. During one of his duties at the airport, he escorted a lady diplomat to the hotel. As they neared the hotel, Qazid got friendly and asked if he could carry her bags to her room. Not noticing anything amiss, the lady agreed. Qazid carried the bags and once inside the room, tried to rape her. The screams and shouts were loud enough for him to beat a hasty exit but the matter got promptly reported to the High Commissioner who wasted no time in ordering his termination.

Such a pity!

The company he kept comprised all the wrong elements that throng the streets of Vasant Vihar and adjoining areas. He had a great job at the Mission, one that afforded him the comforts in a very conducive environment but like most things in Delhi, it does not take long to corrupt and very soon a person is left looking for things that he does not have or would like to possess with little consideration of the overall collateral damage involved. All the misadventures are at the cost of one's family, one's morals, one's values and very soon, one ceases to live and merely exists. Nothing is enough and there is more that one wants, whichever way one can get it.

Maximum for minimum…

# Expatriate Hot Spot

"*Kebab khane chalna hai*. It's been a long time since we went out and had a good kebab meal."

"*Kahan?*" Dinesh asked.

"Khan Chacha."

"Who all are coming?"

"Shalini and Shefali."

"I will get Girish with me. He's been wanting to go there for a long time. You ok with that?"

"Absolutely! Let's meet at two in the afternoon opposite Bahri Sons." And the phone line went dead. It was by default that his friends from college used to connect for impromptu get-togethers such as this one. Dinesh used to always enjoy the plans that came up on the spur of the moment rather than the ones planned a week or two in advance. Ironically, the planned ones were the ones which used to go awry for some reason or another. The impromptu ones always came through. Uday was an expert at this. He was driven by impulse and on one occasion had spent a night out with Shefali in a drunken state. Nothing wrong with that except that Shefali was dating Girish at that point in time. All forgotten, all good.

When Dinesh was employed at the diplomatic mission, he used to run more errands to Khan Market than he used to to the local market in Malviya Nagar. The contrast cannot be starker.

One caters to the refugees from within the country and the other mainly caters to the expats from other countries. The distinction is unique yet similar. Both classes do not belong to the city but form an integral part of its identity. The city and the people both need each other.

Khan Market is located at the heart of the city very close to the famous India Gate. Khan Market was set up in early 1950s to rehabilitate immigrants after partition. The proximity of the Lodhi Gardens leaves the visitor with an impression of greenery. The India International Centre and the India Habitat Centre make it a pocket of cultural activity. The World Wildlife Fund for Nature is also located close to this market. Government residential units ring the Khan Market and a number of bureaucrats and expats regard it as their home and their neighbourhood market.

The land, now housing the Khan Market was originally seed land allotted to immigrants from Pakistan and the North-West frontier provinces during the 1947 partition of India and Pakistan. Today it is one of the most important commercial real estate locations in the city. Many branded products have their showrooms in this market in addition to delicatessens, bookstores, electronics, and kitchenware and fabric stores. The shops including the magazine stores stock more of imported items than Indian goods. Even the basmati rice is from Pakistan. The shops in this market majorly attract the attention of the diplomatic community and it is not unusual to catch fleets of CD cars marked one behind the other on a typical weekend.

As they parked their car behind a CD vehicle, Dinesh saw the driver of the car say something to the parking attendant. The parking attendant ran towards them and in an impolite fashion asked them to move the car.

"Sir*jee*, will you move your car."

"And why should we do that?" enquired Uday as he stepped out of the car with Shalini and the others.

"*Yeh* CD cars *ki lane hai!*" Dinesh could not believe what he had just heard.

"*Pitna hai kya?* CD lane *hai*. Did you make that up yourself or did that driver there tell you to tell us that," Dinesh asked on the verge of losing his temper.

It's a classic example of somebody having something yet wanting that little extra. The parking spaces in front of all residential houses belong to the person staying in the house. The people will protect it with all their might with some resorting to shoot-outs as often happens in Greater Kailash.

"*Thoda peeche le lo,*" said the attendant changing track. The tone had become conciliatory, but the arrogance still showed.

Uday was in no mood to oblige but gave in. They had no plans of screwing up their afternoon over an extra square feet of parking space. "The car is parked here," he proclaimed. "*Hila ke dikha agar hai gaand mein dum.*"

All walked away into the market. This is a place where you could be all by yourself and still have your share of fun watching the harassed house worker run after the *memsahib*, holding on to the shopping bags and the baby, sometimes in a pram, while the woman walks ahead yelling to the house worker to make haste.

"*Kitna* time *lagaati ho tum.*"

"*Bachcha nahin aa raha tha mem'sahib.*"

"Ok, now don't make excuses. Take these bags and ask the driver to bring the car here. Quickly, it's so hot here."

You could watch the foreigners wander around the shops looking bewildered or busily trying to capture the scene on film to carry with them home to stun their friends and relatives. To be proud of the fact they had ostensibly visited a third world country with cows and beggars jostling for space on the same road and street. Stray dogs and urchins squeezing their way with large straw bags while sellers urge you to buy everything from a hairpin to an expensive music system.

The riot of colours and the crowds will keep you entertained for the evening but it was the kebabs that had driven them all the way.

Emerging from a *mohalla* market to a haute *bazaar* with a distinct culinary edge, Khan Market now houses 31 eateries within its 24,000 square feet of space. The cobbled street is what one will now call Khan Market's middle lane, buttoned with various trendy cafes and swish eateries.

The food was delicious and they made their way back to the car. The CD car in front of their car had left by then. They drove off without paying the parking attendant.

As they turned at the corner of the road, the car stalled. The attendant was nowhere in sight but it did not matter. Uday tried to revve up the engine but to no avail.

"What the fuck?" he exclaimed in frustration. It was hot and with the car stalled the air conditioning was a natural casualty.

"Relax," Dinesh replied, "the car has fortunately stalled at the right place."

Car repair and accessory workshops at the opposite end of Khan Market help one service the car or set right a problem within minutes. These shops deal with every known car accessory in the world, right down from stickers to sun film to LCD screens in the car to pressure horns which just force a pedestrian to make way.

They pushed the car to the nearest car repair shop. "That's a way to digest the kebabs," exclaimed Girish. All of them chose to ignore the remark.

The cars were packed bumper-to-bumper yet there was enough space to carry out work around them.

"Out here, even if you fill up each inch of space available, there is still space for more. Look at those guys working under the car."

"Ever travelled by a blue-line bus or a van?"

"No, why?" asked Uday.

"The bus is fully packed with people, with people spilling beyond the footboard of the bus. Some of them would even be in the danger of falling off and coming under the rear wheels of the bus, yet the conductor will ask the commuters inside to make space. *'Itni jagah khaali padi hai.* Please move! Move! You in the red shirt, make space.' The practical impossibility does not matter and all that matters is the pressing need to squeeze the maximum out of the little that is available."

Maximum for minimum…

"*Lo jee,* sir. I've fixed your car."

"What was the problem?" Dinesh asked.

"Nothing, sir. *Kachra aa gaya tha* carburetter *mein.* I have now fixed it and it will not trouble you any more."

Dinesh wasn't sure if that was an accurate assessment but it didn't bother him. They paid the money and since the car was a Toyota, a premium was naturally attached to the fixing charges. Since they were all smartly dressed with women, an added premium was factored over and above that.

They thanked the man and made their way back. As they sped back, Dinesh noticed a Maruti 800 being fitted with a 1,000 watts Blaunpunkt music system. The red car had a fancy sunroof too.

"With the temperature in summer touching 48 degree celsius in New Delhi, the sunroof would surely be useful," he thought.

"And a 1,000 watts music system would surely ensure that nobody would travel in the car any more," said Uday and they all burst into laughter. The customer turned around and glared at them only to discover them well out of the striking range.

It does not matter in a city where it's all about being noticed. People can go to any extent to be noticed even it means making an ass of themselves. Dinesh referred to it as the 'Rakhi-Sawant-syndrome' where the only way to draw huge amounts of attention to yourself is to be more ludicrous and appear more stupid. Be it the loud Louis Vuitton bags that screams LV from every stitch to the Jimmy Choos, from the shopping bags labelled Calvin Klein or Zara carried by most to the casual conversation invariably drawn to the mention of a fine dining experience at the 'Bukhara', they all scream for attention, 'look at me!'

The guy at the Khan Market workshop has the sunroof and a big music system that will help attract attention as he drives around the M-block market in GK I with the windows rolled down hoping that it will catch the attention of the oversized Punjabi young women gorging on *papdi chaat* at Prince Paan Bhandar.

Maximum for minimum… always!

# Lutyens' Arteries

"Come, let me show you the first underground market," Dinesh exclaimed, barely able to hide his excitement.

To him it was always fascinating to be visiting Palika Bazaar especially when it had just been thrown open to the public. He loved to imagine a giant truck or bus moving over his head whist he shopped around in the sheer comfort of an air-conditioned underground *bazaar*.

"Sir, you want stylish belt? Original leather, only ₹20," said one of the shop attendants as he cracked the belt in the air like a whip. As the customer moves on, he comes face-to-face with another attendant who cracks the belt like a whip to even better effect.

Dinesh's first trip to Palika Bazaar was still deeply etched out in his mind. He had gone there with his parents and he remembered being agape with excitement at having seen so many shops buried under the ground.

Rows and rows of shops selling housecoats or gowns that almost all middle-aged women wear regularly, 365 days of the year. It is not the saree, but the housecoat that is the national costume of the country. Whether it is to visit the local market to buy groceries, to buy milk from Mother Diary or simply to walk in the park, the housecoat has become something of an attire worn by most, if not all, middle-aged women in

Delhi. Their raison d' être consists of cutting vegetable on a charpoi atop the rooftop of their house for *achaar* on a warm winter afternoon or to indulge in their favourite pastime, which is knitting. Just as the housecoat has assumed cult status, knitting too has evolved to become the national pastime in Delhi. Like they say it's world famous in Delhi! Knitting a sweater is a full-time job, so much so that a regular job is seen as coming in the way. Most women working in the government offices can be found knitting away in parks that adjoin most government buildings during their lunch hours that start at 10 a.m. and continue until 3 p.m. The others are busy munching away at groundnuts with the shells finding their way into the grass, where they will lie, waiting to be cleaned by a government sweeper who turns up once a month! The women knit and the men play cards. It's all sorted!

Dinesh wondered if the north Indian attire with its curious fixation to the *naarha* had anything to do with the obesity metrics of most middle-aged women in Delhi, especially the ones staying in Sarojini Nagar, Lajpat Nagar, Karol Bagh, etc. The *naarha* does not offer the wearer a sanity check on where the midriff is headed. Be it the *chaddi* or the *salwar*, the *naarha* expands to fill the space available, much like work that expands to fill the time available. If the *naarha* or the much popular elastic gets replaced by buttons or hooks, we might see some hope in the wellness quotient of most.

Punctuating the rows of shops selling housecoats are the shops selling electronic items including DVDs and MP3s. You could get an MP3 with the latest hits for under ₹100 and the quality would be great. After a good round of shopping, one could enjoy a mango shake or even *golgappa*s before returning home. Visiting Palika Bazaar with the family was a joy and over time, the market had made its way to the must see list of most people visiting Delhi. "Let's go to Palika," used to be the common refrain and the Fiat car used to roll out of the houses, fully laden with the entire family and its cargo of excited Indian tourists.

"Sir*jee*, triple X, triple X... latest *wallah,*" whispered one boy as Dinesh walked into the market twenty years later. The transformation was hard to understand. Gone were the well laid out shops and the shiny look of, what was clearly, one of the highlights of New Delhi. The leaking roofs which were almost on the point of giving way because of the seepage were there for all to see at regular intervals. The toilets and the white tiles on the walls smeared red with betel juice. The shops, on the other hand, had all become dens of vice.

What was, at one point in time, a pleasurable family experience was replaced with intolerable moments by young guys strutting around in their fake designer jeans looking for pirated DVDs or any woman that they could lay their eyes on. Dinesh hardly saw many women this time around and it didn't come as a surprise.

"Sir*jee*, latest triple X *chahiye?*" Dinesh was not sure what he meant by the latest in triple X. The same mechanised motions, the same back and forth and the orgasm or the 'pop-shot' as the more trendy preferred to say. How would a latest version change except sink you deeper to the depths of depravity and perversion? "This is in 5.1 surround sound, sir*jee.*" Now how was that going to make a difference? If anybody were to play it at that volume, the neighbours would get a hard on without even having had to buy the CD.

"This is the original one, sir, copied from the master print." Most of these pirated prints were copied with such brazenness that even the FBI warning that comes up at the start of the movie found its way to the screen. Most of the original copies have the FBI warning stating that it is a criminal offence to sell pirated DVDs and that a fine of US $250,000 or imprisonment of up to six months or both could be meted out to an offender. Some of the good copies even have a ticker tape running at the bottom of the screen which states 'Distributor copy, Not-for-sale'. Clearly the menace of piracy starts at a nascent stage in the life of a movie.

The *bazaar* of vice is nestled in the midst of Connaught Place that was designed by Sir Edward Lutyens. The inner circle and the outer circle with internal arteries linking one with the other was still a marvel to Dinesh. He had always admired the design as no two lanes were the same and the beauty lay in retaining this. "Sheer charm," he sighed.

Garment shops, artefacts, restaurants (some dating back to the British era), the ever popular fast food joint called Wimpy's, the much sought after cold coffee from D'Pauls, flavoured milk from Keventers, and shammi kebabs from Wengers among other popular joints made C.P. what it was. During his college days, Wimpy's used to be the rendezvous point to pick up women and the coffee at D'Pauls rarely had any taste to it. Yet, he used to frequent it because it was just so popular and cheap. D'Pauls has become more popular with inquisitive tourists from South India visiting the café to look for an Octopus, little knowing that the name was all that was similar to the real 'Paul' which predicted the World Cup football winners.

There were other stores too: book shops, watch shops, a hobby centre and of course, half a dozen film halls—that was a landmark in itself. That was the time when the Plaza used to screen porn films in its morning shows that started at nine in the morning. Dinesh always thought that anyone wanting to watch porn at nine in the morning had to be stark raving mad and a pervert. But all the shows, even then, used to run to a full house.

For all its illegality, the method used to be as simple as it could be. The theatre owners used to take an unknown, obscure Malayalam film that had been certified by the Censor Board and insert scenes from a blue film at regular intervals into the main film. The film would start innocuously, meander its way through the grind and pow, the porn scenes would start, back to the regular scenes and pow, again! The shows used to play to packed houses and though Dinesh had heard so much about them, he never wanted to nor needed to be part of the madding perverted lot of desperados. Many of his friends stayed away too although he knew of many who succumbed to curiosity, only to come back with total disgust writ large all over their faces. The porn scenes that were inserted were from the south Indian brigade which was anything but interesting. It was crude, vulgar and uninteresting with oversized women and overfed men grabbing at each other in various forms of undress. For a deprived society, deprived of mind and exposure or release, this was a blessing in disguise (read—porn in censored film). The theatre*wallah*s made good money until one day it got too much of publicity by word of mouth. The movie they were screening was a Malayalam film strangely titled *Chora Chuvanna Chora* (Blood Red Blood) and the authorities raided the premises, seized the prints and stopped the shows.

The theatre now shows religious films in its morning shows! There is, of course no taker for religion at nine in the morning. It's only sex that is relevant at any time of the day or night.

Palika Bazaar was replete with shops peddling pirated DVDs, software packages, CD-ROMs, blue films and sex toys. It was not just a family experience any more. Dinesh wondered how an openly illegal activity, such as selling blue films, could flourish in the capital where even prostitution is not legalised. How India, the land of the Mahatma and where the stork still comes to visit a couple, could have such a soft underbelly. Although the existence of such shops is common knowledge, yet the law enforcement agencies do nothing about it. The agencies had conducted a raid once to apprehend the shopkeepers indulging in such acts only to be beaten black and blue by the other shopkeepers who wanted to protect their brethren. The agency officials beat a hasty retreat.

Everything is transitional as periods of strictness get replaced by periodic bouts of nonchalance and frivolity. Episodes of raids result in pandemonium and all the illegal stuff goes underground, only to resurface a day or two later with renewed vigour.

The pirated movies are available on the next day of their release and the Hollywood flicks are available here even before their release in India. The pornographic section is a riot. The variety and range would put Hugh Hefner to shame. There is a Russian collection, a Mexican, even animals, name it and the shopkeeper will oblige. All this priced at under ₹100 and open to bargain. The one with the 5.1 surround sound is more expensive, though.

The sex toys are an addition. Dinesh always thought that these were found in the by lanes of US or Bangkok, but these were now available in the rapidly deteriorating confines of the underground market. A sex doll, priced at ₹5,000 (for a basic model, whatever that means) to ₹50,000 is available here. If you make an enquiry, the shop owner gives you a once over and then barks a command to a *chhotu* who scurries through the labyrinth of shop lanes and returns with a plastic bag.

"*Koi nai* film *aayee hai kya?*" Dinesh asked during one such visit to the *bazaar*. The shopkeeper gave him a once over and then looked at his wife. "What do you want?" he asked rather impersonally. Dressed as they were, they were clearly in the wrong place. Dinesh regretted having brought his wife along, but it was too late now.

Dinesh asked him for the latest Hollywood film and in so saying placed his mobile on the table in front of him.

*"Arre chhotu, dikha de sahib ko."* There are so many *chhotu*s in this city.

These traders have a sense of sniffing out the regular, genuine buyers from the routinely sent decoys of the law enforcement agencies. The traders had a new danger; sting operations being conducted by TV channels that expose the vicious underbelly of a once popular shopping area.

"Where did you buy this mobile?" asked the shop owner, picking up his mobile and scanning the menu. He did not think it necessary to check with him.

"Bought it from Singapore," Dinesh replied.

"Hmmm... nice phone!" Dinesh wasn't sure about what he was up to but it did not take him long to figure out what he was doing. He was examining his phone to make sure that this was not an improvised spy-cam recording the goings-on within the underground market. He moved from one menu bar to the other and then finally came back to the main screen. "Do you have any specific movie in mind?" he sounded more informal and friendlier now as he was now convinced that Dinesh was indeed a genuine buyer.

"Can I see that DVD there?" asked Dinesh's wife pointing to the top shelf out of the line of sight. Dinesh could just read *The Wedding....* The shop owner ignored her. She asked again and again she was ignored.

"What is the guy's problem? Why can he not show the DVD to me? I want to see *The Wedding Planner*."

Dinesh looked up at the guy in front of him. "Why don't you want to show that DVD to my wife?" he asked questioningly and a trifle annoyed at the man for ignoring his wife.

The shop owner leaned forward and whispered in his ear, "Sirjee, that's a blue film. It is not *The Wedding Planner*. It is *The Wedding Nights*."

An embarrassed Dinesh quickly walked out of the store with his wife in tow. How things had changed. How rapidly the underground market had personified the concept around which it was built. The underground market was indeed the place where business of dubious nature was conducted. The market had been true to its name!

As he walked out, trying hard to explain to his wife the reason for his swift exit, he saw a police officer in uniform asking for a DVD from one of the shops. He slipped it into his shirt and walked away without paying the shop owner. As he walked up the stairs, the plastic bag slipped out of the shirt and dropped on to the floor.

Written across the plastic DVD cover with a blue sketch pen was the title of the film, *DPS Kaand*.

# I Did Not Know but Basically

'Ding-Dong. Ding-Dong.'

The doorbell rang incessantly. Dinesh was woken up from his deep slumber at nine in the morning. These weekend binges were something that he needed to get over with. The landlord was at the door with his betel stained teeth and scratching away at the wire meshed door.

"Still sleeping, were you?" he exclaimed not even bothering to apologise for having woken him up.

"I wanted to tell you," he continued without waiting for an answer, "that you have to pay 10 per cent extra rent, since the new year has started. This is according to the initial understanding we had."

"Oh no!" Dinesh exclaimed. "He couldn't have woken me up so early to tell me this!" he wondered.

"I don't think you should have an objection since you would have also got an increment by now," the monologue continued. He could, easily, have had the conversation with himself pretending to acknowledge his unseen presence.

He wanted to tell the landlord that he was not working his ass off sixteen hours a day just to make sure that he could pay his rent. He knew that it would have been an exercise in futility, so without wanting to prolong his presence in the house, Dinesh nodded in agreement.

He smiled a half smile, perhaps half thinking that he could have asked for more and ruing the potential of having lost the opportunity of a possible additional 5 per cent.

Dinesh went through the morning ablutions and then headed to the market to buy bread, butter and eggs for the house. He hated these errands and often wished he had someone who could scurry across and fetch them for him.

On the way, he spotted the usual sight of an open rickshaw ferrying commercial ice to the local sweetmeat shop where a natural extension of trade is also to have a *golgappa* and *chaat* stall. The ice was exposed to all the elements of nature including the dust and the fumes generated by the cars passing by. It would then be hauled onto its final resting place with the aid of rusted hooks and placed on unwashed, weary gunny bags. These commercial ice slabs are broken into smaller manageable sizes and put into the spicy concoction that is poured into a *golgappa* or an ice box containing your favourite soft drink or worse still, your paneer. Paneer, which is a form of cottage cheese or curdled milk (facilitated with the aid of citric acid) and left to hang in a muslin bag to separate the water, is placed atop a slab of commercial ice in order keep it cool and fresh. Not sure if it ensures the second expectation though, far from it. This is the most unhygienic form of water and accounts for the million typhoid cases that the city reports with alarming frequency.

'Honk... Honk...,' and he instinctively moved aside. The car zipped past him as if the driver was involved in a hit-and-run case. Dinesh saw the car move away from the road to the dusty side road and come back to the road in order to avoid the speed-breaker.

One friend named Geoff Pratt, a Britisher, on a tourist visit to India once asked Dinesh whether the people in the country were extremely punctual and time conscious. Dinesh smiled at the incredible thought and asked him why he thought so.

"Oh because, wherever I look, I see people jumping traffic signals, driving on the wrong side of the road, overtaking from the wrong lane, jumping over iron grills and abusing other people who come in the way, not to mention the incessant honking. They must be in a real rush to get somewhere."

Dinesh had looked at him and smiled. "Not time conscious Geoff. Just force of habit."

The market was its busy self and uncaring as usual. Dinesh saw many parents holding their children and leading them to the market. He wondered why the children were always on the wrong side of the road whereas their parents were always on the pavement side. He could understand why the pavements were despised by pedestrians. The pavements were forever occupied by fruit vendors selling their wares or a *mochi* engaged in his trade. There is no space on the pavement and the pedestrian is forced to walk on the road with his or her child on the side of the road where he or she should not be. The pavements provide space options to ones who wish to start a trade such as selling books, selling plastic items, selling fruits and utensils, etc. And the flyovers provide a housing option underneath it. Who says the government does not take care of its poor? Of course they do. That is one reason so many roads (and therefore pavements) are being laid and so many flyovers being built. It is to offer a convenient opportunity to trade and a stay option to the less fortunate.

Dinesh bought the bread and eggs and passed a meat shop. He looked through the front door for a second as he walked. The daily supply of chicken had just arrived and was being offloaded from the Mahindra Apé. Over fifty grilled containers stacked one on top of another and each container stuffed with live chicken barely able to breathe. The grilled containers needed a good scrub as did the chickens inside. It is hard to fathom how these chickens survive the ordeal of travel. He was sure that many of them die en-route but still do get sold anyway. All dead chickens look the same.

He could never bring himself to buying a live chicken and then getting it killed for his *tandoori* nights. Not because of the abhorrent way in which the killing is conducted but more so because he did not want to be the one initiating the killing. The killing was not for him, he would assure his subconscious mind, he only happened to buy it and so he always bought chicken that had already been killed. It made him feel less guilty.

He remembered the first time he had accompanied his father to buy fish and chicken from the INA market, one of the filthiest markets one could buy non-vegetarian items from. There are two lanes of open shops stacked to the full with fishes of all varieties, chicken (some already killed and placed on slabs of commercial ice and others live, awaiting their execution), mutton and some shops also dealing in turkeys (the live ones tied to a post). The turkeys are in high demand during Christmas, whereas the others all year round. Even the fishes can be bought live, especially the catfish. This is one sure way of validating their freshness. Retrieved from the waters and hacked only for your culinary pleasure!

The place stinks to the heavens and is infested with flies. There is a steady flow of residual water from the melting of commercial ice, cleaning miscellaneous items that find its way to the open drains. Surprisingly, there are a majority of foreigners too who buy their non-vegetarian items from here. That was confusing for Dinesh as he always thought that the entire foreign clan buys these items from either PigPo in Jor Bagh or Khan Market. Perhaps not! The men in these open shops wave tattered pieces of dirty cloth over their large display of fish in front of them to keep the flies away, only to allow them to return once they stop. The oozing of blood from the cut pieces of fish ensure the redness of gills of other fish… a sign of freshness!

"Chicken *kaise diye?*" asked Dinesh's father.

"₹80 a kilo," he answered preferring to focus his attention on the foreigners.

"Give me that one there," said his father pointing at the one already butchered and cleaned for consumption.

"How many pieces?" he asked. You usually tell whether you would like to have the chicken cut in eight pieces or twelve.

"*Barah* pieces *kar dena.*"

As the chicken was being cut, Dinesh noticed another gentleman asking for a chicken as well. But he wanted it to be "absolutely fresh".

"Chicken *achcha hai na?*" he asked.

"*Bilkul,*" the shop owner replied. Dinesh wondered whether that question would ever elicit a response like, "No, this is stale but we want to sell it anyway." That's not going to happen. This is common everywhere. "*Sabzi taazi hai na?*", "*Maal purana to nahin hai?*", "*Yeh cheez kharab to nahin hogi?*", etc. A psychological reassurance is always sought, but even a dishonest answer is acceptable as long as they conform to the buyers' beliefs or what they want to hear.

"Give me that one," said the stranger pointing to a large chicken fluttering inside the grilled cage. One of the assistants reached inside and amid the fluttering and the ensuing stampede, pulled it out. Proceeding to pull its wings back and holding the neck back with his index finger and thumb, he reached down for his rusted knife and in one swift back and forth motion had the neck severed. He then casually dumped the chicken into what clearly looked like a dirty, bloodstained wooden box. Dinesh could hear the fluttering sounds as the chicken made a futile attempt to breathe. The fluttering grew less pronounced with each passing second and eventually stopped. The assistant bent down to retrieve it and continued to pluck its feathers before handing it over for the cutting ritual. Dinesh thought he saw the chicken move a wee bit as the last bit of oxygen left its lungs.

"Here you go," said the shop owner extending a plastic bag stuffed with the chicken pieces. Dinesh's father took the plastic bag, paid for it and they left. As they were walking past, Dinesh saw similar rituals being repeated and when they had completed the stretch, he had become immune and more desensitised to the sights and sounds around him. The constant exposure to something, however revolting, always leads to a process of desensitisation.

The mutton in the form of fully skinned goats hung from rusted hooks in each of the shops they passed. Some redder than the other with cut pieces neatly arranged on the slab below. The shop owner was busy cutting the shoulder or the leg part with his knife that was skilfully placed between his big toe and his index toe. The meat would glide over the knife and the cut pieces dropped onto the platform. The platform would be covered with other cut pieces and waste products from the cut meat that was not meant to be consumed and held no nutritional value at all. The shopkeeper would ensure that he maximises his gains even from the waste products. He would sell it as dog food.

That was a long time ago. Nowadays, frozen foods have monopolised the market. With more working couples, there has been a paradigm shift in the way breakfast, lunch and dinner is prepared and consumed. Not so long ago, the breakfast

111

would be a sit down affair with the wife preparing hot *rotis* or bread-toast while one read the newspaper and drank milk from the glass. Lunch would be an essential meal in the day, typically packed by your wife or parents, which one would carry to office in a three-tier container held in place with a locked-clamp at the top. Usually, a metal spoon kept the clamp in place. Dinner would always be with the family and the eldest, usually the father, would ensure that the family always eats their dinner together.

Times have moved to a quick bowl of oats cooked in milk and brought to a boil by the microwave. One either misses lunch or grabs a sandwich from Barista or Café Coffee Day. Rarely does one get to eat dinner with the family because the husband and wife are working and usually do not return home at the same time. Food is cooked and eaten in front of a TV set which is showing your favourite soap at all different times of the night. Since time is never fixed, the frozen foods serve their purpose.

Almost anything and everything is frozen with some even not needing refrigeration. There are frozen peas, meat, rice and other such items that you can buy. The warmth in relationships has been replaced by the heat in this city and frozen foods have led to freezing relationships that once thrived in the warmth of love, care and kindness.

Times have changed to such an extent that you can now cook restaurant-type food at home and there are more restaurants promising you home cooked food. The roles stand interchanged and no one minds it.

# Boot and Reboot—A Hard Drive

A quick drive away from his place in Malviya Nagar is Nehru Place and Dinesh hit it with a vengeance. He was desperately looking for a change after his stint with the High Commission, because he had served over five years in a place that he had grown to love but also grown out of love with. His career curve was flattening and he was stagnating. It was time to move on to fairer climes.

The work life at the High Commission is ideal for any girl or woman who is married or is planning to get married. The fact remains that there was no place more secure than within the premises of a High Commission. One is well taken care of, there is security and unless you are looking and acting desperate, there is no way anyone will cause grief to you by unwanted sexual advances. The work timings are fixed and rarely do employees sit late or expected to sit late. At closure, the diplomat comes around asking you to wrap up as he or she has to close the Mission (only a diplomat of a particular rank or above has the authority to open or close a Mission) and one obliges most willingly. Unlike most Indians, foreigners do have a life outside work!

Though its importance as a financial centre has declined in recent years, Nehru Place houses the headquarters and offices of several Indian and multinational firms and rivals with other financial centres in the metropolis like Connaught Place, Gurgaon, Bhikaji Cama Place, Rajendra Place and Noida. It is widely considered to be a major hub of South Delhi's information technology industry.

Named after the first Prime Minister of India, Jawaharlal Nehru, its main commercial district was built in the early 1980s, and consisted of several four-floor buildings, that flank a large pedestrian courtyard, built over an underground parking. Although poorly maintained, most of the original structures are still in use.

Nehru Place is the hub for all forms of IT hardware, such as personal computers, servers, networking equipment, software, documentation services, and all allied services. Several manufacturers of computer hardware have their authorised dealerships located here, and it is often considered as a computer enthusiast's shopping area. In case you have little knowledge about the products and cannot distinguish the real one from the fake one, the authorised showrooms are the place where you should head, to make sure that you don't make a fool of yourself. Several businesses also build custom-specification personal computers and servers to order on-site, and many others are dedicated to hardware servicing. There are also firms that deal only in used and second-hand computer hardware, as well as small, one-room shops that sell software titles. One can find some of the best deals for hardware here.

One of the unique features of Nehru Place is the pervading informal atmosphere, akin to a flea market or a *bazaar*, in a place that deals in high technology products. You will find pavement sellers selling items such as printer toner cartridges, blank optical media, printer paper and even software from a small stall or cart. The prices of the products vary, depending on their quality as well as knowledge and the bargaining potential of the buyer. Here, you can see the free and democratic competition among hawkers who sell their products to potential buyers in the lobbies, streets and corners. Bargaining is widely tolerated, even expected, as most of the trading is done without proper documentation, such as cash receipts and bills, and it is possible to buy items at a lower price than they are marked with. A vibrant informal economy has developed due to abundant pirated software available for sale, which has led to legal action against many organisations operating from Nehru Place.

There are eateries aplenty. The hottest favourite is *rajma chawal* and almost every other eatery on the ground floor of each of the towers sell it. ₹10 a plate can give you a generous bowl of rice with rajma spread liberally on top of the rice with accompaniment of onion juliennes which are refilled should you ask for it. Great value for money and each of these places remain crowded during lunch hours.

The place is also inundated with placement agencies of all shapes and sizes. 'ABC Consultants' to 'XYZ Consultants' all dot the many towers that form an integral part of Nehru Place. There are specialised placement firms which deal with specific finance, administration or marketing profiles, others which deal with junior, medium or senior positions and so forth.

Dinesh had made multiple copies of his resume and waited patiently at the office of ABC Consultants. After what seemed like an eternity, he was called in, to be interviewed by a certain Mr Singh who kept examining his resume like it was a live bomb.

"So tell me something about yourself," he asked looking most distracted.

Dinesh wasn't sure if should be talking about his black hair, his eyes or that he could play carom well. His mind raced back to his need to make an extra buck that had led him to consider a summer job with a cigarette brand at Nehru Place a long time ago.

"Sir, would you like to try a Chancellor cigarette?" he said as he approached a person with blackened lips.

"No, thanks!" he said as he brushed past him.

This was not the summer job that Dinesh was looking forward to. Clad in a brown T-shirt with Chancellor written across it and with a satchel that contained Chancellor refills, Dinesh was doing his rounds in Nehru Place trying to sell to potential buyers. A couple of his school friends too had joined him as part of a peer pursuit. Both Tavish and Pratip were doing better than he did as they enjoyed the marketing experience. He didn't enjoy it as much.

They had interviewed for this summer job as many college going folks did during their summer break. At ₹50 a day, he could use the money.

He walked around in the sweltering heat partly frustrated and partly embarrassed at the prospect of selling cigarettes in the atrium area of Nehru Place.

"Hello, would you like to try a new cigarette?"

"Hey, Dinesh! How are you?"

His worst nightmare had come true. This was Mohnish, one of his classmates standing before him with a pirated CD in his hand.

"Oh, hi!" he said.

What's this that you are doing?" he asked. "Was he fucking blind or just bloody patronising?" Dinesh thought.

"Just a summer job, dude!" he replied almost apologetically.

"Oh, well all the best! I have got admission to Syracuse University and am leaving for US tomorrow. Take care, bye!"

Dinesh mumbled a feeble 'bye' in return.

He did not report to the marketing office and returned the 'uniform' and the cigarette packs back with Tavish to the marketing incharge the next day. "He is not well," is what Tavish told him.

That would not have been untrue. He felt sick and disappointed with himself.

Not sure why, but he did.

Now at the office of ABC Consultants it was déjà vu.

"I get a hard on when I look at a sexy babe," he almost wanted to say to break the sense of boredom that was writ large on the face of Mr Singh. But he decided against it. Dinesh gave him a brief of his education at Mount St Mary's school followed by the college that he graduated from, and then his jobs leading to his search for nirvana.

He asked him a few more questions and then told him that he would get back to him when a suitable opportunity arises. Dinesh took that as a 'no' and walked his way into another placement consultant. Same story, same response, same action. It was now time for a steamy plate of *rajma chawal*.

Filthy, disorganised and insufferable are some adjectives that come to mind when one is thinking of Nehru Place and the many sellers and hawkers that are visible all over the place. The eateries have no sense of hygiene and stray dogs and cats wander around freely while you are helping yourself to a plate of *rajma chawal* or the omnipresent *thali*. Many customers willingly drop some spoonfuls of the rice onto the ground in an attempt to feed the dogs and cats. The dogs hungrily gobble it up. Some of the dogs get into a vicious fight right in the middle of the eating place making the hungry customers run for cover. A cow stands at a distance chewing cud and dropping dung on the cemented atrium.

The pedestrian courtyard in the middle of the multiple towers is encroached on by pedlars who have set up shops selling everything from pornography to pirated software. To many, this is almost a mini-extension of Palika Bazaar. The parking lots are a personification of chaos unleashed with the most brutal force. Unauthorised parking coupled with the high-handed behaviour of the parking cartels has spelt the death knell of organised and civil conduct. The towers are in shambles with broken windows, leaking ducts, rusted coolers visible from below to the naked eye. Nehru Place has slipped into an abyss of depravation from where it cannot hope to ever extricate itself, just like Palika Bazaar.

*"Kaunsi* CD *chahiye, sa'ab?"* exclaimed a kid who looked to be barely fifteen years old.

Dinesh was surveying the software spread laid out on the pavement right in the middle of the tower area. Just as Palika Bazaar is a den of vice, Nehru Place can be well described as the den of software. Empty sleeves or jackets lie strewn around for you to look. If you appear interested, the boy will pass you an album that has the title and pictorial representation of the available software.

*"Yeh wallah,"* he said as he pointed to an AutoCAD 2007 CD pack.

*"Oye, chhotu,* get this one."

Off scampered *chhotu* to an undisclosed destination and returned with a black plastic bag that ostensibly contained the software.

*"Kitna?"* Dinesh asked.

*"Sau rupaye,"* said the pedlar rather uninterested.

Dinesh bargained for ₹70 knowing fully well that he may well be paying him ₹30 extra, but what the hell.

"Ok," said the pedlar and went to put the pirated CD onto a black plastic bag.

"Do you want anything else?" he asked. "I have the software key as well in case it interests you," so saying he shoved a list into his hand that had the software key to all popular software packages. Dinesh was tempted but declined the offer. The pedlar then went on to give Dinesh a handwritten note which listed the software key for the AutoCAD package that he had just bought. The deal was done for less than two dollars.

Dinesh then turned to leave and reached his car parked barely twenty metres away. As he turned he noticed an impressive tower building situated a distance away from the regular tower blocks.

Curious to know, he asked the parking attendant running in his direction to collect the parking fee of ₹10. "Listen *bhaiyya*, which office is this?"

"Oh, that's Microsoft," he said with an air of disdain.

# Made in Anywhere—Here

*"Roshan di Kulfi khane chalna hai."* It's been a long time and Dinesh also wanted to pick up some dry fruits from Roopak stores.

Until about 1930, the Karol Bagh area was an undeveloped jungle. The area was mainly residential with a large Muslim population until the exodus of many Muslims to Pakistan and an influx of refugees from West Punjab after partition in 1947, many of whom were traders. There also remains a sizeable Tamil-speaking population. Karol Bagh was home to a large Bengali community too, and has one of the oldest Durga Pujas in the city, though their numbers have now dwindled.

It would not be wrong to define Delhi as the metropolis of malls and marts. It boasts of markets of all kinds—if it has glitzy malls, it also has stately shopping arcades such as Connaught Place. But Ghaffar Market, in Karol Bagh, has always been in a different league.

This is the grey market for all those seeking 'imported' goods at less than the 'official prices'. Just like Nehru Market is a grey market for all kinds of software and hardware and Palika Bazaar for most things sleazy. The market, where many shops have no names, witnesses a horde of buyers almost every day. The goods are all imported through unofficial channels and all these goods eventually find their way to this market where nothing sells except *phoren* goods.

Any new launch can be found here even before its official launch in the country. The iPhone was available in Ghaffar Market much before its launch in Europe. Similarly, PlayStation 3 (PS 3) was available at Ghaffar a month before its launch in India. "It is a market for those who do not look for bills or guarantees, but wish to stay ahead," says a shopkeeper. And while talking to people, it seems there is no dearth of such customers. There is no fear of law here, sadly.

But while the prices are a steal in Ghaffar Market, one needs to be a skilful negotiator and a risk-taker to get the best deal. There are no warranties and you need to have a great degree of faith, hope and trust when you buy these imported goods from this imported market.

Dinesh bought his first Casio digital diary from here. Those were the days of Nintendo pocket games which were so well flaunted in schools and colleges alike. And if you had one of those, then you were ahead of the times. There were no mobile phones at that point of time and a digital diary was quite sought after. After much bargaining, he had managed to get one for ₹1,800.

Earlier while he was working at the South African High Commission, one of his friends had bought a locked mobile phone for him from South Africa and Dinesh did not know what to do with it. "Take it to Ghaffar," said his friend, "and they will unlock it for you." He paid heed and went to Ghaffar, identified a shop and handed the guy at the shop the new phone.

"What is the problem?" he asked as he examined the phone with a certain sense of disdain. He was obviously used to dealing with more high-end expensive phones.

"It is locked," said Dinesh, not knowing how to technically represent the problem he was faced with and for which he needed a solution to.

The shop-owner smiled. "So you need the key?" he said and laughed at his own attempt at humour. Dinesh did not react. "It will cost you ₹300."

"I can pay ₹200," Dinesh countered.

"Ok, then it's done for ₹250," he said and went into the darker recesses of his shop without even waiting for a response. He returned ten minutes later and handed Dinesh the phone. "That will be ₹250," he said.

Till some time ago, Ghaffar Market was famous for garments, cosmetics, crockery, electronic gadgets, toys and shoes. Now it is better known for being an imported electronics market. The market is also a favourite with domestic tourists who form the largest chunk of the customers today.

Dinesh had an unexplainable aversion to the place. Apart from the fact that it was disorganised, scary with a million shops crammed into one another and by-lanes that hardly existed, he dreaded to think what would happen if a fire or a bomb were to explode here.

Karol Bagh was the target of a terrorist attack when a bomb exploded in Ghaffar Market. At least 18 people were feared killed and over 100 injured as New Delhi was rocked by serial blasts in three busy market places. Two blasts took place each in the central Connaught Place area and a market in the Greater Kailash area, whereas one blast took place at Ghaffar Market in the Karol Bagh area during rush hour. Three unexploded bombs were also recovered near India Gate, Regal cinema hall and Central Park in C.P.

Indian Mujahedeen, an Islamic militant group, claimed responsibility. An email sent to local media outlets just before the blasts read, 'You are going to get message of death.'

Frantic and desperate searches went through the city hospitals by the relatives of the victims of the bomb blasts that rocked Delhi on a Saturday evening. Some got lucky while others continued their search knowing deep down that this was going to be a futile search, however hoping. There is great strength in hope in this country. We hope that things will get better, we hope that the politicians will do something, we hope we will not forget such instances of cowardice but it takes only weeks, sometime only days, to move on with our lives without so much of an insinuation of such an act ever having taken place.

One of the Dinesh's neighbours in Malviya Nagar bought an impressive Sony music system from one of the audio shops in Ghaffar. The music system for all its hype died down on him a few weeks later. He took it with him to the shop in Ghaffar from where he had bought it and the shop-owner was quick to replace it with another system without even asking him once for a receipt or any document that evidenced the sale. No questions asked. A few more visits and a few more buys from the same shop and you enter the shop owner's circle of trust. All deals here are conducted in cash but there is an unwritten code of ethics that is hard to beat.

"Sirjee, can we also start this business?" Girish had asked after having purchased his 3G iPhone from the same shopkeeper from whom he had earlier bought an HDMI enabled DVD player, a home theatre system and a Sony Bravia LCD TV.

"*Oye kake*, it is not that easy. You youngsters think it's easy to start something like this. These kinds of businesses take years and years to perfect. We travel out to many of the select and identified foreign locations to buy the displayed items. Ok, here is the secret. We bring them in through a well established network with the custom officials without paying any duty.

The settlement with officials happens every month and both sides are happy at the end. We also get regular travellers who approach us and offer to sell some stuff which has just recently been purchased from abroad. Both systems work fine and both make a decent profit. You kids should enjoy life and leave these businesses to us," he said and chuckled to be joined soon by some of his colleagues.

"Do you think that you could get me a handycam from Singapore?" asked Hitesh, as Dinesh sat having a drink of rum and coke with him. He had since moved on from the advertising agency he had been working with for some many years and landed a job with another advertising house. He seemed to land a plum job almost instantly. Dinesh did not hold a grudge to what he had done to him earlier. He had done what he thought was right and if it had not been Hitesh, it could well have been someone else who Dinesh did not even know. At least this devil had a face and was not a faceless stranger. After he had moved on, Dinesh had met him and told him of what he knew. He had then apologised and stated that he did what he did to survive in this city where options were running out fast. Dinesh had decided to forgive him.

Dinesh was scheduled to go to Singapore in a week's time on an official assignment and had walked into his house to borrow a suitcase that he could carry with him.

"Sure," he replied. Dinesh had no intent of picking one for himself so this request seemed easy to accommodate. Anyway, Hitesh was paying for his stuff. "Which one? Do you have a specific model or type in mind?"

"It's a Sony, model no. E7654. Should cost around ₹20K or so there, but out here it is priced at over ₹30K." This was so quintessential Hitesh. Always after the latest gizmos and gadgets. His wife Maya was nowhere to be seen and Dinesh did not want to ask him either lest the issue of Nisha cropped up again.

"Ok, sure," Dinesh replied as Hitesh looked at his watch impatiently. Dinesh reckoned that this was his polite way of asking him to get lost. He got up as Hitesh bid his bye with his mobile cradled between his head and his shoulder. As Hitesh walked into the other room, Dinesh thought he heard the name Mahira. "Wasn't that the name of his immediate boss he used to work with at the advertising firm?" he let the thought pass.

"So what?" Dinesh thought. "What's the big deal?"

Little did Dinesh know that it was indeed a big deal.

Dinesh and his wife had a great trip to Singapore and after having purchased the handycam from the SunTec Mall in Singapore, they were on their way back after a week of fine living at the Four Seasons hotel in Singapore. As they arrived at the New Delhi airport, Dinesh turned to his wife.

"I think I should head for the Green Channel and tell them that I have this handycam valued around ₹24,000. Since we are allowed ₹12,000 each as duty-free, I do not think we should have a problem. What do you say?" Dinesh told his wife. She nodded in agreement since they had not purchased any other dutiable item from Singapore. Little did they realise what was there in store for them.

Dinesh boldly strode towards the Green Channel in a misplaced sense of confidence. As a custom officer turned to look at him he said, "Hello, sir. I have this handycam that I have purchased in Singapore and it has cost me around ₹24,000.

125

I have the bill too. This would be duty-free, isn't it since both my wife and I have a ₹12,000 duty-free allowance available?"

The customs official looked at each other and then looked at him. He thought one of them was trying to stifle a laugh.

"It does not work like that," he said it matter-of-factly. "Each of you have a ₹12,000 duty-free allowance but you cannot combine the individual entitlement against one product of the combined value. You will have to pay the duty difference."

Dinesh felt like an arsehole and the ground beneath him seemed to give way. All that he had to do was to have walked past them confidentially and they would not even have bothered. Instead, here he was in front of these vultures, voluntarily asking them to take his rear. He tried to plead innocence but knew that they had him by the short and curlies. The custom officer continued, "Which model is it?"

"I have the bill."

"Oh we know how bills are made," he replied as he referred to a thick manual which listed out the current prices of all audio and video equipment. He had not even bothered to look up and acknowledge Dinesh's integrity. The default assumption being that every person is a crook and deserves to be treated as one. Guilty until proven innocent.

"That will be ₹7,000 as duty," he said as he concluded the assessment. "You want to pay by dollars or rupees."

Dinesh thought of calling up Hitesh and appraising him of this development which would invariably add to his 'landed cost' but decided against it. He was too tired and just wanted to get over this never-ending ordeal.

"Please, I cannot afford so much. This is for a friend. Let's settle for ₹4,000 as that is all I have," he said most truthfully.

"Ok," he said. "You will have to pay it in rupees then, not in dollars."

"But I only have dollars," Dinesh said most exasperated. "I have just landed and have yet to change my currency."

"You see that Thomas Cook counter there?" said one of the customs officials pointing to the blue board behind his counter. "You can change your money from there."

Dinesh walked to the Thomas Cook counter where the desk clerk changed the money for him. He walked back to the customs official and offered the money.

"Keep it down," he hissed. "Don't give it to me so openly. Put it inside the passport and hand over the passport to me. You see, the vigilance guys might be around." Dinesh did as was told.

Barely had the passport been given to him that he returned it, but this time the money had magically disappeared.

"You are free to go," he said in a hurried tone.

"But what if I get stopped at the gate?"

"Just tell them that you have met with Mr Sharma. He will understand," he said with a knowing wink.

Dinesh's wife was seated most patiently on the chair and once the ordeal was over, he motioned her over. She joined him as they wheeled the trolley that had two castors wanting to go in two different directions. Everything and everybody seemed to be having a mind of their own except himself.

Predictably, he was stopped at the gate. *"Kya laaye ho?"* asked the customs man at the gate as he examined his passport. "Laptop, video camera, etc."

"I have met Mr Sharma already," said Dinesh most obediently as he was tutored to say. He looked up towards the customs booth that he had left hundred feet back. Mr Sharma seemed to be waiting for the look as he waved animatedly as a gesture of acknowledgement and indicating that he be let go.

He reciprocated the acknowledgement. "Ok, you can go," he said without a second thought as he handed his passport back to him.

Dinesh pushed the trolley through and as he was exiting the main gate, he looked back at the scene that he was leaving behind. He saw a Sikh gentleman wheeling in his oversized trolley stacked to the top with a 42 inch Sony Bravia LED, a Panasonic music system, and two laptops in full view and stacked one on top of another. He passed through the Green Channel, gave a knowing nod to the custom official manning the gate and walked through without even so much as a pause.

"I would probably get to see those items at Ghaffar Market tomorrow," Dinesh murmured to himself.

The traders have an operation that is similar to the Russian women who transit India (mainly Delhi, Mumbai) regularly. For the traders, the items bought by them sell in the markets and for the latter, it is the Russians themselves who are traded.

The Russians, Chechens and many others from the CIS nations regularly travel to India on cheap airline tickets and a tourist visa, and are available either as escorts or for the night at clubs and farmhouses where they perform for a private audience connected through a common agent or pimp. These advertisements, in colour, are regularly printed in all reputed newspapers and the intent is evident. The operation is conducted in a streamlined manner to such an extent that a Diners card or an American Express card that is rarely accepted by any commercial establishment is accepted here without even a service charge. The money they make during this short 'business trip' is more than adequate to fund their air travel, stay and yet leave a sizeable margin of profit at the end of their stay. They then go back to their country and return after a period of time to make more money and the cycle continues. Occasionally there are raids at the better known farmhouses and they are arrested, only to be released the next day once the right price has been delivered to the police in-charge. For all the money that they make, the risk is worth taking.

It is the Indian fixation for a fair skin that drives this behaviour and ensures that the 'world's oldest profession' never goes out of business. Most of the advertisements that appear in the classifieds openly mention "5-star" or "7-star" service suggesting escort services with Russians, Mexicans, Arabs and the like. The Russians are much in demand as they are fair and as one of his friends told Dinesh, aggressive in bed. For most Indians, this is a great combination, used to as they are to a more subservient, docile woman at home, this presents an irresistibly inviting contrast. The prices are affordable too as a customer gets to have a *phoren* babe without having to shell out an exorbitant sum that he would have had to pay if he were to negotiate for an Indian model or an air hostess. The *phoren* alternative assures them of the best bang for buck—economy and satisfaction guaranteed. Maximum for minimum...

Dinesh handed over the handycam to Hitesh a week later. He could not go personally so he had it sent through one of the office helpers. He tried calling Hitesh over his mobile but it was switched off. The office helper returned in the evening and Dinesh sought a confirmation from him. "Sir*jee*, Hitesh *sa'ab to nahin the*, so I have handed over the handycam to his wife," he said.

"I hope you gave it to the right person at the right address."

"Yes, sir. The woman said she was his wife and that she would hand it over to him. She was a tall and *gori aurat*. I have even taken a receiving note from her," the office helper continued, appearing worried at the looming possibility of having given the handycam to another stranger.

"Tall and *gori*. That did not sound like Maya," Dinesh thought. "Maya was dark and that was something Hitesh always held against her. Then who was this?"

"Show me the receiving note," he said to the office helper.

Scrawled across the piece of paper that was handed over to him by the office helper were the words, 'Received one handycam, thanks'. Signed with a flourish underneath was the name, Mahira.

The 'whites' had once again triumphed over the 'blacks'.

# Slip between Third Leg

"Pakistan *Murdabad*, Pakistan *Murdabad*," roared the crowd in unison.

Dinesh looked around, partly bewildered and partly confused. Not because he was immune to such slogans one hears almost every day at every nook and cranny of New Delhi, nor because he wanted to feign ignorance of the obvious hostility so unabashedly expressed during every cricket match between India and Pakistan, but because this was not an India-Pakistan match. Not by a long shot. The match being played at the Feroz Shah Kotla maidan in New Delhi was a one-day international between India and England.

"Indiaaaah, Indiaaaah," roared another section of the crowd as they made a futile attempt to recreate the Mexican wave.

Dinesh took in the sea of people around him. Most were seated on the topmost hard cemented stepped section. Some were seated a bit lower on plastic chairs while the VIPs were sprawled on maroon sofas as waiters did the rounds with cold drinks.

"*Jeetega bhai jeetega*, Indiaaaah *jeetega*," roared yet another section of the crowd. Standing on tiptoes, they waved wildly and chanted. This was India playing and the Feroz Shah Kotla had not witnessed a cricket match of this kind in a long while and not one involving another giant cricketing nation, England!

"Man, for a capital city, this stadium sucks," moaned Girish who was seated next to Dinesh. Old buddies, they had decided to spend the day in the company of boisterous cricket fanatics more interested in directing their lung-power against their neigbouring country than in the ongoing match.

"At least we have a stadium," replied Dinesh. He was right. The capital city had been practically a stadium-less city till the Asian Games were hosted in the city in 1984. Stadiums magically appeared during the Asian Games in 1984 as did some of the more reputable hotel chains that found a convenient parking space in the city. With time, the stadiums were a picture of neglect and ruin as it led an orphaned existence much like the athletes who were deprived of their training facilities and seen serving tea and coffee to their bosses who ran the sports federation.

"There isn't much scope for sports in this country. Where is the infrastructure to promote them?" Girish continued his lament. "Apart from cricket, we do not focus on anything else, yet hockey is supposed to be our national game. *Chutiapa hai yaar*. Look at this stadium. Looks like a village maidan in a concrete enclosure."

Dinesh nodded in agreement. The stadium was old and badly in need of a make-over. In fact, building a new one would make better sense.

Someone hit the ball for a four and as it went spinning towards the boundary, the crowd roared with delight. The sheer energy in the stadium, a one-day international between India and England and a generous dose of Pakistani bashing kept disrupting Dinesh's discussion with Girish.

"Nothing much has changed," continued Girish once the din around him subsided a bit. "The Feroz Shah Kotla Stadium was first a fortress, built by the emperor to house his version of Delhi—Ferozabad. The irony is that it still looks like that despite having been converted into a stadium… full marks to the guys who built it. They have retained the original look alright. Concern for heritage and all that, I guess," he chuckled to himself. "Did you know that this stadium was established in 1883 and is one of the oldest cricket stadia in India? It had also hosted the first ever test match in independent India."

Dinesh did not dare challenge the facts. He knew better than to argue with someone who breathed, lived and slept cricket, like many others in Delhi.

"Who manages this stadium?" asked Dinesh as a brilliant catch ended Rahul Dravid's tenure at the crease. The crowd fell silent.

*"Kaise khel raha tha yaar,"* yelled the man sitting next to Dinesh.

"You mean, who mismanages it?" retorted Girish with a smirk. "Currently, the stadium is being managed and maintained by the Delhi District Cricket Association. The irony is that this is one of the many cricket stadia in the country that has played host to many cricket matches watched by few on the ground."

"Why is that?" exclaimed Dinesh.

"It draws the crowd and the interest is immense. However, by design and intent, the true cricket aficionado perpetually finds himself at the entrance holding a valid ticket which…"

*"Abe,* hit the ball *saale… gilli-danda khel raha hein kya … gaandu,"* someone shouted at Virendra Sehwag, one of the most belligerent batsman the country had ever seen. Girish stopped for a bit, and then continued with a smile on his lips.

"The guy would, almost have bought the ticket from the black market as you hardly ever get tickets through authorised outlets. They are sold even before they are put up for sale.

Yet, despite all the money the poor chap would have spent to watch a live cricket match, he will be denied entry by a portly and mostly impolite set of unruly police officers manning the stadium gates. *Haraami hai saale… sabko apni jebein jo bharni hai…* they all want their cut."

Girish was right, to an extent.

The umpire raised his hand to signal the commencement of the drinks break and as the drinks were wheeled into the ground, most spectators in the general stands started making a beeline for the portable loos parked next to the stadium. One of them hastily unzipped his trousers as he queued up and reached within the folds of his undies. *"Isse toh zor se lagi hai,"* Dinesh thought as he followed Girish in the surge to the loos.

"Good crowd turnout," Dinesh said looking askance at Girish, getting ready for a mouthful. Girish did not say a word and Dinesh could tell that he wanted to complete the task at hand and head back to the seating area as he could lest it be usurped by another. "A cricket match at the Feroz Shah Kotla will usually have a crowd comprising and limited mainly to influential bureaucrats, DDCA officials, MCD officials including clerks and peons, officials from the Delhi Police, members from the Archeological Survey of India and lastly, if lucky, the true cricket fan who would have managed to sneak into the stadium after bribing a cop."

Dinesh was noting the guys as they exited the loos. "Just look at some of them," he told Girish pointing towards one youngster in a fancy French Connection T-shirt. He was rubbing his penis through the folds of his trousers. Girish pointed towards another who seemed to be enjoying the rub, his face showing an orgasmic expression he had never experienced before.

"He looks like he is about to cum," laughed Girish aloud and Dinesh joined in. They reached the loo and as they exited, they noticed that an equal number of expectant pissers were lined up against the bushes and the trees. The shake at the end of it all resembled a Shakira moment. Dinesh started humming 'Hips don't lie'. And Girish smiled at him as they headed back.

Their place was taken as it was expected but they managed to find another seating space near a floodlight pole.

The crowd had slowly started to return and soon the stadium was packed to capacity.

"*Saale*, this stadium has a seating capacity of close to 30,000 spectators. I believe it has now been renovated, expanded, etc., to accommodate over 50,000 spectators but the seats that are made available to true-blue cricket enthusiasts are less than 1,000 in number! Even before a cricket match is announced, the seats are 'booked' by people who know people. This breed of 'connected' people, and incidentally, the only breed who make it rich in Delhi, pass the passes (no they do not pay for them) on to their *chacha*, *mama*, sister *ke bhai ke bete* and so on, till the stadium is but a gathering of families spanning generations captured and ensconsed in one oval frame... a brilliant Kodak moment. We are after all family oriented and since every friend or stranger is an uncle or an aunty (*beta*, uncle *ko namaste karo*), the family increases exponentially with each passing year without fail. Abou Ben Adhem (may his tribe increase!)."

"C'mon Sachin! Smash them!" Girish yelled. The match had begun and Sachin and Sehwag were at the crease.

As if on cue, Sachin swung the ball hard for a boundary. The crowd went berserk; in their uncontrollable frenzy, some even hurled their empty mineral water bottles at the English fielder who had come to retrieve it. Most other cricketing nations hold their matches without barricading spectators behind iron grills. In Australia, the crowd lazes around on the green with beer with only an occasional streaker to pep up matters. In England, the crowd remains seated behind a waist-high barricade. In India, a passionate game followed by equally passionate fans unleashing their animal instincts without much provocation perhaps demands that they be confined and secured behind head-high metal fences.

This was 2003 and the crowd in Delhi was at its vocal best. Crowds and individuals have to be at their vocal best. Over 10,000 police officers waved their lathis menacingly in a bid to rein in the crowd.

"Sit down, *behenchod!*" The recipient of the almost religious expletive pretended not to have heard anything. In *saaddi dilli*, the 'b-word' is used as often as the heart pumps out blood into the body. Not a thing really to be noticed.

Mercifully Dinesh was spared the 'b-word' and the charge of the lathis. He looked decent and well-groomed in his designer wear. A privileged spectator, he worked for an MNC that had paid a hefty fee to ensure exclusive rights to a corporate enclosure dedicated to it and referred to as the 'Corporate Box'. It was a box all right! The top honchos from the MNC that authorised the payment, and other invited guests, ensured that all the seats were occupied. There are, of course privileges attached to such pleasures that make the experience worthwhile.

The enclosure in which Dinesh and Girish were seated had a set of four corporate houses; each allocated a square that together constituted one section of the stadium. Dinesh's corporate enclosure was next to three other major corporates—Pepsi, British Airways and ABN Amro. At least one was assured of a VIP viewing experience without having to dislodge someone's elbow from one's floating ribs as perhaps would have been the case in general enclosures.

In most countries corporate enclosures are a given but in others, they come at a price. DDCA officials agree albeit reluctantly to allow a certain areas of the stadium to be used as corporate enclosures, which is surprising since that would surely bring in good revenue. So when Dinesh was designated to book the corporate enclosure, he was excited and rather keen to get it right. An appointment with the concerned official was sought immediately. Three days later, Dinesh was at the stadium on time.

"So which is the area that will be allocated to us?" Dinesh asked rather gingerly during a quick round of the stadium, not wanting to offend the official who seemed to be drunk on power.

"That side," said the official with a sweep of his hand that spanned a wide section of the stadium and half the sky.

"Which side?"

"That side," he repeated with the same expression and the same sweep of his hand but this time extending beyond the skies to a land far away.

"What about the snacks?" Dinesh enquired with a certain degree of trepidation since bringing food items into the stadium could be considered a security risk, in which case the official would be within his rights to not grant permission to do so.

"Since you have a corporate box, you can bring in the snacks," replied the official puffing on his Gold Flake cigarette.

Dinesh was elated! Finally something was going right and there was light at the end of the tunnel. The light was that of an incoming train that would soon go over him.

"But," the official continued, "you need to buy the snacks or food items only from Bengali Sweets in Gole Market. Here,

137

take my card and hand it over to Mr Gopal and tell him that I sent you. Give him your requirements—snacks, cold drinks, and water, whatever. He will manage everything. You will not have any problems with the security here. I will manage it."

He smiled and winked at Dinesh. Dinesh reciprocated and felt like an idiot.

Dinesh had taken pains to check that all arrangements were in place, right down from signing the documents to ensuring that his bosses, colleagues and subordinates arrived at least three to four hours before the start of the match, since having a ticket did not guarantee entry. A ticket was a mere claim to entry! The rest depended on how inclined the cop felt to say *chal hat madarchod* after seeing your face.

Dinesh had been born and raised in Delhi. Forty years in the city had taught him the art of survival. If you can survive in Delhi, you can survive anywhere in the world. He had mixed feelings about his interactions with the DDCA... like watching your mother-in-law drive off a cliff in your new car... The flip side was that he had met interesting people from other corporate houses at the DDCA, people with profiles similar to his, doing the same things he did and feeling equally screwed and hopeless.

That was where Dinesh first met Rahul. Rahul managed corporate accounts at the DDCA and was Dinesh's 'point's man' for all things related to booking the corporate enclosure. That was also where Dinesh met Lancy from ABN Amro who was much entrusted with the same task that Dinesh had. Three people bound by a common purpose in a purposeless environment.

But there was something else.

This was where Dinesh met someone almost fated to be a dear friend. Susan, Lancy's colleague, was Australian, and had a welcoming demeanour that was most endearing. Dinesh and she had got talking and it wasn't long before the official interaction at the Feroz Shah Kotla turned into a friendship that would span Hong Kong and Australia, and time. Susan was a person with her heart in the right place. Unlike most people who had made Delhi their abode and found it frustrating to survive in spite of having lived in it for years, Susan found it unique, different and lovely in the limited time that she spent in the city. Dinesh found her approach to things appealing.

There was, however, something amiss with this friendship and, it snapped after almost close to six years in the most bizarre fashion and for the most bizarre reason. But more of that later, much later!

"Side *hatt, madarchod,*" exploded a cop as he roughed up someone inside the stadium. Sensing India's imminent defeat, the crowd slowly began to leave. At least they had managed to watch an exciting match, braving among other adversities, bursting bladders, and the final walk back to the parking lot that seemed to be in another city.

Dinesh and Girish decided to go to a local restaurant to grab a bite before heading back home. On the way, they passed a board which read 'Delhi District Cricket Association'.

"What do they do?" asked Dinesh.

"Hmmm… nothing, actually! It's an art they have perfected over the years," said Girish. "The DDCA is the local authority in Delhi which controls and manages the cricket scenario in Delhi. The Board of Control for Cricket in India (BCCI) is the authority on what should happen and how in Indian cricket. Established in 1929 and predictably, like most things in Delhi, this apex sports body is managed and run by a motley group of politicians and 'me too's' with little or no knowledge of the game. But they sure are a hardy bunch of survivors."

"What makes them so powerful?" Dinesh wondered.

"The people of India, my friend," responded Girish. "The millions of Indian fans who watch this game with such passion that the divorce rates have skyrocketed. That translates into an ever-expanding sponsor and advertiser base which gives the BCCI tremendous power. Remember without the BCCI's endorsement, no competitive cricket involving Indian players can be hosted within or outside the country." Both Girish and Dinesh nodded in agreement as they walked into a nearby Udipi restaurant and ordered their snack-cum-dinner: *masala dosa* with filter coffee. It tasted better than the one supplied by Bengali Sweets.

# *Tussi Great Ho—Hai Nee!*

*"Hai Nee,"* screamed a sticker at the rear window of a red Maruti 800. A classic sight in West Delhi. These stickers are like windows to the driver's area of residence. They come in handy in identifying cars from different parts of Delhi. *'Hai Nee'* is classic West Delhi followed by *'Sonu teh Monu di Gaddi'*. As one moves to South Delhi, one catches glimpses of better looking cars with more stately slogans or just a 'Harvard University', a 'MIT' or a 'GB' sticker planted firmly next to the number plate. It most 'humbly' boasts of the many trips the owner may have had to Great Britain. North Delhi prides itself on the smaller cars and can be identified by the passengers inside, and car slogans almost do not exist for East Delhi.

Regardless of which part of Delhi they are from, almost all new cars will have the plastic wrapped on the new seats with some even retaining the ribbon stripes on the bonnet that came with the car when it left the showroom. They will, rarely, be taken off before a month. The point is that it is not enough to buy a new car. It is equally important to tell the world that it is a new car.

Dinesh travelled to Pitampura regularly on work. You do not go to West Delhi for pleasure. It is a place that has some of the best and some of the worst mansions inhabited by the rich, true-blue Punjabis. Most of them, if not all, are business persons. As he passed one particular mansion that seemed to never end, he asked the rickshaw-*wallah* if he knew who it belonged to. "*Haan*, sir. *Kabaadi-wallah ka hai.*" The owner of that mansion makes a living selling garbage! It was only later that Dinesh got to know that he was in the ship-breaking business. Big money indeed, but still a *kabaadi-wallah*. Perhaps the only country in the world where one gets paid for trash. Trash is therefore valuable and therefore something to be treasured.

Tilak Nagar is predominantly a Sikh colony. Indeed Delhi has its areas where a particular community establishes its majority presence. Tilak Nagar for Sikhs, R.K. Puram for South Indians, Old Delhi and Nizammuddin for Muslims, Chittaranjan Park for Bengalis, and Janak Puri for everybody else.

One of his friends from school, Tavish, who moved to the US used to stay in Janak Puri, as did Pratip. The three were inseparables from school and used to spend time together either trying to complete a school project together or hanging out at Kadimi for a plate of *pav bhaji*. Janak Puri was perhaps the biggest colony that Dinesh had set his eyes on. Tavish used to stay in an address which read C1A 52B. One can understand the scale of the colony. First you have a 'C', then the numbers followed by another 'A', followed by another number followed by another alphabet. A trainee postman would go mad and would never make it to the stated address in time.

They used to spend time together either on a fun mission or when they used to get together to study collectively for their Boards. Both Tavish and Dinesh used to have a healthy sense of competition between them. With the arrival of the Board exams, they planned to spend the night together and study. Sounded like a great idea; only that it had fundamental flaws. Tavish was a morning person and Dinesh a *nishaachar*. Each one tried to overcome it but it was not meant to be. It didn't take long for the inevitable to happen—Dinesh was the only one studying at his house at one in the morning while Tavish snored.

On one occasion, he woke him up and persuaded him to go out for a walk just so he would lose his sleep. As they walked, sharing a cigarette between them they were stopped by a cop who was on his routine rounds.

*"Hawabaazi kar rahe ho?"* he asked in a menacing tone. "Where do you stay?"

"We were studying and decided to take a walk around the colony. My friend stays here round the corner, adjacent to the playground," Dinesh answered.

"Go back home, *saalon*. This is no time for a walk," he said as he advanced towards them baton firmly in hand. The two of the three musketeers scampered back home, safe in the knowledge that they were secure.

Just adjoining Janak Puri is Tihar Jail, the biggest prison complex in Asia.

Tihar Prisons, also called Tihar Jail and Tihar Ashram, is Asia's largest prison complex and one of the largest in the world. It comprises nine prisons in the Tihar complex with a total population of around 14,221 inmates against the sanctioned capacity of 6,250 inmates. About 80 per cent of the inmates are awaiting trial.

The original Tihar Jail was built in 1958 and was proposed to be a maximum security prison run by the State of Punjab. Almost ten years later the control was transferred to the National Capital Territory of Delhi. In 1984, the year when Indira Gandhi was assasinated, additional facilities were incorporated and the institution was renamed as Tihar Prisons.

The first-time offenders' ward is separated from the long-term prisoners' area. The long-termers, typically those charged with murders, rapes, terrorism and the like, are under constant supervision. Other sections of the prison are reserved for women inmates and adolescent prisoners between the ages 18-20. Instances of adolescents being sodomised are fairly common and typically perpetrated by the long-termers. Many women inmates also suffer at the hands of the lesbians who inhabit their prison cells. There are also rampant cases of drug abuse, sexual harassment and violence and the jails remain overcrowded resulting in problems of hygiene, cleanliness and sleeping berths. The more 'influential' inmates enjoy the comfort of a good bed and 'ghar ka khana' within the prison while the others have to make do with *chapati* and *lauki ki subzi*.

One international drug peddler allegedly ran an international criminal syndicate supplying ephedrine—a sought-after chemical precursor in the illicit manufacture of Ecstasy and Ice that are popular at all-night dance parties from within the confines of his jail cell. He lived a lavish life and seemed more at ease in captivity rather than out in the open where he would need to worry about any potential attempts on his life.

Some criminals end up behind bars and many more operate out in the open. Confining someone within the prison walls does not amount to much and does not alter what happens regardless. The prison walls do not offer much protection either. You are a marked man outside the prison walls and once within, you are equally marked. The only difference being that if the underworld did not get to you outside, the police will make sure that they will get you inside in the form of custodial deaths!

The bars and grills of the confining kind, not the lounge bar, distil in the minds of most Delhiites too. It is not the prisons alone that have bars on them. The concept spills beyond prisons to mark a presence in most of our day-to-day activities, and is a constant reminder that we need cages to control ourselves.

The grilled concept is prevalent in most things that Dinesh had seen. Be it the telephone billing and payment counter, the alcohol stores or the cricket stadiums, the way we transport our chickens or the way we transport criminals, it all happens within the confines of grills and iron bars. With each grill, we constantly reaffirm to ourselves that we have not moved too far from the Neanderthal stage and that we need to collectively do much more to consider ourselves to be a part of the human race.

At the cricket stadium, it is to prevent unruly mobs from storming the stadium and jostling the players that necessitates the need for bars. Nobody wants to wait or observe civility in their conduct. During a recent Indian Premier League match, the cheerleaders had a tough time as they had to bear the lecherous looks and comments, not to mention the gropings of the libido laden spectators. It is not just enough for one to have paid to watch the cricket match. Each one is in pursuit of getting that little bit extra. Standing in line is not an option; one needs to get ahead of others, get more for less effort. Maximum for minimum…

'Keeping up with the Joneses' is an adage that seems so true in this city. It was hard to be in Delhi and not have at least four essential things required to transport you to a certain societal acceptance level. One is a good address in South Delhi. Second is a nice fancy car, third is good school which you send your kids to (preferably in a chauffeur driven car), and lastly a dog. Since the first three seemed a distance away, Saahil decided on buying a dog.

It always amused Dinesh when he saw dogs with bulging bellies from lack of exercise being taken for walks by bored housemaids who were more worried if their make-shift dwelling under the flyover had escaped the demolition drive by the MCD squad and whether she and her children would have a place to stay at night after she returned from work. The dog on the leash, left with no option of walking anywhere, yawns and shits on the pavement area meant for early morning joggers or old folks taking their morning walk. The walk invariably exercises the maids more than the dog.

Rarely do people buy dogs that suit the environment. A great dane or a labrador would look great in a farmhouse or in a house in Jor Bagh or Amrita Shergil Marg, but to find such dogs in DDA colonies such as Vasant Kunj or Vasant Enclave had left Dinesh much confused. How can you have a dog that is bigger than the house? These kind of dogs need to be exercised, they need to run to be kept in shape. But Delhi being what it is, it is not so much the love for the dog but the fact that a dog is the right thing to have. That helps establish a certain standing in one's self-created society, even if it be so in a DDA colony in R.K.Puram. A dog with its head out in the car symbolises affluence, and the bigger the head the better even if the car has to be parked on the service road adjoining the DDA colony for want of parking space. Parking on the road is the only option since your DDA colony does not allow you with enough parking space. It does, however, provide a closed garage space to park your two-wheeler. The assumption being that a DDA house-holder can only afford a two-wheeler. But then the two-wheeler garage is rented to a press-*wallah*, who would keep a stray dog for company. How are either any different from a societal standpoint now. The owner and the press-*wallah* both equalised in their positions by a canine which was larger than what their habitat would allow.

Saahil began to go through the many classifieds on this subject. He saw one that interested him and quickly called up Dinesh to accompany him for the purchase. A doberman was exactly what he was looking for. Although priced at ₹5,000, it seemed to be a good buy with a Kennel Club of India (KCI) class I registration. The address was that of Punjabi Bagh and it wasn't long before they parked their car outside the very imposing gates of a *kothi* which bore the listed address.

The security guard let them in after checking with the owner on the intercom. As they made their way into the house, they couldn't help but admire the neatly manicured lawns. They were greeted at the door by a dark complexioned maid who led them inside and had them seated. "Will you have water?" she asked in a much rehearsed tone. "No, thanks!" we replied. "*Sa'ab* will be here in a minute," so saying she scampered in the direction of one of the rooms.

Mr Singh walked in clad in a *lungi* and with a glass of whisky in one hand. "Hello! How are you?" he said in a very rehearsed way as well.

The maid followed him and kept a basket in front of him. It had a beautiful litter of four pups.

"Which one would you like to buy? They are all so beautiful," he said in a rather over-eager tone. Perhaps it was the whisky.

"My wife looks after them and she is away to Dubai," he offered.

Dinesh did not see how that was relevant. After all it was the doberman pup they had come to look at and buy, not his wife.

"I have to look after them till she returns," continued Mr Singh. "By the way, my name is Harbir Singh Panesar," he said offering his hand once again. "Would you like to have something?"

"I will settle for the black and tan coloured one," Saahil said pointing towards a rather docile pup which was crouched a distance away, busy nibbling at its own tail.

"Sure, why not," he said.

He handed over the pup to them and Saahil examined the pup with great care, just to be sure.

"Do not worry, sir*jee*. This is top quality," exclaimed Harbir as he took another swig of his whisky.

The money changed hands and Mr Singh handed over the relevant KCI registration papers. All things seemed to be in order. They thanked him and left.

On their way out, they passed his large fleet of cars which consisted of a Skoda, a Sonata and a Tata Sumo. They were all parked under his red porch. The security guard gave a salute as they left the premises. Salutations and 'Sirs' are so easy to come by in this city.

The pup cried all night. Probably the withdrawal pangs of having moved to a smaller accommodation.

# Forgotten and Erased

"Moolchand, Bhogal, *Neoda, Neoda, Neoda*," hollered the conductor of a blue-line as his hand banged on the side of the bus.

An urchin selling peanuts tried to board the bus only to be kicked in the face by the conductor. "*Hatt, behanchod!* Wants a ride free, *hain? Saala bhonsadika!*" he guffawed and the other passengers joined in. They all shared a common bond—that of insensitivity. Why did it seem fit to the conductor to abuse an urchin, and for others to share a laugh? Was it arrogance or a misplaced sense of appearing tough? If only it was about being abrasive, abusive or kicking an urchin in the face. "Toughness was more about appreciating the strength within you and drawing upon it at times of adversity," Dinesh let his thoughts trail.

The urchin managed to save himself from coming under the wheels of the bus but did not appear frightened. This was what he was being subjected to on a daily basis. Over a period of time, this city had stripped him of any remnants of self-respect that he may have had. It had desensitised him to most things that would have revolted many. But not him. Constant abuse without an option to alter the status-quo would have left him frustrated and devoid of any hope for the future. He had no choice but to embrace and cooperate with the inevitable.

Dinesh had parked his car on the kerb and was standing next to the bus stop. As he helped himself to a cigarette from the kiosk that adjoins most bus stops in New Delhi, he noticed a refrigerated water trolley parked on the footpath. Almost all bus stops have a 'refrigerated water' dispenser selling water for ₹1. The ice used to refrigerate the water could be from any source. The last time Dinesh had seen commercial ice being transported in the summer heat was in an open cycle rickshaw. It stopped at a traffic signal and the rickshaw-*wallah* had taken off his *gamcha* and wiped his sweaty brow with it. He had then placed it on top of the three ice slabs that he was carrying. Seconds later, a young group of beggars, aged anywhere between 4-7 years surrounded the rickshaw and placed their grimy, sweaty and dirty hands on top of the slabs to cool themselves. Dinesh had quite seen enough and he had driven off in disgust.

He looked at the urchin as he dragged his bare feet on the hot bitumen to reclaim his place next to the footpath. As he moved amidst the various people who were awaiting their turn to board the bus, there were many who picked on his peanuts without paying for it. He did not say anything. This is a classic of any vendor selling fruits, peanuts or vegetables. As the items are being weighed or put into plastic bags, the buyer will invariably help himself to some additional peanuts to munch on, or he will pick a couple of grapes to eat as his 100 gms of grapes are being weighed, or he will simply break the tip of the ladyfinger to check its freshness—totally unmindful that the act had rendered it unsaleble. Carrots will be picked up and eaten while the vegetable vendor is still weighing the other vegetables that are bought. Once the purchase has been completed, the customer will always ask for the additional freebies!

*"Thoda dhaniya or mirchi daal de na yaar."*

*"Sirjee dhaniya aaj kal mandi se mehenga aa raha hai.* It is now ₹30 a kilo and we cannot now afford to give it away free."

*"Koi baat nahin yaar.* Just put in a small bit along with the *mirchi.* Total *kitna hua?"*

"That will be ₹33."

"C'mon *yaar,* make it thirty. *Yeh le, tees rakh."*

The vegetable seller will grudgingly oblige and as he hands over the plastic bags.

As the buyer hands over the money to him, he will invariably pick up some peas to munch on the way back to his vehicle.

Maximum for minimum...

"Uncle, want to buy some peanuts?"

Dinesh looked down and it was the same child. His eyes were glazed and smeared with dirt but expectant that somebody would eventually pay. He seemed to have lost his childhood somewhere and the childlike innocence had been replaced with a blank, expressionless visage that had been injected into him through years of deprivation and hopelessness in the streets of Delhi.

He did not look a day beyond six years, but had been buffeted enough to carry the street smartness of a 20-year-old. Dinesh did not want any peanuts but could not bring himself to say no. He was reminded of a girl-child he had met in G.B. Road and the similarities seemed to hit him. He could not remember the name.

*"Kitne ka hai beta?"* he asked.

*"Le lo,* sir. ₹5 for 100 gms."

Dinesh asked for 200 gms. The urchin seemed to show a glimmer of happiness. Perhaps he was happy at the prospect of finally getting to have lunch after many days. Perhaps he was happy that he is not being forced to give it away for free.

Perhaps he was happy that he will be able to give something to the *seth* who was running this racket.

Organised begging that involves the abduction of children— known as the begging mafia—is common in India, with the states of Tamil Nadu, Kerala, Bihar, New Delhi and Orissa having the most severe problem.

Dinesh recalled a report by India's Human Rights Commission which said that these stolen children were "working as cheap forced labour in illegal factories, establishments, homes, exploited as sex slaves or forced into the child porn industry, as camel jockeys in the Gulf countries, as child beggars in begging rackets, as victims of illegal adoptions or forced marriages, or perhaps, worse than any of these, as victims of organ trade and even grotesque cannibalism."

Most of the victims are between two and eight years of age. They are often not fed so that they cry continuously, enticing passers-by to give them money. After being abducted, the children are taught begging techniques. "They are taught ways and nuances of begging such as the most appropriate place to beg, the kind of people one should approach, the kind of dialogues and mannerisms that would make everyone sympathise," said Mufti Imran, a researcher with the non-governmental organisation *Save the Children*. "The more a person is tortured or tormented, the more unfortunate he looks—all this will invoke more sympathy among the people who will then give them alms and religious places are the perfect locations to extract more," he continued explaining why the beggars seek out places of worship.

Child beggars do not get to keep their takings but rather have to hand them over to the group controlling their area at the end of every day. "On an average, a beggar earns two to three US dollars. They get food in temples and *masjid*s and sleep in public places."

Adults are also kidnapped and forced into begging. Often, to entice empathy among potential contributors, their limbs are amputated or they are disfigured with acid. Sometimes blood vessels are stitched to block blood supply to parts of the body, bringing about gangrene.

In 2007, Indian news channel CNN-IBN conducted an undercover investigation of the doctor-beggar mafia connection. Three doctors working in government hospitals in Delhi were filmed by hidden camera striking a deal with the beggar mafia. Police filed charges against the doctors who had been given $200 to amputate the limbs of individuals who were abducted.

Thankfully, the urchin in front of Dinesh had been spared the torture but would still remain a forgotten child.

"*Yeh lo*, uncle," it was the same boy again. Dinesh took the paper cone from his hand and gave him a twenty rupee note, aware of what he was doing, the grave mistake that he was committing. The urchin looked up at him and said, "Uncle, *change nahi hai.*" There was a mixture of hope and desperation on the boy's face. *Hope*, that the Uncle would ask him to keep it, and *despair* that the Uncle may return the peanuts back … many emotions to battle everyday at such a tender age.

Dinesh asked him to keep the change. He looked up at him and asked him if he could give him two ten rupee notes. Dinesh was puzzled and asked him why.

"I will give a ten rupee note to my father as he is too old to walk and earn. He can buy some food for himself. I will keep the other one to buy a storybook. I love storybooks. I cannot read but I love seeing the pictures with all the colours," he replied. Dinesh looked at him even more closely. A colourless existence seeking joy in a colourful world of make-believe.

He gave him what he wanted and the urchin scrambled off lest Dinesh changed his mind. Dinesh was not going to and tried to make sense of the little figure running, barefoot in the summer heat of May in Delhi, to a tent like structure at a distance. Hair tanned with the heat and undernourished to the extreme, yet not losing the childlike interests of reading a storybook... surely he could read some lines. Dinesh wasn't sure. Perhaps it was simply to go through a journey of colours that would cast a resplendent hue on his otherwise monochromatic existence.

Dinesh got into his car and drove towards the boy. He was not to be seen but he did catch a glimpse of another boy trying to squeeze a drop of juice from a tetra pack that somebody had thrown. He managed a drop and seemed to relish the taste.

Maximum for minimum...

The winter months has its own set of challenges but it was a season Dinesh really enjoyed. His friend from the US was here and on one night they were returning back after a late night drinking session at a friend's place.

"*Yaar*, can't we pick up a girl from somewhere. You are from Delhi and should know where these things can be arranged."

"This is not US," Dinesh reminded him. "And you are asking the wrong person," he lied.

"*Chal hatt, gaandu. Sau choohe khake billi haj ko chali,*" he laughed out loud. He was not too wrong, though!

He always chose to be critical when he is in India and Dinesh could never understand that.

"Fuck! These roads are bad, man," he exclaimed.

"You can always walk," Dinesh said. "Aw c'mon man! Don't get so serious and uppity," the friend replied. Dinesh did not reply back.

As they approached a traffic light, it turned red and Dinesh stopped the car. They were immediately surrounded by a group of young beggars tapping on the car window and another cleaning the car bonnet with a dirty piece of rag. Dinesh was reminded of the urchin he had met some months back. Hopefully, he had managed to get the story book he so badly wanted. Hopefully!

"This is crazy, man. Fuck off you guys," Tavish shouted out from within the confines of the heated car.

"Ignore them," Dinesh said. "Do you realise that they barely have a piece of rag on themselves to keep them warm. Let them be."

The urchin, from whom Dinesh had bought peanuts many months ago, was barefoot in the summer heat on the roads in Delhi. In complete contrast, these urchins, some learning to walk, were barefoot in the cold wintry months in Delhi. Both situations would help in the desensitising and numbness process, numbness to the emotion of pain and numbness to the environment around them.

The response seemed to have hit home and even though Tavish was inebriated, he reached out to his hip pocket and pulled out a ₹500 note.

"No," Dinesh said. "You will only be encouraging them to beg."

Tavish chose to ignore the comment. By this time, all the beggars had moved onto the next car after having experienced his friend's initial outburst.

"Where have they all gone?" Tavish enquired.

"They are behind us, preying on the other car," Dinesh said.

He proceeded to put the money back into his wallet.

"If you really want to give anybody anything, then spare a thought for that small girl there," Dinesh said pointing to the fancy car parked alongside them at the traffic light. The girl, not a day beyond five years stood in front of a Honda Accord with her palms pressed against the headlight. Seeing her, Dinesh was reminded of Vandana.

"Oh the one fiddling with the headlight?" he asked.

"Yes, that one. She is not fiddling with the headlight. She is using the heat of the headlight to warm her hands in the cold."

Tavish beckoned to her and handed over the money. Neither of them spoke all the way back home.

# Ho! Ho! Ho! and a Bottle of Rum

As Dinesh celebrated his 35th birthday, he had a certain feeling of accomplishment. Having come through a series of events, some momentous whilst some downright heartbreaking, he was proud to have survived in a city that could have robbed him of his own identity and could have left him desolate, if given half a chance. Actually, he did not give the people in the city the half chance that they needed because the city in itself would have taken him under its wings as it does to millions of others who set up base here. It's the people and not the city that takes away from you. The people from all walks of life, rude and obnoxious in their demeanour and loud and appalling in their appearance, set to extract the maximum but offering little or nothing in return. There are the exact opposites as well, diametrically opposed to the concept of being rude and unbecoming. They are, however, in a sad minority.

Dinesh had paid his share of collateral, though. He would have loved to have his parents, especially his father, witness his ascendancy both socially and financially from where he had last left him; in a government sponsored Type IV flat in Netaji Nagar with a job that paid him equivalent to a lower division clerk in the government. Alas, that was not to be. His father had paid a very heavy price in the city and Dinesh had an ominous inkling that he would be called to pay the price too in a matter of time, over and above the interest he was paying in the form of a never-ending EMI called lifestyle.

It was a family that most would have been jealous of, too good to be true. A family of four conforming to the family planning slogan of *'Hum do, Hamaare do'*. The father, a joint director in the Ministry; mother, a home-maker; a sister, married to an engineer in Delhi, and a grandchild on the way. It was, indeed, too good to be true and over a period of time the stuff that dreams were made of came crumbling down like a pack of cards, leaving Dinesh to fend for himself.

His father was charged by the CBI for allocating grants to a fictitious NGO and his sister's marriage broke off on account of irreconcilable differences. Both the incidents came like a bolt out of the blue catching his father and the family off-guard. The events caused irreparable damage to his father's psychological and mental framework and he decided to take voluntary retirement while the case was still in progress. Being in suspension was killing him and although he was allowed to continue work after a two-month suspension, he could not bring himself to walk the path again in perceived shame. After all, it was the path that he had so carefully nurtured. He could not believe that he had been framed on a charge which he had allegedly committed while he was attending his daughter's wedding in Kerala. How could that even be admitted in court! How could his daughter be divorced from someone who he had so carefully chosen as the most suited!? He kept asking himself these questions. Questions to which he found no answers. Dinesh's mother only compounded the problem. With her fetish for all things material, she found the source of her overindulgent ways dry up with her husband's voluntary retirement announcement. She sought monetary refuge with her son-in-law and jeopardised the daughter-son-in-law relationship as well. All things came down crashing in one big heap.

Back home in Kerala, Dinesh's father moved to his wife's ancestral home, a decision he regretted ever since. At her mercy and command, he saw all that he held dear lose its significance including Dinesh. Dinesh's mother would chide him constantly for the sarees he could no longer afford to gift her, humiliate him since he was staying in her house, and ridicule Usha, Dinesh's sister, who was now also staying with them post her divorce. "Some people are made that way," Dinesh thought as he spoke to his father over the phone every month and realised the futility of trying to wish that it would all be like before. The wounds so inflicted over time would never heal. He tried to augment his father's pension with occasional money dispatches to help satiate his mother's burgeoning needs but soon realised that it would never be enough and that he too had a family to run. The lifestyle that he had and the debts that he had run up in his pursuit of a larger life had squeezed Dinesh's ability to be a better son.

Fate had landed such blows that Dinesh's father had lost faith in almost everything and everybody including his son Dinesh. It was an irreversible development and Dinesh could only watch from the distance. However, one development held promise. His father saw a ray of hope and a will to live when his first grandson was born. He found an alternate to Dinesh who was physically absent and was increasingly getting to be mentally distant as well. His whole life began to revolve around his grandson and he would inadvertently refer to Dinesh also by his grandson's name. Like his sister, Dinesh too had been divorced by his father because of irreconcilable differences. His father had set up a separate world, a world that did not include him. Caught in the rat race with little time to pause and think, Dinesh had ignored and paid the price of distance and proved the adage 'distances make the heart grow fonder' wrong. With his nephew to substitute his physical presence and giving his father immense joy, much more than he practically could, Dinesh did not feel the need to alter the equation. He thought it best to cooperate with the inevitable.

"Side *ho behenchod, saala bawli gaand,*" yelled a killer blue-line driver as his repeated pressure horns elicited no reaction from him, thereby *forcing* him to overtake Dinesh from the right side of the road.

Dinesh was snapped out of his reverie in a flash but he was instantly aware that he was in Delhi. Home to the beautiful Lodhi Gardens, majestic Rashtrapati Bhavan and India Gate, historically significant Connaught Place, incredibly lively nightclubs, convenient flyovers, arrogantly interesting Gymkhana Club and Delhi Golf Club, enlightening India International Centre and the haven for lip-smacking delicious food, Old Delhi; all do not let you forget that this place is still worth living in.

He had, over ten years managed to buy a penthouse and two apartments for himself and was also the proud owner of two cars. This was from a point from where he had to borrow from his boss, around ten years ago, to make a down payment for his bike. He did not steal nor did he achieve this through covert means and that is what made him proud. It's so easy to make money in this city, as everything has a potential to be corrupted.

"In Delhi," Girish had said, "One needs to have the following if you want to make a decent existence. Chiefly, it will be a South Delhi address. The South Delhi address does not refer to any of its poorer cousins such as Vasant Kunj, Vasant Enclave or Greater Kailash 4 but to the true-blue South

Delhi address, namely Vasant Vihar, Shanti Niketan or extend it a bit more to Jor Bagh, Amrita Shergil Marg, Aurangazeb Road or Prithviraj road and the like. Second, a good range of cars, imported of course, should line the driveway. Third, the *ayah* should be there to take care of the children who would in turn be students of G.D. Goenka or Modern School. Eating out should be in restaurants in five-star hotels (you should not know of restaurants outside five-star hotels), the bills for which you settle with your Platinum or your Centurion card. The food should not be Chinese (that is so middle-class), it should preferably be tapas or exotic and you speak with an accent that is far removed from being typically Indian, *"Bhaiyya, gaadi bahar nikalo."* Not to forget that you should be armed with a Vertu mobile while your kids play with their iPhones or get their sense of sport with a Wii. You have then truly arrived and belong to this city.

*"Yaar,* I have given two phones to my driver. One is for their personal calls and the other only to receive my calls."

"Who pays for his personal calls?" Dinesh asked not wanting to sound middle-class.

"I do, *yaar.* Who else? *Ek, do hazaar mein kya farak padta hai."* The difference between *ek, do hazaar* is exactly *ek hazaar* but for some the difference does not exist.

And of course, the crowning claim to fame would be having a membership of a club if not two, and the more exclusive the better.

The Delhi Gymkhana Club is one of the oldest clubs in India. It moved to its present location on the 3rd July, 1913. It was called the Imperial Delhi Gymkhana Club and Mr Spencer Harcourt Butler was its first President. The club is located in the heart of Lutyen's New Delhi occupying 27.3 acres of prime land as per site plan made on the drawing board by Sir Edwin Landseer Lutyens as part of his grand design for imperial celebrations. When India gained independence in 1947, the word 'Imperial' was dropped and it was simply known as Delhi Gymkhana Club. So selective is the membership criterion that the usual waiting period for membership is about 50-60 years.

Dinesh was celebrating his birthday here through the generous obligation of a dear friend. You need to have a member check you in. As the drinks and the smokes enveloped the room, the group made their way out of the closed area into the open.

"What's the matter? Surprisingly, no rush tonight," enquired Saahil of one of his friends who was more regular at the club than at work.

"Not sure, maybe it is the recession," Uday wasn't sure that the people frequenting the Gymkhana would worry too much about recession. "Surprisingly, that babe is not around today."

"Which one? That backless babe?"

Nobody responded but everyone looked around. Dinesh wondered why the club was not making money considering the reputation it enjoyed.

"Pilferage, *yaar*. Alcohol gets pilfered regularly. Also with the prices being so low, there is not enough to make a decent profit."

That's the irony. The richer you get, the more are the extra discounts and freebies available to you. The Emporio at the Nelson Mandela Marg has a store that offers free champagne to each of its potential customers. Considering that each of the items in that store are upwards of ₹75,000, a glass of champagne holds no attraction for the 'been there, bought that' shopper. The rationale eluded Dinesh. It would, however, attract most who consider shopping at Sarojini Nagar and Lajpat Nagar as a value for money experience.

Clubs such as the Gymkhana or the Delhi Golf Club offer drinks at subsidised rates. At least subsidised from a market rate perspective and Dinesh could not understand the need to do that. The funny part is that the influential and wealthy clientele of the Gymkhana or the Golf Club take snobbish pride in just being there. Perhaps it is the ambience or what it does to you.

"I always thought that clubs need to have a high price tag for all their services and facilities to be considered upmarket and niche," Dinesh said. "Waiting for 30 years to get membership is the only niche the Gymkhana or the Golf Club enjoys. The rest is pedestrian. Have you even been to the Congressional at the Bathesda in the US? That is where Tiger Woods and his ilk hang out. That is class personified."

Uday and Girish agreed but did not say anything. As the toasties arrived, Dinesh let his gaze survey the place and his ears pick up any gossip. He never denied that he enjoyed a good gossip.

"Do you know Mr Kataria? The same guy who has now moved to Canada?" This was a middle-aged gent in a middle-aged company.

"Wasn't he in the Ministry at some point?" replied another.

"Yeah, yeah. That's the one! The fucker is now back in India and wants to pick up a good place and set up something. I know of this good deal on the road to Shimla."

"*Arre*, did I tell you that I just picked up a great villa in Goa for a steal. Got a little work done but now it is perfect. You must check it out the next time you go to Goa. You must stay there and tell me what you think." Offers for a free stay in Goa and Dinesh was instantly reminded of his Bihari landlord who other than extracting rent had also got him to pay for part of the electricity consumed by him. And that wasn't even Goa!

163

"Sure, *yaar*. I may plan to go there sometime next month. *Mein* phone *karoonga*." Somewhere along the trail of this conversation, the poor Mr Kataria got lost. Goa became more relevant, replete with an offer of a free stay.

The live band started and some of the elderly took to the dance floor with their spouses or significant others. It was hard to tell because the level and intensity of emotion that they showed on the dance floor did not alter with the change in partners. It remained the same.

"Let's go to some other place after this, what say?" suggested Girish.

"I agree," Uday concurred, "Not much happening here. Let us just finish off our drinks and head for the Smoke House Grill. It's Dinesh's birthday and we have to make sure he remembers it."

Everybody laughed.

"I forgot my pass today and I had to ask Rahul to use his card to let me in and order the drinks and food," exclaimed Saahil, as everyone stood outside inhaling generous puffs of low tar and nicotine emanating from his Davidoff Lights. It was not fashionable enough to be smoking Marlboro Lights.

"He is a great guy," Saahil continued.

"How do you know him?" asked Nachiketa.

"Oh, we were in school together!"

"He is not all that good. He is a fucking son of a bitch!"

One could clearly see there was enough anger and venom in him as he said that. Taken aback, Dinesh looked at Nachiketa and then at Saahil not sure whether they were, in fact, talking about the same person.

"Why, what happened?" asked Saahil.

"*Saala*, I did not know him initially but over a period of time we became friends. He is a regular here like me. It usually happens that when we see a familiar face we smile, acknowledge each other and over a period of time start chatting up. That's what happened in this case too," Nachiketa paused to inhale the smoke and take a swig of his Whyte and McKay. "After we go to know each other, I opened to him further and told him of the separation that I was going through. Although I still loved Shikha, there were many issues that came up between us and try as we might, we could not resolve those. So we separated. I was still trying to make things work between the two of us. I introduced him to Shikha, who also comes to the Gymkhana occasionally, so that there was a neutral party that could make her and me look at things differently."

"Hi guys, wassup?" it was another acquaintance of Saahil. He paused to shake hands, exchanged a few pleasantries and then left.

"One day," Nachiketa continued, "I decided to visit Rahul so we could then drive to the Gymkhana together. I kept trying his mobile but in vain. I reached his place at Sujan Singh Park and saw that his car was parked there. I thought I recognised the car parked next to it as well but ignored it and ran up the stairs. I rang the doorbell and after a considerable wait Rahul opened the door dressed only in his jeans. I barged in as all of us friends do and was just in time to see Shikha make a quick dash to the bathroom adjoining the bedroom which could be seen from the living room." He paused as he took another puff. "Here I am trying to make it work with my wife and he steps in to act as a 'good samaritan'... *saala haraam zada.*"

All in the group thought it best to change the subject. And Dinesh, taken in by the sudden change in the tenor of conversation, let his eyes wander around.

"Oh hello Bhatia *sa'ab*! Good to see you. *Kaisa chal raha hai?*" said yet another middle-aged gentleman acknowledging the presence of another member.

"Nothing much. Just planning to visit my son in the US next week."

"Oh, good good. He got married last month, right? Mandira did mention to me and we wanted to come for the wedding but *mujhe achanak* London *jaana pada* on some work. I did try to connect on my return but you know what it is like. Something keeps coming up."

"*Koi nahin*. You must drop in sometime."

"Sure *jee. Aur sab theek?*"

"All izz well!" and they both laughed out loud.

Dinesh and his group decided to wind up. With not being allowed to smoke and the use of mobile phones forbidden inside the main hall, the place was getting claustrophobic and offered a contrarian perspective of enjoyment to the group.

The live band switched to LaBamba and some more couples joined in the dancing. As Dinesh munched on the delicious *keema* naan with *hari* chutney, he began to wonder what it takes to lead a life in this environment all the time. Is it enjoyable or just seems to be enjoyable. He knew his father would never jell well with this crowd inspite of being a senior bureaucrat. To start with, he did not drink and this company and set-up was not him. Also, there were enough issues that his father had been presented with that would normally take many lifetimes to resolve and he had only one. There was just no time that he had to sit back and reflect on life. The pace of life had kept up with him and provided fresh challenges at every step he took giving him no time to reflect. Here was his son, happy in this set-up, enjoying the company of friends over drinks, having to face little or no challenges in life; it was almost as if his father had been the sponge that had taken it all away from him.

"What are you thinking, Dinesh?" Saahil asked.

"Oh, nothing," Dinesh shouted back over the increasing sound of drums emanating from the live band. His father kept coming back to him in his thoughts. "C'mon, let's have our last drink and head out elsewhere."

"Sounds good. We better hurry. It's quarter to eleven."

The waiter came, quickly took the order and returned in a flash. The crowd was beginning to dwindle now. It was nearing 11 p.m.

"See that guy there," said Saahil gesturing with his eyes towards a guy standing next to the bar counter.

"Yes," replied Dinesh. Nachiketa too listened in with rapt attention. "He is separated from his wife and the funny part is that it is his wife who is the member in this club. The guy is now seeing another babe who too is a member." Saahil smiled.

"For some people club membership is the prerequisite to any relationship that they got into," wondered Dinesh and looked at the person more intently.

"The funny part is that the woman's husband also happens to be in the club tonight," Saahil announced and the group let out a hearty laugh.

"All the makings of a grand orgy. C'mon, let's go."

Such tales you encounter regularly at most clubs and the Gymkhana was no exception. The talks would start with the weather outside, move on to politics, gravitate towards the general scene in Delhi and then eventually find its way to the dark recesses of the mind habitated by deals and sleaze.

The group returned to a dark hall. It was 11 pm and the staff at the club had diligently gone about switching off the lights. "*Abe yaar*. At least wait for us to leave," yelled someone from across the hall. Nobody heard him.

# Expected to be 14 Hours Late

It was raining cats and dogs that day. Dinesh was expecting to see his father who was coming down from Kerala after a long time. Some people refuse to change with time and his father was no exception. Having spent his lifetime in the government service and having lived a non-pompous existence, he refused to let the facilities that come with a price tag colour his perspective of life. For him, travelling from one place to another still meant travelling by a DTC bus. Dumping an old *Tempo* and buying a new *Futura* pressure cooker was not an option, but getting it fixed after a wait of over an hour in a shanty store in Sarojini Nagar was immensely gratifying for him. Three cheers to the old order which was and remains so much less complex and devoid of complications. The life charted on the roads of modernity on the other hand has a different story to tell though.

"I will come to pick you up," Dinesh said over the phone. "What time is the train, what is the train number, and station?"

"No need for you to come," his father replied, "I can come to AIIMS via bus and you can pick me up from there. Guess that will be more convenient for you."

"No, no, I will come."

The weather was bad and Dinesh had to abandon his plan of taking his car. It's one thing to be able to afford a car, but to be able to drive it and park it in a proper place is a separate story altogether. In a city like Delhi, one can never take anything for granted. Just like buying a ticket to a cricket match is no guarantee to enter inside the stadium, having a car is no guarantee of being able to drive it when you want and keeping it dent-free, especially at the New Delhi Railway Station. Even if you are lucky enough to have managed to squeeze the car between a space that can possibly accommodate a scooter, you can be rest assured that you will return to a car that has been nudged, pushed and caressed in all directions.

After driving to his friends place in Saket so the car was parked in a secure place, Dinesh hailed a taxi which was so well ventilated that he could see the road through the car floor. The floor of the car was rusted and there were perforations that left him worried and edgy. The driver, unmindful of any defect or hazard, drove the taxi with the stereo belting out *'too cheez badi hai mast mast...'* As the rain increased in intensity and the roads got flooded, Dinesh noticed that the driver had not activated the wipers. He seemed to be in a blissful state, was unperturbed and had the heart to hum a song in spite of the near death situation he and his passenger were exposed to.

After a while the rain quietened down and reduced to a minor drizzle. Sometimes a drizzle does more to your vision than a full-fledged rain does. The raindrops dotted his windscreen in a million places. At a traffic light, the driver bent down and pulled out a rod. As Dinesh peered closer, he could make out that it was a wiper which had probably broken off from its intentioned position.

He reached out from his side window and wiped the window clean of any raindrops with some quick swishing movements of his hand. Mission accomplished, he dropped the wiper back inside the car. Dinesh reasoned with himself. Why would he want to fix a wiper when he is comfortable in the existence of such an arrangement? Why would he want to buy a new one when this works fine? The law does not punish you for this. When was the last time you heard of someone getting challaned because the indicators were not working? That would pretty much be the whole of Delhi. *Jab tak chalta hai chalne do...*Maximum for minimum...

The New Delhi Railway Station is the main railway station in New Delhi. It is the second busiest and one of the largest in India. It handles over 300 trains each day, from 18 platforms. The New Delhi station holds the record for the largest route interlock system in the world and probably also does for the largest number of visitors that depart from here every day.

As the taxi made its way to the front of the New Delhi Railway Station, Dinesh was amazed to see that time had stood still around the area that led to the railway station. It has always been like that and he had not seen any change over the past 30 years. You will find it overcrowded with vehicles of all shapes and sizes that jostle for space with pedestrians, cows, bulls and dogs, the frustrated traffic cop sitting on one side smoking a *beedi*, the beggars in abundance, the drug addicts smoking their way to heaven and hell, and young girls robbed of their childhood as they are routinely raped or are forced into prostitution for their own survival. These street girls suffer from different sexually transmitted diseases for which they cannot access hospitals for treatment. The girls have no idea of bodily functions—pubertal and adolescent changes, knowledge about sex and sexuality, reproduction & HIV and AIDS & STD prevention; it's all here, a veritable canvas of the ugly underbelly of New Delhi, all on a single road strip leading to the New Delhi Railway Station.

The main road running parallel to the Panchkuian road is flanked by *dhaba*s on one side and stalls of earthenware on the other side. There was, of course, no footpath as it had all been eaten away or devoured by the *dhaba-wallah*s or the stall vendors. The *dhaba*s were curiously similar as almost all of them would have a series of shining large steel vessels kept in the front with ladles or large spoons referred to as *kharchi*s kept on top of these utensils. One of the *dhaba*s had a big board in front of it which said:

SAI Restaurant
Only Vegetarian
Breakfast, Lunch and Dinner available.

There were many others with a similar message in front of them and most of them are open 24x7, like the call centres in Gurgaon. Call centres and *dhaba*s are similar in operation. The only difference being that the *dhaba*s were all poorly maintained and low on hygiene. Dinesh could see an urchin washing the utensils on the road adjoining the footpath. The used steel plates were dipped rather hastily into a filthy bucket and taken out in a flash and kept on the side to drip-dry. After some dips, the water was just as filthy as the plate that was being cleaned but it did not matter. It did not matter to the customers inside who were perched atop sun mica laminated chairs and tables. The price being what it is and if a good meal comes for under ₹20, then everything else can be compromised. Hygiene, cleanliness, is all inconsequential after a point. For a villager trying to make two ends meet, this is no less than a five-star hotel.

As you take your place inside these *dhaba*s which are almost always referred to as a 'restaurant' by the proud *dhaba-wallah*s, water in a steel glass will be kept on the table with a bang. A laminated menu card will be handed over to you. The menu card will be impressive in its range till you figure out that it is only the vegetables that are different to each dish; the gravy that is mass produced remains the same. The *roti*s will come fresh from the *tandoor* and do taste great until you see the urchin behind a worn out curtain, knead the dough inside what looks like a kitchen. He will occasionally pause to wipe the snort from his nose and continue with his task of kneading the dough. Dinesh presumed that was what added to the taste! The salad comprising of onion juliennes, radish and carrots with a spray of *chaat masala* or rock salt will arrive automatically and is complimentary.

"*Thodi aur* salad *dena,*" yelled one customer. It is, of course, religion to ask for a repeat of anything that is free. A complimentary salad item has to be repeated just as the *golgappa*s.

After you have finished a hearty meal at under ₹50, there is even some *saunf* or mouth fresheners. All this and the *dhaba-wallah*s still make profit. The point is that there is practically little or no infrastructure cost. The *dhaba* is unauthorised, the power connection illegal, the urchin staff are paid in kind with a meagre quantity of free food and rarely money, so clearly there is no overhead cost. What you produce is what you make money on.

Dinesh passed the *dhaba*s and entered the gates of the railway station. For all its size and scale, the lack of parking facilities is an abysmal example of the myopic planning that is ignored year after year. The cars are pushed into the confines of what seems like two rows of pavements. He couldn't help but notice that every car parked had a dent or two almost as a confirmation that it had been to this parking lot before. The parking attendant tore off a parking slip and handed it to the taxi-driver. The slip was handed over to Dinesh as he was responsible to pay on the way out. The slip boldly stated that nobody would be held responsible for any loss of items within the car and the car was being parked at the owner's own risk. What was the slip for, anyway? Dinesh knew the answer. It was to reinforce the fact that the responsibility of any damage or loss was that of the car owner. Without the slip, one may not be sure.

Dinesh headed towards the main station entrance. He looked at his watch and noted that he had arrived 15 minutes ahead of time.

The entry point to the main station was, like always, littered with people. Many were lying down with their belongings doubling up as pillows. There were other groups who were also squatted on the floor and many others who had their lunch or snacks open in front of them, while each member in the group helped themselves to a *roti* which was then rolled into a cylinder and eaten up. There were many stray dogs too which sat beside some groups hoping to catch any food item that would be thrown their way. The groups on the floor did not have eating habits that were significantly different from what was being practised by the dogs. Same method... same approach.

As he made his way to the platform ticket counter, he was shoved a couple of times by passengers who were running late and were on the verge of losing their train. He ignored them and stood in what seemed like a queue to buy a platform ticket. No matter how short a ticket line is, there will always be someone who will try to move into the queue from somewhere in the middle or try to ask someone already in line and closest to the ticket counter to buy the ticket for him. In doing so, he will be reprimanded by the others behind him, refused by most, abused by some and will eventually end up spending more time requesting for some assistance than he would have had had he stood in line in the first place. It's the illusion of being able to get something out by making minimum effort that is the fundamental driver of such actions.

"*Abe oye* Bihari, can't you see the line you motherfucker?" The state from where the person hailed had become an abusive term. The person standing in line was obviously incensed with the other trying to get in or hand over the money to someone in line to purchase a platform ticket.

"*Gaali kyon de raha hai?*" he retorted. "You buy the ticket, I am not stopping you."

"*Saale*, I will beat you so hard that you will not be able to shit for the rest of your life. Get back in line," he sounded menacing enough for the man to move to the end of the line obediently.

"*Saale*, these bastards will never change."

Dinesh purchased the platform ticket that was thrown at him from within the glass counter as he looked beside him to overhear an interesting conversation between a ticket aspirant and the ticketing official at the next counter.

"*Sirjee*, I need to go to Sonipat," stated the harried passenger.

"What are you going to do in Sonipat?" asked the ticket official. "There are no tickets available."

"*Sirjee*, I have to go. My mother is no more and I am going there for her last rites."

"I can't help you, why don't you go to Moradabad instead? I have tickets available."

Now, why would anyone want to go somewhere simply because the tickets were available? The reasoning did not matter. The passenger will still travel to Sonipat. The only difference being that the system and the absence of sound advice has ensured that he will travel illegally without a ticket. The system ensures that we break the law. The mother's last rites had to be performed. That could not be compromised, and that could only be performed in Sonipat, not in Moradabad.

Dinesh took his platform ticket and walked through the main gates. He had to go to platform no. 9 and that was a fair distance away. Since he had arrived much before time, he decided to look at some magazines that were available at the kiosk on the platforms.

There was a time not long ago when 'A.H.Wheeler' were the only booksellers that were found on the platforms of any railway station. Lalu Prasad Yadav decided to change all that as it was considered western. The name was too English for Lalu to digest and in a misplaced moment of patriotism, he decided to cancel the A.H.Wheeler contract for all the railway stations and put it up for open bidding.

A.H.Wheeler has been synonymous with Indian rail travel for over 125 years. The threat to A. H. Wheeler & Co., which published Rudyard Kipling when he was all but unknown, was announced live on television when Lalu Prasad Yadav, the then railways minister, delivered his budget.

He departed from his prepared text to say in Hindi: "Wheeler, Wheeler, Wheeler, Wheeler. Why do we have a bookstall by that name everywhere? The English have left this country long back."

While A. H. Wheeler sounds quintessentially English, the company is an Indian-owned enterprise that was founded by a French author, Emile Moreau, and an Indian business person in 1877. The only English thing about the company is its name, which was thought to be good for business in those days. Records show that Moreau borrowed the company's name from successful London booksellers called Arthur Henry

Wheeler's. Mr Moreau had so many books in his house that his wife demanded he get rid of them and the bookstores that used to dot almost every railway station under the name A.H.Wheeler was born. When Dinesh was a child, he used to wonder why there was a Wheeler stall at every railway station. He grew up reading their books on every journey he embarked, only to realise their uniqueness. It had 258 bookstalls across India and provided employment to 10,000 Indians. It stacked a variety of books from Mirza Ghalib to Nick Carter, aside from daily newspapers and magazines.

Above all, it instilled a reading culture among the travelling Indian masses and moved it beyond the standard game of cards that was prevalent amongst the bored and ticketless passengers.

As he walked from one platform to the other, he began to wonder and doubt Lalu's sense of prioritisation or the lack of it. There were more striking features to the railway station that needed strong attention, that is the filth, the beggars, the unusable loos, the unhygienic food vendors, the rude coolies, the list seemed endless.

He reached platform no. 9 and looked at his watch. With 15 minutes to go, the announcement over the 'Ahuja' speaker confirmed that the train was on time. Dinesh looked around and could see a sea of humanity waiting to welcome their near and dear ones. *"Cho chweet,"* he chuckled. This was the standard procedure. A dozen people to see off somebody and half a dozen to welcome them at the other end.

His father had noticeably changed in all these years. With multiple bypass operations, he had turned frail and seemed weak. It was hard for Dinesh to internalise this transformation. As a healthy man working as a 'Cabinet Secretary' with the entire world around him, here he was getting down from a train with just one person to help him with the bags. It was hard for

Dinesh to digest this change and he was sure that it was the same for his father too, just that he refused to acknowledge it.

As he got down from the train, Dinesh helped him with the baggage, an old duffel bag that he had been carrying around for years which he refused to part with.

"How is everything, *beta*?" he asked as he hugged Dinesh.

"Moving along, papa," Dinesh replied with a smile. All these years had got him accustomed to that response. He looked at Dinesh and patted him on the shoulder. Dinesh could sense that he was the only thing that was going right in his life. The rest was all in shambles.

"How is work treating you?" he asked.

"Not too bad," Dinesh replied and they walked towards the main exit point, pausing at regular intervals since his father could not keep up with him post his multiple surgeries. "Not too strong now, *beta*," he said almost apologetically and smiled partly as he paused holding the stair railing for support.

They did not speak too much but they did understand each other in their silence. Distances had created an uncomfortable unfamiliarity between them. The father that had left for Kerala post retirement was a different man compared to this form that he was now in. Almost defeated and reconciled to whatever life was throwing back at him.

His father was a contradiction of the fact that good deeds beget good outcomes. Without having ever smoked or consumed alcohol, he ended up with testicular cancer, a weak liver and two bypass operations. Without having ever touched a cent that did not belong to him, he was charged by the CBI for allegedly granting loans to a fictitious NGO, a charge that kept bringing him back to Delhi almost every three months for an appearance at the Patiala House courts where the case was being heard. Having always wanted his children next to him all

177

the time to a stage where his son stayed over 3,000 kms. away. His daughter, whom he always wanted well settled and married ended up staying with him, only as a divorcee with a child whose father later absconded. A wife, who did not understand him and therefore ridiculed him at every stage only because he did not have the earning capacity to fulfil her fancy wishes for Kanjeevaram sarees. Deep down Dinesh knew that his father would have loved to fulfill every wish that she had, but the means to achieve that end had miraculously vanished. The pension was just enough to pay for the trips that he had to make for his court appearances. In one way, the government was taking away from him what it was giving him. All his friends had left him when he needed them. And yet, he had no regrets. It was hard to understand that all this was happening in the lifetime of one individual. The city takes away more than it gives you.

"Sirjee, taxi, hotel, *aur koi cheez...*" enquired a cab driver as they exited the main gate. As Dinesh was walking ahead with his father's bag, the presumption was that he was a visitor and therefore would need transport.

The banter continued, "Taxi, want taxi… good guest house … all facilities." Dinesh looked at the man and he had a slight grin on his face. *"Naya maal aaya hai, sahib… bilkul virrgen."*

His father was still a fair distance away, walking ever so slowly down the stairs, pausing with every ten steps looking up occasionally to smile at his only son, an apologetic smile that kept telling Dinesh that he was sorry for not being able to keep pace. Dinesh had to turn his face away. "No, thanks!" he replied.

*"Sasta laga denge sahib,"* he continued. Somewhere along the conversation, the line between humans and vegetables

blurred and Dinesh was not sure whether the wretched form in front of him was trading in vegetables or human beings, and probably minors.

"*Nahi,*" he replied in an angry tone. The driver got the message and moved on to another traveller.

Amid the filth and stink of unkempt and uncleared garbage bins, uncouth autorickshaw drivers eyeing women passing their way, he helped his father into the car. He seemed relieved that he could finally sit down and rest. Dinesh sat in beside him as the driver started the car. After what seemed like eternity, the driver managed to turn the car from between the million other cars that had sandwiched his taxi. There were a couple of bumps but it did not seem to matter.

As the car exited, Dinesh paid the parking attendant ₹10 as he noted the duration of time the taxi was parked inside. He took the money and motioned it to go.

"How much did you have to pay?" enquired his father.

"Ten rupees," Dinesh replied.

"I am making you spend money *na, beta*? The taxi and all this. What to do, I cannot help it." Dinesh did not know how to respond. It had always been like this. His father concerned at the amount of money Dinesh had to spend on his account. In all these years, Dinesh thought that he had sent sufficient money to his father each month as a good son should and suddenly it all felt insufficient. He felt sick in the stomach. Was it because of the city and its trappings that he had failed to recognise this fact. This feeling made him feel naked with shame. He was so caught up with his own life that he had taken the comfort of his father for granted. At that moment, Dinesh vowed to change that.

It had stopped raining and there was less dust all around. The overflowing drains bore testimony to the fact that the rains would be remembered for many more days. The taxi passed the *dhaba*s which were doing brisk business. The utensils were almost empty and the urchin was busy cleaning the used utensils outside on the pavement. The water flowed relentlessly to the drain alongside. The vehicles ploughed through one another and negotiated their way alongside the tongas and the bullock carts. The horse seemed least agitated as it was well trained in the art of chaos or more specifically in the art of thriving in chaos. Alvin Toffler would have been proud.

The taxi made its way through the traffic and jumped the red light. An autorickshaw passed Dinesh just then. He thought he recognised the face in the auto, but wasn't sure. They continued to rumble through the potholed roads and waited as a traffic policeman motioned the traffic to stop. Dinesh wondered why he did so and moments later saw a convoy of Ambassador cars pass through Connaught Place outer circle area. A VIP movement and the city had come to a standstill. Some minutes later, they were back on their way.

The autorickshaw which he had noticed was parked a couple of cars ahead of them. His father was silent and thoughtful, so Dinesh did not think it appropriate to intrude into his thoughts.

As the taxi drove past the autorickshaw, Dinesh peered in and saw the same man whom he had met at the exit point of the railway station with an offer of a *virrgen*. Alongside him, in the autorickshaw, was another man chewing betel leaves and nestled in between them was a young girl, no older than 14, looking petrified and almost in tears.

# Dis-order Dis-order

Dinesh's father had come to attend a CBI hearing case in which he was the co-accused. The case had been dragging on for the past twenty five years with no outcome in sight and promised to carry on for another twenty years. Of the five co-accused, three had already died and one had gone insane. His father was the last man standing, literally.

He was up and ready to leave at 5:30 a.m. Dinesh could never understand as to how a consistent pattern was obvious in the way the older generation lead their life. Early to bed and early to rise and all that! So much of discipline in all that was done and said. We now have a scenario in which life for most starts at 9 p.m. with dinner being served in front of a TV set, or an evening out followed by some TV and off to bed by 11 p.m. if not later. He, for one, could never think of getting up, having a bath and being ready for the day by 5:30 a.m. Many of his friends did that but Dinesh was a night person, as Tavish had learnt to his discomfiture while experimenting with all-night study with him a night before exams.

"I will have the car ready to go at nine, papa," he exclaimed. "Is that ok?"

"Why do you worry about a car for me? I can take a bus to Patiala House. It is not a big deal." Dinesh did not say anything as the so called inconvenience was nothing compared to the inconveniences that his father had to face.

They had had this discussion more than a million times but there seemed to be no end to it, so he continued to keep the tradition alive. "No, papa. I will have the car sent, so be ready. Is nine ok to leave?" he repeated.

"Yes, that will be fine," his father relented.

The Patiala House Court Complex is situated in the palace of erstwhile Maharaja of Patiala near India Gate. The criminal Courts at Patiala House Courts Complex deal with cases pertaining to New Delhi, South and South-West Districts. The Delhi Legal Aid Authority also has its office at Room no.1 in Patiala House Courts Complex. It provides free legal aid to poor litigants and under trials who cannot afford to pay for the services of lawyers. The authority also organises Lok Adalats for expeditious disposal of cases.

The car stopped in front of the many gates of the Patiala House Court. The parking, similar to the New Delhi Railway Station, was an improvised mix of strategically placing the car between the space meant for two cars and then parking another car at right angles to it. Lost in the equation somewhere is the presence of a footpath which has another set of cars parked on it forcing the pedestrians to walk on the road and risk a possible hit-and-run. Even if there is a hit-and-run, Dinesh knew, justice was right next door.

Dinesh asked the driver to stop and they got off. As they walked through the gates, there was a loud horn as a rundown car tried to make its way through the gates. The guard manning the gate opened it with reverence and the car moved in. The windows were tinted and Dinesh could not see who was inside. There was a sticker on the front and the back windscreen. It was that of a collar with two extended bands in black-and-white. It signified that the occupant of the car was a lawyer, an advocate or a judge—by all counts an untouchable.

There were many two-wheelers parked inside and Dinesh held his father's hand as they walked through the compound to the lawyers chambers. Flanked on one side of the premises were food stalls similar to the ones that dot the roads leading to the railway station. Equally filthy, with the only difference being that the *dhaba*s near the railway station allowed you indoor seating whereas the ones in the court provided you with rickety benches to sit on, out in the open.

In spite of a law which prohibits smoking in a public area, there were any number of kiosks and stalls selling cigarettes, *bidi*s and *gutka*s. There were people and constables alike indulging in a nicotine break as the policemen held their captive prisoners in a unique vice like grip. There was one policeman who had his captives in handcuffs. The handcuffs were then linked to a chain which was held by him, much like a dog on a leash. The more serious criminals were held in chains whereas the less heinous ones were moved around in an interlocking grip with the policemen.

The courts were absolutely packed with people seeking justice or bystanders and escorts. It bothered Dinesh to think that the criminals were being escorted through this crowd of teeming millions. "What if…" he dared not think any further.

A backlog of cases has become a big problem for the Indian judiciary—from the Supreme Court to the subordinate ones. At the current speed, the lower courts may take 124 years for clearing up 2,50,000 cases. The number of cases pending in Delhi courts last year stood at 9,42,429. There are more than 12,00,000 cases pending in the five district courts of the capital which are fighting hard to clear the backlog. At present, as many as 12,02,130 cases are pending among which as many as 5,08,660 cases relate to dishonoured cheques. The figures reiterate that there was fat chance that any serious crime would ever see the light of day.

"*Aayeeye* Nair *sahab. Kaise hai aap?*" enquired the advocate who was entrusted with fighting the case out on behalf of Dinesh's father.

"I am ok," Dinesh's father replied. "What is going to happen today?"

"Nothing, sir," responded the advocate. "Another date," he smirked.

This has turned out to be some joke. Attendance in the courts had turned out to be another date fixing exercise. With another date given because of lack of witnesses or absence of the CBI official or absence of the judge either because of leave or strike, the case had continued for over twenty five years with no end in sight. The punishment had already been meted out by the inefficiency of the judicial system by which Dinesh's father, had suffered for over twenty five years hoping each time that justice will prevail, only to see it move about another date time and again. He was beginning to lose faith in the whole exercise and although Dinesh had seen traces of expectancy each time he came to the court in the initial days, it was increasingly dulled with the passage of time. Their attendance in court had become merely an exercise in the futility of expecting deliverance of justice.

The court was in session and the judge was seated listening to the arguments and the counter arguments of the prosecutor and the defendant. Dinesh looked around the courthouse. It had many steel almirahs which had stacks of files that had turned brown with the passage of time. The almirahs served as a barricade as well as a storage device.

As the judge read out his decision either for an extension of date or an interim order, the assistant seated next to him typed furiously on his old typewriter trying hard to keep pace with the proceedings.

Dinesh saw his advocate wink to the assistant and an acknowledgement followed. The file was placed on top of the stack which ensured that they would have to wait less for the next extension date. True enough, the judge took four minutes to declare that the case would be further heard in four months as all the accused had not presented themselves in person.

As they exited the courtroom, the advocate inched closer to Dinesh and asked if he had fifty rupees to spare in change. Dinesh asked why and he replied that he needed to give it to the clerk who had so conscientiously placed their file on top and ensured that they did not have to wait for another hour. Dinesh gave him the money and saw him hand it over to the clerk. A bit of back and forth followed as the clerk expected more but it was quickly settled.

"What was that for?" Dinesh's father enquired.

"Just something to keep your file moving," Dinesh replied knowing fully well of the response to follow.

"That's not a legal thing to do and you should know that," came the reply. His father still upheld his sense of belief and refused to accept the fact that the world had transformed to a place which did not have time to acknowledge his presence any more.

"Give side," exclaimed a police officer as he escorted a man in handcuffs through the court corridors. Dinesh moved aside and held his father's arm. It seemed like a procession as the accused in handcuffs was followed by his friends and relatives including a woman who had her head and face covered with her saree. She was crying and was pleading with the cop to release the man.

"What's this?" Dinesh asked his advocate.

"Oh, this man murdered his father-in-law as the latter objected to his drinking. In a fit of rage, this man hacked him to death with an axe."

"And who is this woman with her head covered?"

"That's his wife," he replied matter-of-factly.

Strange are the equations that keep changing with the passage of time. A wife is seen pleading with the cops to release her husband who had killed her father, a daughter who murdered her mother and showed no remorse, a young son who killed his father because the latter objected to his obsession with pornographic films. An action preceded the relationship and such instances were rising with alarming frequency. We have become less tolerant and more accepting of the violent ways of our relations. Property, money, passion all formed the genesis around which the seeds of violence and intolerance have nurtured. Dinesh remembered the time when he used to buy a bottle of Old Monk rum and wrap it nicely in a newspaper or a black plastic bag so we could carry it back without anyone noticing it. The bottle used to be safely hidden and if a bag wasn't found, it would slip into the shirt or forced into the trouser pocket. Not any more. These days it's no longer taboo to be seen with a bottle of alcohol. Any place, anywhere is a good place to consume your favourite beer. The cars with their air conditioning switched on are the latest mobile whisky vends, and it is not unusual to see a group of three or four sitting inside their Hyundai Santro and pouring their drink and soda while a *chhotu* fetches their chicken-tikkas from a nearby *dhaba*. It's almost standard operating procedure to have these mobile vends in any marriage reception. The marriage would be solemnised inside a giant pandal while a motley group of youngsters gather round a car with its boot open and helping themselves to generous helpings of whisky and soda, not to ignore the loud pulsating beats of *"Beedi jalailey..."* blaring from their ill-equipped car stereo.

"Sir*jee*, my fees," it was the advocate. He may forget to come to the court for an appearance before the judge but he will never forget to take his fees. Dinesh opened his wallet, careful not to reveal the full extent of its content and gave him ₹500. This is one thing that Dinesh always ensured; that he had just enough money in loose change to be able to give in denominations of ₹100 so he saved the flexibility of scalability. If he were to offer a currency note of a larger denomination, there would be no way the balance would be returned. Work expands to fill the time available. Similarly, the fee expands to accommodate the money being offered.

"Sir, please give me ₹100 more."

"Whatever for," Dinesh asked.

"There are many people I need to pay off. They will be expecting this. Remember that your case file was the one right at the top. At least I can buy them lunch and they will remember to accommodate you in the same manner the next time around."

Dinesh gave him the money not knowing if any alternative existed. His father stood at a distance looking around him.

The advocate thanked Dinesh and vanished through the corridors. Dinesh escorted his father through the broken iron gates and got into the car. The driver struggled as he wrestled with a million cars that were parked alongside. Finally, he managed to pull away.

As they were being driven off, Dinesh saw their advocate seated with a police officer engaged in a deep conversation.

He got up and bought some cigarettes, gave one to the police officer and offered a handcuffed person the other cigarette. The handcuffed youth took it and the advocate lit the match and offered to light their cigarettes as well. Soon enough, the merry threesome were puffing out smoke. The man in handcuffs was the same person who had killed his father-in-law.

So another trip to Delhi for yet another court hearing. Dinesh wondered about why it was referred to as the hearing when everybody had preferred to stay deaf for over 25 years. Like all things Dinesh's father had begun to get used to, this was just another. The case had gone on for over 25 years and with each passing year, it slipped further into the recesses of routine. The Fifth Pay Commission had ensured that his father could now come for the hearing by plane. In a way the government had made it more convenient for him to attend hearings. Since it was nearly impossible to discharge the case, it had thought of the next-best choice and that was to make it convenient and less time-consuming for him.

"It is much faster to travel by plane, *beta*," his father said as Dinesh received him at the airport. The simplicity of his father never failed to humble Dinesh. "I will check into the India International Centre this time." Before Dinesh could even show his protest, his father continued, "Chandu wants me to stay there this time. Perhaps, this is his own way of thanking me. I had to accept or else he would have felt bad this time."

"Always wanting others to be happy!" Dinesh thought.

Chandu was from the same village in Kerala and had moved to Delhi around the same time that Dinesh's father was appointed as the joint director in the Ministry. For months

188

he struggled to find a job and Dinesh's father intervened, swam against opposition from his wife who would not want to help anybody without something in return, and secured him a job as an Assistant. For this, Chandu remained eternally grateful to him. He had no means then to repay him but over time the tides had changed as events ensured a balance, equilibrium. Dinesh's father was coming back to the city he once ruled as Dinesh used to say, but in a state that was not even remotely close to the status he once enjoyed. This time Chandu had managed to convince his saviour to stay and he had reluctantly accepted.

"It is perhaps convenient too as I have to go to Patiala House and this will be so much closer." Dinesh just nodded. "Can you do one thing for me?" he asked.

"Of course, papa. Please tell me."

"Why don't you stay with me for the night? I will be gone tomorrow and this way at least I would have had a chance to spend some time with you."

Dinesh was thinking. How could he say 'No'? He idolised his father but could never bring himself to expressing it. One look at his father and he would become speechless, partly in sorrow and partly in confusion. Sorrow at the sight of what had come to pass and confusion at the thought of how it could happen to his father.

"Ok, I will stay. I will quickly go over to my house and get the night clothes and some things to eat."

"Ok."

Dinesh dropped his father at the India International Centre and went home. He knew his father would be well taken care of since Chandu was at the gate to receive him. "At least papa would get the flavour of what he was used to getting all the time at the Ministry, again," thought Dinesh.

He returned a couple of hours later. It was almost 9 p.m.

"What kept you?" asked his father waiting at the door just as he used to when Dinesh used to leave for school.

"Oh, the food took longer. I have also packed some *golgappa*s. You enjoy it, don't you?" asked Dinesh.

"Oh yes. Thank you, *beta*. I have put you through some trouble, haven't I?"

"Not at all, papa. Please do not say that."

He had merely smiled but his face betrayed a million emotions. Dinesh could tell that he was thrilled at the prospect of his son having dinner with him and staying the night over. It, in his mind, compensated for the hundred and one requests he had made to Dinesh to come to Kerala. All of which Dinesh had been unable to accomplish.

It was nearing 10:30 p.m. and Dinesh had laid down on the floor while his father slept on the bed.

It was two hours later that the pain started.

"Dinu, Dinu..."

Dinesh was woken up from his deep slumber immediately and he turned to look at this father now sitting on the bed, clutching his heart. He was sweating profusely and Dinesh knew that something was majorly wrong. He quickly got up and held his father. It was in a matter of seconds that he had his father up and in the car being driven at breakneck speed to the Safdarjung Hospital.

"The doctor is on his way," stated the bored clerk without even bothering to look up and roughly annoyed that Dinesh had disturbed his sleep.

Dinesh did not say anything as he rushed back to his father who was seated on the metal chair. He smiled as he saw his son approach. The doctor came an hour later and assured Dinesh that everything was alright. He suggested they should keep Dinesh's father under observation for a day at least. Dinesh nodded. "Is he going to be alright, doctor?" he asked but the doctor had already left as his shift drew to a close. Dinesh sighed at the hopelessness of it all.

"Only general ward is available, sir*jee*," said the same clerk again.

"Is there no deluxe room or premium room available?"

"No, all sold out. *Bataiye* sir, *itna* time *nahi hai*."

"Ok, give me what is available. I can be with him through the night, right?" Dinesh asked knowing fully well what the answer would be.

"Not in the general ward. You admit him and then you can come back in the morning at 10 a.m."

Dinesh did not want to leave his father alone. He had done that all his life. His father was smiling at him and nodded that it was all right.

After completing the documentary formalities and wheeling his father into the general ward, he, careful not to step on a dog in the corridor, reached the bed numbered 12. It already had a patient sleeping in it. He looked around for the attendant and there was none. Someone came in ten minutes later.

"Excuse me. My father has been allocated bed no. 12."

"So, *yeh toh raha na!*"

"Yes, I know," replied Dinesh, "but there is already a patient sleeping here."

"Nothing we can do. There is a shortage of beds and it has to be shared," saying so the attendant left.

"That's ok, *beta*," it was his father. "It's just for four hours! I will manage. Don't worry. I will be all right. You go and get some sleep."

"C'mon, please move out of here," it was the irritating attendant again.

191

Dinesh held his father's hand and looked at him. He was lost almost wondering where he was and trying not to have Dinesh worried.

"You go, *beta*," he said hurriedly.

Dinesh turned to go as his father seated himself next to the patient who was fast asleep. As he walked past the door, he turned to look at his father one last time. Seated on the bed, with his head bowed down, Dinesh thought he saw a picture of defeat.

A million events, a million issues, and only one heart!

A pale shadow of his former self, his inner-world had allowed him to survive this long while the external world let him down so helplessly, mercilessly.

Never had the words that had been uttered by his father when they met at the airport held a greater degree of significance in Dinesh's life. *"Why don't you stay with me for the night? I will be gone tomorrow…"* The realisation that he would now not need to visit Kerala and fulfil his father's long-standing desire, that his father now did not need to worry about court hearings any more, that he did not need to worry about his daughter or his grandson, that he did not need to worry about fulfilling his wife's ever increasing demands for expensive Kanjeevaram sarees. All this, and a lot more, had become irrelevant.

His father passed away in his sleep that night to an inner world, safe and happy in the thought that he would not trouble anyone, any more.

# The Other Side

Years passed and like most things in life, time healed everything and their gathered momentum on their path to normalcy.

*"Purani Dilli chalna hai,"* it was one of Dinesh's old time friends, Manoj, from the days he used to work with an American desktop publishing firm. "We can have *aloo poori* and *halwa* and wash it down with *badaam*-milk," he laughed his loud laugh.

For long they had cherished the thought of having breakfast in Old Delhi on a Sunday morning. Although they had all left their college life far behind, they still nursed a desire to go to Old Delhi for a meal. Dinesh was reminded of Old Delhi for two reasons, actually three. Firstly, for its rich traditional food outlets replete with *ghee* that drips from every dish. Secondly, for the phenomenally popular Karims that serves the most delicious *burra kebab*s that can put any KFC to shame and thirdly for G.B. Road, the only official red-light district in Delhi and home to the one girl Dinesh had found hard to erase from his mind and whom he wanted to meet again.

"Yes, let's go," Dinesh replied almost instantaneously, little realising that this one trip would be instrumental in closing an open loop in his mind that he had long wanted to close.

In fact, his only strong recollection of G.B. Road was when he had gone there with Nisha almost over five years back as her consort on a story that she was doing. When the reference of Old Delhi came up, his mind instantly raced towards G.B. Road and the girl by the side of the door named Vandana. It is strange how life had moved on without its baggage of such a touching recollection of that beautiful, childlike, blue-eyed girl, who had made a grab for the chocolate bar that he had given her.

"What would her life be like now? Is she still there?" Dinesh wondered and reached out to what Mayank Austen Soofi had to say on the life for a sex worker in G.B. Road. Mayank had visited the place on research work and had used the time to explore the real life as lived by a sex worker in the area. Amid his research, he interviewed one such sex worker from Bangalore.

*"You will perhaps never invite me to visit your family, for I am one of the 4,500 sex workers who live and work at Garstin Bastion Road, the city's red-light area. No pity, please. I have no objection to selling my body for the sake of roti. Besides, I have become used to this neighbourhood. My three boys were born here. The best friendships of my life were made here. My six co-workers live together like sisters. This kotha is my home.*

*"G.B. Road has 20 buildings. Dark corridors with steep stone stairs lead to kothas (96 in all) on the first and second floors. Mine is on the first. I usually wake up around noon. The bustle starts an hour earlier when the shops downstairs roll up their shutters. They say it is Asia's largest hardware market. It could be true. Stores are forever stocked with pumps and paints, tiles and toilet seats. But what's there for us? No parks, no playgrounds, not even a beauty salon. It is the pethi walla who brings nakhun-polish and lipsticks around midnight.*

*"We face many problems here. The kerosene sold in the ration shop is so diluted that we are forced to buy it in black*

*from Kamla Market. The sweepers demand a monthly bribe of ₹500 or else they dump rubbish on our stairs. If latrines get choked, plumbers ask for ₹2,500. We can't even complain to the authorities. There is always the risk of harassment.*

*"While we entertain customers throughout the day, evenings are busier. We dress up, apply powder, body lotion, and lipstick; and stand out in the balcony. By then the thoroughfare has started teeming with cars, scooters, rickshaws and pull-carts. Men stare up at us while the women, passing by in rickshaws, throw discreet glances. Sometimes, when we spot photographers, we take out our sandals and threaten them.*

*"Our daily customers have gone down from 15 to 2. That we are growing old is not the only reason. A few dalaals, in the payroll of wealthier kothas, solicit for customers in front of our stairs. Occasionally, they snatch the mobile phones and wallets of our regulars. When we ask these goons to go away, they dare us to complain to the police.*

*"Nowadays we are able to get a good number of customers only on select occasions—like Republic Day, Independence Day, or during political rallies when men come visiting the city for a day or two. However, it is the immediate future that appears more worrisome. The government is bringing in a law that will class our clients as criminals. Who would then come to us? How would we earn? What would become of our children?*

*"There's an MCD school here but I send my boys to the one at Minto Park. G.B. Road is a dangerous place and I don't want them to keep the wrong company while away from my eyes. Teachers are sympathetic and understand our problems. They have promised not to disclose our address to anyone. You see, my boys are always worried about their friends discovering where they live. Babu, my oldest, wants to be a maulana, and Chhotu, a lawyer. I try to bring them up well. A tuition master*

*comes in the evening to teach them Maths and English. The rest is up to their kismet.*

*"Money is always a problem. Out of my monthly earnings of ₹5,000, I spend ₹1,500 on my children and another 1,000 on new sarees and makeup items. The monthly rent of the kotha is ₹500. I also regularly send a money order worth ₹1,500 to my parents in the village. But it becomes difficult to sustain your income as you grow older. Some women manage to save and start a new life outside G.B. Road but I will have to stay on."*

Most get into prostitution to provide for their family. The family that they have left behind. It was for their older parents and younger brothers or sisters who need to be taken care of. "Even the prostitutes had a greater sense of responsibility than he did," thought Dinesh.

*"Aaja* hero," gestured a woman from atop the many decrepit balconies from where the prostitutes conduct their marketing exercise in G.B. Road. Dinesh looked up and saw a dark complexioned woman gesturing for him to come up to the *kotha*. He was on a cycle-rickshaw with Manoj and headed for some breakfast at Chawri Bazaar. They were passing through the hardware shops that conduct their business from the ground floor with the brothels located on the top floors. At hindsight, both hardware and software appeared up for grabs and ready to use.

He was being drawn to this place and what had happened with Nisha around five years ago flashed across his mind. Suddenly, he was gripped with the insensate desire to meet Vandana. He did not want to walk away although it had been so long. He wanted to catch a glimpse of her before they headed for their breakfast at Standard Sweet Shop in Chawri Bazaar.

He told his friend what he was thinking. Manoj looked at him incredulously and did not answer. After a while, he spoke,

"*Chup chaap baitha reh gaandu.* If you show your interest, they will make sure that you do not leave without striking a deal. *Apna lund sambhal ke rakh,* it will come in handy but not here."

"It is not the interest in them that is making me go there," Dinesh said as he quickly recounted the incident that had happened to him five years back. "I just want to see her one more time and…" saying so he trailed off. "I do not want to fuck anyone."

"But get fucked myself by going there again, right?" Manoj interrupted and laughed.

"No, you wouldn't understand. It is beyond sex and trade, it is to know about the life, or the lack of it, she is forced to lead. I do not know…"

"*Itne saal ho gaye.* Are you sure that she is even there? Do you even know which *kotha* she was assigned to?"

Dinesh did not like the term 'assigned to' in what Manoj had just said but humoured him nevertheless. There was no way he could have been in this place without the company of a local who knew the place well. Manoj was a local and he knew the place very well. He looked at Dinesh one more time and very reluctantly agreed. They stopped the rickshaw, paid the rickshaw-*wallah* ₹20 and walked towards one of the *kothas* marked no. 65.

As they walked up the stairs, Dinesh was accosted by one of the pimps. "*Kya chahiye?*" Dinesh realised why he was profiling them. Dressed as they were, he assumed that they would be the type who would be humping women in five star hotels or the types who would be browsing through the massage parlour advertisements that appear daily in the morning newspapers. '5 star or 7 star service. Full satisfaction guaranteed.'

Dinesh explained what he had come for. The pimp shooed him away warning, "If you want to fuck her, then pay first and talk later." He continued in an aggressive tone, "*Saala*, you want to waste time talking and seeing what it is like inside. Are you a fucking reporter? *Subah-subah dhanda kharab na kar.*"

"No," Dinesh said. But continued with his entreaty, "I will pay for the visit. I do not want to lay anyone. Just want to have a look inside and meet Vandana, the blue-eyed girl. Is she still here?"

It was 10 a.m. and the number of clients were low so the pimp turned less dismissive.

"*Achcha*, you want to meet Vandana? How do you know she is here?" the tone was a mix of annoyance, anger, anxiety and nervousness.

"I had seen her while my friend was humping a prostitute in the same *kotha* many years ago. She seemed to be eight years old and was carrying a cup of tea inside for someone. She had blue eyes and I have remembered her from then. She must have become ripe now for the picking." There was no way Dinesh could have told him the truth. He couldn't have said it any other way without arousing any suspicion.

The pimp's eyes lightened up, and Dinesh knew that the burst of vitriolic expletives which followed was more endearment than anything else.

"*Haan*, now let's talk business," Dinesh said firmly. He was beginning to feel repulsed at how the reference base for Vandana was being established. "Is she here or not?"

"Yes, she is. A teenager now, she will be expensive and will cost you ₹5,000 for a hour," he said.

"Ok," Dinesh replied and the deal closed. Manoj looked at him incredulously but remained silent, clearly not knowing what to do. It was too early in the morning for him to seek another for his own comfort.

*"Dekh lena sahib, hamaare pass aur bhi young ladkiyan hai.* If you like someone inside, then we can negotiate a discount. There is some fresh stock that came in last night from Nepal," he let out an evil laugh through his betel and *gutkha* stained teeth. Dinesh was instantly repulsed but Manoj egged him on. He wanted to end this as fast as he could.

Dinesh handed over the money to the pimp and he counted each note making sure to examine the watermark on the ₹500 currency note. Once he was through, he beckoned that they follow him.

They wandered in through the narrow hallway which had a row of rooms on one side with a dirty overused curtain providing an illusion of privacy. In one room there were at least a dozen young women huddled up. The place was suffocating and it resembled a pigsty. These minors looked not more than 14 years old but they said they were 20 years old. They had the documents to prove it.

The entire place was submerged in an uncanny ambience. The dark compartments in various parts were camouflaged to look normal from outside. Dinesh had not seen these when he had last visited the place with Nisha, the attractive journalist who had laid him for vested interests and beyond. Maybe he just did not want to look at anything else now. Those dark compartments were called *tehkhana*s in the local parlance. *Tehkhana*s are hidden safe places between *do-chatta*s (mezzanine spaces narrowing down from the roof of a big room). These *tehkhana*s are convenient to hide child prostitutes whenever there are raids or visits by social workers.

Dinesh was looked at suspiciously by each of the occupants of the *kotha*s, and by some clients who walked out buckling up their belt. A commercial sex worker, as long as she is 18 or above and solicits voluntarily keeping her activity outside the

199

vicinity of public places and notified areas is not punishable under the law. However, running or abetting a brothel, living on the earnings of prostitution, procuring or inducing or taking persons for prostitution, carrying out prostitution around public places, and seducing or soliciting for the purpose of prostitution, are all punishable acts. The law dealing with prostitution is ambiguous. While on the one hand it does not prohibit prostitution, on the other hand it penalises those prostitutes who are caught soliciting customers whether by words or gesture or wilful exposure of her person. A sex worker can legally practice her profession inside a house but cannot solicit clients on the streets.

The law has many loopholes and inadequacies. It does not punish the client and it does not make any provision for the rehabilitation of women and children who are rescued from brothels. There is no single legal entity which oversees its implementation. That's what gives birth to a hundred Vandanas every day.

As they walked and surveyed the area, the pimp nudged Dinesh, "You were talking about her, right?"

They turned their heads in the direction he was pointing to and there she was.

Dinesh knew it was Vandana as soon as he saw her. She looked older than her age but had the same look in her strikingly beautiful blue eyes. He was staring at her but she did not seem to recollect anything. Not that he expected her to. Now taller with a faded frock hiding her somewhat frail body, she looked clean. She stared back and then returned her gaze to the toys in front of her, she seemed to be looking for something, perhaps her lost childhood or the remnants of it.

"Yes," Dinesh replied to the pimp before Manoj could answer. He was trying very hard to hide his excitement.

"*Tu marvayega yaar*. Let us get the hell out of here," said Manoj. He was beginning to feel uncomfortable and Dinesh could sense it, but he had unfinished business to close.

The pimp then led them into a stinking room smelling of cheap Charlie perfume. They did not want to sit anywhere. The twelve year old Vandana looked at them and asked them how they would like to do it. "*Dono saath mein, ya alag alag?*"

A part of Dinesh died when she asked them that. She could be any school student studying and wanting to be part of the society that had discarded her. She could have been his daughter, she could...

Dinesh could tell that she'd been 'initiated' into the trade for some time. The childlike innocence was fast waning but it was still there. She did not recognise Dinesh and he did not try to help her recollect. Dinesh looked at Manoj as both did not know how to continue next. Dinesh was not sure whether he was speaking to a child, a teenager, a prostitute, or a mixture of all three. He looked around the room. There was a small colour TV set in one corner with V-shaped antennas jutting out from the back. A small table lay parked with many books kept on top of it. A shelf on top of the table had a picture, perhaps of her as a child, Dinesh thought, to remind her of the childhood she never had. Next to the picture were local-made Barbie dolls. Dinesh looked at Vandana in turn. It was evident that she had tried to dress up as Barbie. Dinesh got up to examine the books.

"*Bolo seth*. I do not have time to waste. Others are waiting. Do it fast, whatever that you want to do," she interrupted.

Dinesh continued towards the table and saw that these were Amar Chitra Katha books. This was one side of her. A side that was her own, to be shared with no one. The side she wanted to show was not what Dinesh wanted to see. On one side of the wall lay the evidence to prove that she was still a child. On the other side was a bed with posters of naked women cello-taped on the wall. Two sides of the same coin and each one so much in contrast. One side depicted childhood and the other side depicted the state that she was in. In the middle, where we sat was the balance.

Dinesh turned to her and she agreed to talk after much persuasion. It took her a while to internalise that they were there for a talk and not for her flesh. That, to her, was an illusion and unbelievable. After much time, she agreed to tell them her story.

Her unfortunate story unfolded as a series of missed opportunities. She was from West Bengal. Her parents, with a meagre income, had many children to support. It was difficult to survive. She said that she got abducted at the age of nine. "Someone promised me a job," Vandana said recalling her past.

"I was sold in Sonagachi in Calcutta before I even went to a proper school. My mother was left all to herself after my father was killed by the *babu*s for demanding payment for the meals they had eaten at his *dhaba*. With three sisters and two brothers, she had to sell me off to a man for ₹500. He took me by train to this place and sold me to a madam here."

The small dingy room in the brothel next to where they were seated had at least twenty five young women; some shouting abuses, others simply chatting. Dinesh had to strain hard to fully understand what she had to tell him.

"For three months, the *malkeen*'s *babu* assaulted and raped me to prepare me for this trade," Vandana continued. "One day there was a police raid in the brothel where I was living, and I was taken into police custody."

Suddenly she bared her legs and showed a deep scar. "I was put behind bars. There at midnight a police officer came and tried to squeeze me out of the lock-up. He could not do that and my legs got entangled in the iron bars. While I was stuck between the bars, the police officer raped me. My legs were injured and were bleeding profusely but he did not care. I was shouting but there was no one to listen."

Vandana continued with her tale of horror but a part of Dinesh had stopped listening.

"I was staying in a caged brothel for three years. When there was no client, we were pushed into a cage and locked in."

Dinesh could not take it any more and motioned to Manoj to leave. As he got up, she reached out to the coat-tails and held tight. Dinesh looked down at her and could see fear personified in her eyes.

"Sorry, *seth*. Are you angry with me? You will not complain to madam, will you?" she asked as they were leaving with fear writ doubly large on her face.

"No, we will not. Don't worry," he replied trying hard to fight the teary film that was fast forming in his eyes.

She walked towards the bed, lifted the dirty thin mattress and took out what looked like a condom pack. She quickly ripped it open, took the condom out and threw the silver foil on the floor.

"They look for proof. An unsatisfied customer means loss of repeat business. We have to do it whether we like it or not," having said that she walked across to the latrine and flushed the unused condom down but left the condom pack cover lying on the floor. That was her evidence of survival and life. She did it without any hesitation or doubt. The way she handled the condom and flushed it down the toilet was a mechanical act. An assembly-line type of action. There was no sensitivity or even an awareness of what she had done. This was her side of survival, survival for the world so she could survive in her world, her world of Barbie dolls, Amar Chitra Kathas and her childhood.

Dinesh took one last look at her, reached out to his coat packet and took out a Mars chocolate bar.

He handed it over to her and she took it without a moment's hesitation. "You are a nice man. Can I call you *bhaiyya*?" she asked.

"Of course," Dinesh replied, not knowing what he was saying but more with the intent of helping her overcome her feeling of utmost dejection. Battered and bruised, she still pined for those rays of hope that could lift her out of this well of despair where each day a part of her died. There would be many more like her but he was not sure what it was that drew him to her, that did not allow him to forget her even after so long. Was it the blue eyes that still yearned for those elusive moments of hope? Was it the first time he saw her that cemented the bond? He would never know.

Manoj and Dinesh walked out through the door. Dinesh looked back one more time and saw that she had returned to her Amar Chitra Katha with the Barbie doll nestled next to her side on the bed. Dinesh was still reeling from this visit and Vandana had already moved on to her real world.

They exited down the stairs and stepped out in to the corridors of the hardware market, pausing for a brief moment as Manoj withdrew money from HDFC bank's ATM.

"I need to do something for her," Dinesh said as he looked at Manoj who was busy counting the dispensed notes.

"Just relax! I am never going to come back here again," Manoj replied. Dinesh ignored him.

On the way, he stopped to buy a cigarette from the *paan-wallah* who was managing his kiosk. Dinesh had to calm himself down. Manoj waited.

"*Kya hua sahib*? You look worried and disturbed. Wasn't she good enough for you?" asked the *paan-wallah* as he spread a thick coat of *chuna* on the betel leaf he was holding in the palm of his hand.

"Nothing, nothing at all," Dinesh said but continued to tell him about what Vandana had narrated to him, about herself and the experiences that were now a part of her life, getting repeated day after day, night after night.

"That is a common story here, sir*jee*. Everybody here has a story to tell and we cannot do anything about it, except hear them. Vandana is a nice girl but she has aged so much over the past many years. When I look at her, I feel so sad but these pimps just do not think so. All they can think about is the next customer that she will have to sexually satisfy."

Dinesh winced. "Do you know this girl, Vandana?" he asked. Manoj was looking at him impatiently and he could see that he was worried about them and the place. But Dinesh was curious to know more.

"Of course I do! She comes here every day in the morning to buy *paan* for her *malkeen*. I usually give her some sweets. She is after all a child. Whenever she comes here, she narrates a story to me from one of the comics or books that she has read. These *kabaadi-wallahs* are nice to her and usually give her some old books and comics from their stack."

"One day she narrated her story to me and I was overcome with grief. I thought I will do something to save her from this mess, but it not possible. I have to survive. If any of the pimps find out that I helped with the escape, they will simply kill me and make life impossible for my family. Anyway, there are so many of them. *Kis kis ko bachchayenge.* But what are people like you doing here? You seem to be from good families."

Dinesh proceeded to tell him the story and what had drawn them to the place. His conversation with him was interrupted a thousand times by customers wanting a *beedi*, *gutkha*, *khaini*, etc.

"She was here when she was barely nine. She reminds me of my daughter but her plight is something that I would not wish on my worst enemies."

"Let's go," said Manoj getting concerned about their safety.

"Thank you!" Dinesh said as he gave the *paan-wallah* ₹100. He did not bother to wait for the change. Everything seemed so inconsequential in perspective.

"Sir*jee*, you have forgot to take the balance," the *paan-wallah* was shouting after them as they had turned to leave.

"Buy that girl something with the balance money," Dinesh said as he turned to leave.

As he was walking away, the *paan-wallah* shouted out, "*Sahib*, please see if you can do anything to help." Dinesh knew what he was referring to and knew that he cared. What was not clear to Dinesh was whether Vandana would be happier or sad in any other place. Whether any other place would allow her the freedom to exercise her double identity. Both her worlds seemed to coexist amicably.

Dinesh nodded nevertheless and joined Manoj on the cycle-rickshaw. Neither of them spoke on their way back. They needed to get their thoughts back in focus and he had to do something for Vandana lest he forgot her just as time had forgotten her.

"What could I do?"

The answers had so far eluded him.

The breakfast was great. *Aloo poori* finished with *halwa* all dripping and soaking wet in *ghee*. There were a few customers and an unending fleet of luxury cars outside Standard Sweets.

The drivers were all lined up outside with small slips of paper in their hands. "*Sahab* has ordered this," said one as he passed on the slip to the man seated behind a huge pan of hot oil, deep frying the *pooris*. Hardly had the *pooris* come out of the pan, were they passed on to the unending line of customers. Business was brisk.

Manoj and Dinesh asked for *badaam*-milk to wash down the over infusion of ghee in their palate. The place was run down with tables with sun mica tops. Dinesh was instantly reminded of the *dhaba*s opposite the railway station. "Strangely, the food at all these small-time joints seemed infinitely tastier than what one gets to eat at fancy restaurants," Dinesh said. Manoj agreed.

They walked away after paying a paltry sum of ₹65 for the entire meal for two. Dinesh even got it packed for the family. Old Delhi rocks even without an earthquake!

It was well past 12:30 in the afternoon and almost time for lunch. They bid goodbye and promised to meet again soon for a repeat. They drove their separate ways and as they passed India Gate, Dinesh was suddenly reminded of Vandana.

How quickly they had forgotten her, yet again! How quickly they had forgotten a girl who was robbed of all her innocence at the age of nine. How at the age of twelve she had all her life robbed away from her with no hope in sight. The police officer who could have provided her with a ray of hope was quick to diffuse it for his moment of sexual gratification. In the pretence of doing his job, he had extracted all that he could possibly extract from whatever source he could. It did not matter whether the girl was nine or nineteen. The fact was that she was in his power and in a misplaced sense of power, he had chosen to exploit her in the only way he knew best: rape. That she had her legs entangled between the rods of her jail cell had only helped further his bestial pursuits and made his task easier. He had her in his clutches and he could satisfy his perversion with minimum effort.

Maximum for minimum...

For some reason, Dinesh believed that he would be meeting Vandana again. He only hoped that it was sooner rather than later.

# Part II

Part II

# South of Delhi

"Uncle, *hum* shift *kar rahein hain*," Dinesh told his Bihari landlord. The landlord did not say anything at first and let out a loud burp. He looked around for a piece of cloth to wipe his mouth and then looked up at him.

"Where are you going?" he asked.

"I have bought a house in DLF, in Gurgaon," Dinesh exclaimed with an air of triumph.

"How big is it?" the landlord asked.

"Well, it is a four-bedroom duplex," he replied. The landlord was taken aback. He was perhaps thinking that Dinesh would have managed to save a bit over the past many years in spite of the rental that he had been charging and the electricity that he had helped subsidise. The saving that he could have laid his hands on if he had charged extra rent. "Damn, missed opportunity!"

"Good. When I was your age, I used to be as focused as you are. You have done well. You came here just as you got married and now you are leaving after five years into your own house. This house is obviously lucky for you as you got a new job, bought a new car and now your own house. Good!"

Dinesh could see that he was proud of him. Over the past so many years, he had come to view him in a different light. He apparently viewed him as a son figure as he had none of his own. In a Bihari household, it is so important to have a male child in the family. A family without a male child is just not complete. When Dinesh had moved in, the landlord had wasted no opportunity to tell Dinesh that a child was a must to complete a family.

"You should have someone who will crawl around, keep you awake at night, pee on the bed and call you 'Papa'. Isn't that something you would like to hear?" Dinesh had to agree that it did seem to be an emotional thought and something he mentally accepted although not perhaps in the way the landlord had tried to market the 'concept'.

"Of course, uncle!" Dinesh replied, "We will want to extend the family with a child but that will not be soon as we need to settle ourselves first."

The Bihari landlord continued, "Make sure it is a boy." Dinesh was not sure if he had any control over that unless the landlord expected him to choose the right sperm and direct it to go and penetrate the egg at that right moment. Presto, it's a boy!

"Why does it have to be a boy?" Dinesh asked.

"You have to have a boy now to balance the girl and make the family complete," he said. "Every family should have a boy," came almost as an afterthought.

"And what happens if there is a boy? Does it need a girl to complete the family?" Dinesh asked rather sarcastically.

"No, no. A boy completes the family as it ensures that the family lineage carries on."

Clearly, he had chosen to ignore the fact that there does need to be a woman at the other end to complete the cycle of procreation. Masturbation does not lead to babies.

The view as expressed by the landlord was not in the least an isolate view as almost over 80 per cent of the country endorses the view that a girl is typically a good second child to have. Dinesh had a theory here and it was so uncannily true. You will see that mostly in cases involving parents having two children, the first one will be a girl and in most cases having more than two children, the majority will be girls. The quest to have boys as an essential in the family drives the behaviour of producing more till such time that there is a boy in the family. There is an increasing tendency to select boys when previous children had been girls. In cases where the preceding child was a girl, the ratio of girls to boys in the next birth was 759 to 1,000. This fell even further when the two preceding children were both girls to 719 girls to 1,000 boys. However, for a child following the birth of a male child, the gender ratio was roughly equal.

Dinesh did not have the heart to continue this conversation any longer as it was empty of any logic, intellect or right thinking. As Thomas Hardy had once said, "I am but a fool to argue with a fool."

One of the primary reasons for the skewed sex ratio in the country is the rampant killing of the girl child either at birth or eventually during its life. A mid-wife in Bihar is paid more to facilitate the birth of a boy than she is for the birth of a girl child. She is then paid even more to kill a girl child than to bring it into this world. Dinesh couldn't comprehend a woman having the heart to do this to another woman to be...

Plenty of couples try to subvert the rules of nature in a less drastic way and are happy to pay for the privilege. The author of *How to Choose the Sex of Your Baby* retired to Las Vegas on the proceeds. In 1991 modern science had shifted the figure to 929 females to each thousand males. Gandhi's goal of a nation in which, intellectually, mentally and spiritually, women would be equivalent to men has not been realised.

"*Achcha*, so when would you like to leave. Remember you have to give me one month's notice?"

"So much for the father-son equation," Dinesh thought with a smile. "I would like to move out in 15 days."

The man looked at his wife who gave an understanding nod. He seemed reluctant at first but mentally reconciled.

"Ok, give me 15 days rent and you can go. Do not forget to visit us once you are settled there."

He said the last words in such a hurried manner that Dinesh did not know how to react. The emotion was beginning to show from beneath the strong façade of a 'don't care, don't give a damn' crude demeanour. It was almost like he was trying to hold back something. Something he did not want to be seen lest it expose his vulnerability. Strange man, he had so many contradictions in one frame.

Dinesh thanked him for all his help (there was none, though) and walked back to his rented accommodation on the second floor. As he walked up, he paused for a second to look back.

He thought he saw his landlord wipe a tear as he walked into his bedroom. There was an underbelly to all this.

"Sir*jee*, do not forget my commission," said Jitender. Jitender was the broker who had helped Dinesh get his house in DLF. Like all brokers, he had assumed a larger-than-life significance once he had introduced Dinesh to the seller. As with all brokers, it is not openly apparent about whose side they are. The broker is yours but invariably ends aligning with the seller.

"I am expecting ₹17.5 lacs for my house," Tripurari said, as she sat in front of Dinesh surrounded by her husband and a couple of other relatives. The relatives manage to find a prime place and position in the affairs of the family however distant.

Whether it concerns them or not, it doesn't matter. A point of view is always available for the asking and opinions assume the status of arseholes, everybody has one!

"I am afraid my budget does not allow that," Dinesh replied in a matter of fact tone.

They were at the seller's house in a dilapidated part of Munirka, opposite JNU, and were being served Rooh Afza, *namkeen* and biscuits. She looked askance at the broker almost seeking support.

"C'mon sir*jee*, why don't you increase the budget a bit," said the broker.

"Why don't you pay the difference then?" Dinesh snapped back, "Or better still, why don't you forgo your commission."

"Don't get upset, sir. I am here to help."

"Help my ass," Dinesh thought. All he was interested in was his commission. It did not matter how the deal closed and whose side he ended eventually.

They finally closed the deal at ₹16.90 lacs which was ₹10,000 lower than his final estimate. Life had taught Dinesh to never start with the final figure, whether it was shopping in Sarojini Nagar or Lajpat Nagar, or buying fruits and vegetables or closure of deals. Save the best for the last.

As they left the house, Jitender caught up with him on the way to his car. "Sir, do not forget my commission. It is 1 per cent of the total value, including registration and stamp duty."

"Fuck off," Dinesh said. "You do not expect me to pay you a commission on top of the selling price. You want to include the registration and stamp duty as well. Will you facilitate the sale without the stamp duty papers to help me save the brokerage? That is the money I have to pay over and above the cost of the house," Dinesh was beginning to lose his patience with the vulture.

He did not get too affected. He knew that this was part of a standard operating procedure. Start higher so the final commission figure, which is the norm, appears lower in relation. The approach of saving the best for last that Dinesh had learnt seemed to be a freely downloadable approach for all to use.

"Ok, sir. We will adjust as you please. Let us close the registration formalities at the earliest. Remember the registration cost is 14 per cent of the cost of the house. This will be on the declared white value," he said with a wink.

The reference to the black component in property deals is so common that it has lost its distinction and the line between white and black money is so blurred that it is nearly non-existent.

"I thought the registration cost was 12.5 per cent," Dinesh said with an air of pseudo-intellectualism most commonly found in Bongs.

"Yes, sir, it is 12.5 per cent but we have to pay another 1.5 per cent to the dealing clerk to ensure the papers get processed in a timely and quick way," Jitender grinned.

Dinesh vowed to fight this practice and landed up at the Registrar's office the next day. Tripurari came accompanied with her brothers and uncles in tow, presumably to guard the black component of the deal that would be exchanged once the papers were signed and the deal formalised. Once the papers were signed, they were submitted to the dealing clerk who made the obvious pretence of examining them with complete diligence.

"*Mubarak ho*, sir!" he exclaimed through the grilled window.

"Thank you," Dinesh replied. The clerk continued to look at him askance. After some time, he turned his face away and asked for the fees to be deposited.

"By the way, is there any way you can reduce the 1.5 per cent that you are going to take for the processing. I am not sure that I can afford to pay that much," Dinesh stammered.

"No problem, sir," the clerk replied without a moment's hesitation. Dinesh was most elated and stared back to Jitender who appeared surprised.

"You can pay me whatever you want," he exclaimed while continuing to examine the papers, "but you will have to complete the documentation first. The registration form is still not complete and the copy of the agreement to sell is not notarised. This will take time so perhaps you can bring this to me tomorrow and we can go through this one more time".

Dinesh got the message and quickly offered to pay him the 'processing fee' of 1.5 per cent. He smiled at him and asked him if he would like to have a cup of tea. Dinesh politely declined, certain that he may charge for that too.

"Although, there are some missing entries and papers, I am sure I can take care of that," he continued. Dinesh quickly handed him over the money which magically disappeared.

"Here you go," the clerk stated. "The papers are complete and you can take this slip. Bring the slip in tomorrow and I will have the stamped and formalised copy handed over to you."

Dinesh did not even feel the need to thank him but he did. He had never experienced his resolve to not pay anything extra dissolve so fast. There was no way that anyone could beat the system since it is not the clerk alone who ends up richer. It is a chain and one that goes right up to the top. The clerks even refuse promotions as that would entail bidding goodbye to all this money that comes to them from under the table or through a grilled window. They are richer than even their bosses as they make more than their monthly salary through the 1.5 per cent they get for every deal.

Rumour has it that the PA to a senior member in the Ministry once dropped into the Registrar's office to register a property for a Ministry official. He too was asked to pay the

1.5 per cent. Incensed, he refused to pay and stormed out. The clerk couldn't care less. Once back at the senior officer's office, he narrated the entire incident and recommended that the clerk be transferred. A resounding slap was planted on the PA's face by the officer, "If you ask that the 1.5 per cent be waived for you on my behalf, then someone else who hears of this will demand the same treatment and then more and more will follow. If that happens, how in the world would I get my monthly cut of ₹5 crores, you *behenchod*." The PA quickly vanished and was seen at the Registrar's office making the payment to the clerk who had the 'I-told-you-so' look about his face.

Dinesh collected the slip from the clerk and looked at Jitender who could not help but control his snigger, "Sir, I told you that this is the practice and it will not change. When can I take my commission?"

As Dinesh settled down with his wife in DLF, he began to understand the subtle differences between living in Delhi and living in NCR. The area in the house was significantly larger. What makes up a couple of rooms in DLF is what makes up the whole house in New Delhi, and the comparison being among the better areas and not the poorer cousins. The cost of living is much more and the gentry consist mainly of MNC executives. You have to have your own mode of transport to survive in DLF as the public transport does not exist and even if it does, it was of little use to people like Dinesh who did not wish to resemble a subway sandwich while travelling in an autorickshaw. The high rises with its 24 hours of power back up, water and security is a boon to most and Dinesh began to enjoy his moments.

DLF City, an identity in itself, is an ultimate branding phenomenon in Gurgaon. You have people who stay in

Gurgaon and you have people who stay in DLF. This is a fact that is recognised even by the media. If you look into any of the TO-LET classifieds that appear in the prominent newspapers, there is a separate section for Gurgaon and a separate section for DLF and the private colonies. DLF are the only real estate giants who build skyscrapers valued at over 20 million rupees but are arrogant enough to not have any sample flats. They still sell and there are buyers aplenty. Many of these flats are bought for investment purposes by NRIs who are based out of the US or Dubai.

Innovation knows no bounds and neither does competition. One of the non-DLF builders acquired the land adjoining the DLF Golf Course and built a towering apartment complex overlooking the course thereby trying to maximise its property value on somebody else's landscape. The marketing literature proudly announced apartments with a golf course view. DLF did not like the fact that the apartments were being sold for a premium because of a feature owned by them. Shortly after that, Aralias was launched under the DLF banner right next to the other apartment tower. Now Aralias had the golf course view and all the other builder got was an apartment block that faced the rear side of the apartment tower built by DLF.

Sometimes innovation crosses the realms of practicality. A new concept called 'expandable homes' was launched with just open halls and no rooms. One could choose the size one wanted and have them custom-built. These were priced even higher than the finished apartments. Shining Audis or BMWs ease their way through the imposing gates of the DLF Golf and Country Club while fruit sellers outside sell fruits on the road leading to the course. There is enough room for everyone and each one can coexist.

No matter where you stay, it is hard to beat the perspective distortions that are carried in the minds of all. If you drive a big car, you obviously live in a bungalow, little knowing that the car has been bought on EMIs that is nearly breaking the owner's back. It is all *showbaazi* in Delhi and the *Dilliwallah* thrives on it. It is the contrary in Mumbai. Even the richest bloke will be travelling in the electric train jostling for space with a junior executive in a small firm. Dinesh was comfortable eating *kulche chhole* from a *redi-wallah* which would be impressively titled 'Amritsari Kulche', but he could not be seen doing that by the roadside for fear of retribution in case he was noticed by any of his Delhi friends whose idea of a good meal did not spill beyond the Italian marbled corridors of the Aman. It is misplaced, but Delhi does that to you eventually. Having *golgappa*s at Prince Pan Bhandar in GK II is acceptable, but not in Lajpat Nagar because it is where the wannabes hang out. Significant location ensures societal acceptability.

One of the classic examples of perceptive distortion took place when Dinesh decided to look at some of the fancy penthouses in Gurgaon, just to get a feel of what they look like. He could at least look at it and savour the experience, and feel the aura of walking around a penthouse overlooking the golf course. The best part was that there was no price tag attached to this experience.

Maximum for minimum…

He had heard of some of the good ones overlooking the DLF golf course where the top floors have every bedroom overlooking the golf course. He was not sure as to why it was so important to have the bedroom overlooking the sea or the golf course or the harbour. The bedroom is a place where you would want to sleep unless the idea is to experience the sheer joy of humping someone with the golf course or the sea in

the background ... lends a definition to humping perhaps...
a perfect experience set around idyllic surroundings ensuring
the best bang for buck.

"Hello, Narinder speaking," Dinesh had dialled one of the
brokers from a classified listing in the newspaper. Someone who
specialised in penthouses and premium apartments.

"Hello," Dinesh replied. "I am looking to buy a penthouse,"
he lied. There was no way he was going to tell him the truth.
The brokers will be least accommodative in case you are looking
for a house or apartment without of the intent of buying.

"Ok, sir," suddenly Dinesh had been knighted! "Which
area are you looking for and what is the budget?"

"The budget is not the issue. I am looking for something
near the golf course area."

"I have just what you need, sir. When would you like to
see it?"

"How about tomorrow at 10 a.m.?" he asked.

"Sure, sir, no problem," he replied with utmost earnestness.
An enquiry for any other property would have elicited a far
more lukewarm response.

"Done! Let's meet at gate no. 2 of the DLF golf course
then," Dinesh continued.

"Sure, sir. I will be there," he replied.

The next day Dinesh parked his Maruti Zen at the DLF
golf course gate just behind a shining Hyundai Sonata at sharp
10 a.m. He had got used to the part where nothing happens
on time especially in Delhi and being on the suburbs, could
Gurgaon remain untouched. It is a contagious thing. It was
ten minutes past 10 and Dinesh was beginning to get restless.
He reached out to his mobile and dialled Narinder's number.

"*Haanji*, sir," he replied almost instantaneously, almost as
if he was waiting for his call.

"Where are you?" Dinesh asked in an annoyed tone.

"I am parked in front of the DLF golf course road, sir," he replied sounding worried.

Dinesh had seen the driver of the car in front of him put his mobile to the ear as he had dialled the number.

"I am in a Sonata, sir. It is light blue with *gujjar boy* written on the back window," he said proudly.

"Ok, I am coming," Dinesh replied and drove his Zen alongside his car.

As his car drew alongside, Narinder looked sideways and saw him for the first time. Dinesh smiled and he gave him a half smile as he gave his car a once over.

"I will follow you," Dinesh said and he half nodded. Suddenly the enthusiasm and eagerness had been replaced by a look that screamed, "What the fuck?"

His car stopped after a distance and he got out with the mobile planted in his ear. He was talking to someone as he motioned to his sidekick to lead Dinesh to the house as he reluctantly followed him. The enthusiasm, the interest and the gung-ho disposition that was evident from the previous days phone call had disappeared only to be replaced with a dull, uninterested, must-go-through the motions kind of approach.

The sidekick opened the main door and led Dinesh through the doors of the amazingly beautiful penthouse while the broker remained glued to his mobile. The sidekick then proceeded to open the bedroom door and Dinesh had a look inside. Dinesh finished surveying the same and reentered the main hall. The sidekick then looked at his broker or master who had finished the call.

"Shall we go?" he enquired.

"What about the other bedrooms?" Dinesh asked. There were still three more bedrooms to see.

"Oh, they are all the same," he replied with absolute disinterest. "You have seen one, you have seen them all."

That was the end of the search. Dinesh's social standing had been mapped onto a mental grid by the Zen car that had dared to drive in with. The mental grid did not allow a Zen and a penthouse to coexist in the same frame. Needless to say, Dinesh decided not to pursue such exercises in the future.

As the years rolled on, Dinesh observed that the cataract in his left eye had actually begun to mature and it was perceptibly growing in size. The cops and robbers game in school and the after-effects had reared its head yet again after almost ten years.

"What is that white thing in your eye," Dinesh had a few ask him. He did not pay heed until this began to bother him. In any conversation, he felt that the people were staring more at the white spot in his eye rather than listening to what was coming out of his mouth. He developed a unique style to counter this and would invariably hold his left hand up to touch his temple and partially cover his left eye whenever he engaged in a conversation. It seemed to work but he knew that this white spot was damning his confidence. He was reminded of *Macbeth* 'Out damn spot. Out!' as he often chanted mentally at night. It got too much for him to bear and one fine morning he left for Dr Shroff Eye centre to get it examined. He just did not want to go to AIIMS again and be told that the cataract had reached adolescence but still had a further long road to traverse before it achieved 'enlightenment'.

He secured the appointment and awaited his turn. The place was bustling with patients; each one looking at the other with sympathy, concern and an in-built sense of voyeurism. The more serious the case, the greater would be the look at concern. Each one looking at each other's eyes, Dinesh was beginning to get worried.

Dr Naushir Shroff walked past and stopped just as he passed Dinesh. He retraced a couple of steps and now stood directly in front of him.

"*Jara uthna, beta.* Just get up," he said.

Dinesh stood up and he reached out and held his chin in between his thumb and his pointing finger. "How long have you had this?" he enquired looking into his left eye.

"Sir, around ten years," Dinesh replied not sure what he was going to say next.

Dr Shroff gave a gasp of disbelief and asked him to come in next, out of turn.

"I can't imagine a young boy like you can be so stupid as to wait for ten years to get rid of a cataract that can be removed in twenty minutes flat."

Dinesh was sitting in his chamber as Dr Shroff examined his left eye. "How did this happen?" he asked.

Dinesh recounted the story of the cops and robbers in school and how he was asked to wait for the cataract to mature before anything further could be done. Dr Shroff shook his head. "Please fix a date for the surgery at the desk outside."

Dinesh thanked him and fixed up for a surgery date after five days. There was no earlier date. He was totally booked with almost five to six surgeries a day.

With an ever increasing sense of anxiety, the day finally arrived for Dinesh and he got admitted. The surgery was scheduled for the afternoon but there was a medicational ritual that needed to be conducted. After his eyelashes were cut and his left eye intoxicated and marinated with different varieties of eye-drops, he was wheeled into the operation theatre for the surgery. Here he was injected with local anaesthesia that totally numbed the left side of his face. There was enough anaesthesia to last for half an hour—all the time that was required to remove his cataract once and for all.

Twenty-two minutes passed and the cataract had yet to be removed. He was injected with extra doses of anaesthesia and was beginning to worry. Over his semi-drugged state, he muttered out as to what had happened.

"We were trying to destroy the cataract through the laser," he heard someone say, "but have not been able to. After so many years, the cataract has calcified and had almost turned to stone."

After what seemed like eternity, the cataract was removed in under forty-five minutes. Dinesh caught a glimpse of Dr Naushir Shroff when he was wheeled out. He thanked him over a slur and he smiled and waved.

Life took on a different turn from then on and everything looked great. The leaves looked greener, the flowers more colourful, even the underbelly of Delhi looked beautiful. The choked sewers during the monsoons seemed like flowing rivers and the people appeared more polite, well-mannered and nice. Things seemed to be back on track and from concealing the white spot he would actually look into the eye of the person in front of him. However, little did he know then that he would be visiting Shroff again soon for a far more traumatic reason.

'*Jai Jai Shiv Shankar*' played out loud on his FM radio as he was driving to work one day. The figure of a pot-bellied man partly clothed and grinding '*bhang*' as Rajesh Khanna and Mumtaz gyrated to the music flashed across his mind. Before he had even begun to savour the music, he was stopped en-route by a pot-bellied traffic police officer. Dinesh leaned out of car window and asked him what the matter was.

"*Kanwariye aa rahe hai*. Don't you know how to read?" he said as he pointed to the countless billboards which announced the march of the *kanwaria*s.

Each year, one is subjected to this ritual in July and August and although he was used to seeing this since his schooldays,

225

it was only now that he had begun to get bothered by it. He was also intrigued as what this was all about. He used to remember his schooldays, when he would see the motley group of three and fours, all clad in their saffron attire in a march with their *kanwar*s perched atop their drooping shoulders. Some of them had their feet bandaged and some appeared unwell but they continued their march.

*"Gaadi peeche kar behan ke lund,"* shouted the traffic police officer and Dinesh obliged. He was momentarily taken aback by the physical impossibility of the expletive the pot-bellied police officer had just mouthed but that did not matter. He then saw the endless stream of many groups of *kanwaria*s walk past his car.

The annual *kanwar* pilgrimage taken up during the Shravan month (July-August) is one of the toughest pilgrimages in north India on all holy occasions mentioned in the Hindu almanac. Millions of lord Shiva devotees, popularly known as *kanwaria*s, visit Haridwar and during their return, they carry *kanwar*s, a bamboo stick with two small pots hanging on both ends, on their shoulders. Lakhs of *kanwaria*s from as far as Rajasthan, Haryana, Delhi and Uttar Pradesh, tread long, tortuous and undulating paths to fetch Ganga water from Haridwar against all odds.

There are different types of *kanwaria*s apart from the regular ones walking the entire route like *Dak kanwaria*s (marathon runners), *Khadi kanwaria*s (in which *kanwar* is to be kept on the shoulders), *Jhula kanwaria*s (in which it can be kept on a stand while taking rest) and *Baikunth kanwaria*s (with least restrictions).

Every year, the Haridwar-Delhi highway gets choked with a steady flow of *kanwaria*s with alarming regularity. Cheap loudspeakers on the roadsides and those fitted to the vehicles of all shapes and sizes blare out bhajans sung by a motley crew of self-styled saints ably led by Narendra Chanchal, some set to the tune of raunchy Hindi film songs. The frenzy of the *kanwarias* knows no bounds. They do a jig and a jog to keep the festive mood going even as the older pilgrims quietly utter their prayers as they head towards their destinations.

Determined and focused, they are relentless in their pursuit of their goal, which is to set out from the villages of North India in the hinterland of Delhi, go to the nearest source of the Ganges, typically Haridwar and then fill the pots and then come back home. They are a strange mix of tradition and modernity—men wearing Reebok shoes and gaudy saffron vests walk or trek and occasionally stop to take rest. The resting-places are audible before they are visible, with loud, garish devotional music being played over cheap amplifiers. A number of *Shiv bhakts* can be seen there squatting or resting on makeshift tables or cots and engorging themselves at the *bhandara*s sponsored by the local traders as music belts out from cheap T-series cassette tapes. In another time and era, it would have represented the rigour of the faithful devotees, but today often such a crowd represents the madness of a mob.

As India evolves, its religiosity is evolving too. There was a time when religion was supposed to be the concern of the senior citizens and it was a matter of worry for the parents that their children were indifferent to the ancient traditions. There were weekly trips to the temple which the family took on themselves as matter of routine. Given the number of young people chatting and trekking in their saffron T-shirts, the twenty-first century's ritual of a religious pilgrimage has evolved as a large hairy monster.

*"Chalo,"* shouted the cop almost sounding so annoyed with his job. He motioned his lathi and tapped on his car bumper egging Dinesh to move faster. He moved and was instantly stopped ten feet later as the traffic signal turned red.

He sat motionless tapping on the steering wheel and looked at the rear-view mirror at the sound of some commotion behind him. He could see a rickshaw driver being beaten by 3-4 *kanwaria*s since the rickshaw had unknowingly come in the path of their smooth progress. The rickshaw driver did not say anything but simply endured the beating with folded hands. After some time the beating stopped and the *kanwaria*s proceeded their trek having relieved their frustration and aggression on the hapless rickshaw driver. Dinesh drove on. The pot-bellied police officer was nowhere to be seen.

# I Will See You...
# You Don't Know Me

Coincidentally or by divine intervention, Dinesh always ended up with a job located close to his residence. With almost all known MNCs housing a swanky office in Gurgaon, it was not an impossible likelihood. As he grew with time, the needs went up and so did the sense of wanting to achieve something more. It's strange that with each passing milestone, there appeared a Hundred more that he wanted to cross, just to make himself feel useful and acknowledged.

Dinesh had sailed past the interview and got himself a plum position in a renowned MNC. Great place, great money and some real downright nasty politics. The challenge was great but the politicking almost killed him. It's something else when you can confront somebody with facts on stories that they may have spread about you, but when the perpetrator works behind the scenes in cahoots with the executive assistant or the CEO then it's a known fact that the combination is hard to beat. Having endured an experience with Hitesh and Nisha, Dinesh was doubly cautious of two things. Trusting people and falling in love too easily. Both were so easy to happen.

This was like a classic soap opera full of politics and sleaze but minus the *saas* or the *bahu*. One of the directors had his favourite boy in to work as the financial controller, another director had his muse all the way from Ahmedabad to work for him in Gurgaon. The financial controller had a pact with the housekeeping boy to supply him with women while he portrayed a sagely image of a man happily married with one kid, and a politicking widow who had a lesbian relationship with the executive assistant to the CEO. A widow in a lesbian relationship is almost enough to titillate a pervert mind but there was more to this soap. The CEO himself had a great thing going with one of the junior business executives.

"There was enough material for a Madhur Bhandarkar film," thought Dinesh. Enough material for the makers of vivid videos. He thought of the possible titles—*Black Widow*, *Lesbian Thespian*, and *Widow Libido*. How about the Hindi titles—*Widhwa ka Badla*... and that was enough. Dinesh had rather he not think beyond this.

The expats ran the show well. They knew the business well and had a practical approach to most issues. As part of an expat relocalisation plan, an elaborate blueprint was prepared to replace the expats with local talent over time. The fancy farmhouses in Westend Greens, Kishangarh, Chhattarpur were not sustainable beyond a point but for the expats for whom it was nothing short of living in Beverley Hills 90210. They lived life to the hilt and with each farmhouse coming with its own private swimming pool and a tennis court; they couldn't find reasons to complain.

Earning in dollars or pounds and spending in rupees. Where in the US or UK can you get a bottle of beer for under a dollar or half a pound? Most of the expats came in single with their wives firmly planted in the country of origin. Left alone, with all the infrastructure and money at their disposal, the expats had little to do but to dine out, party out, get into relationships with Indian women who were only too happy to be accommodating given the white man syndrome. Even in their wildest dreams, they could not have imagined that they would be living a life surrounded by immaculately manicured lawns set against the sylvan backdrops of the Aravali Range, with servants even ready to wipe your arse for you. A fleet of cars at their disposal, which was used for personal purposes or to transport women under the cover of darkness. The driver played such an important role here. Be it the High Commission or the MNC, most diplomats and expats found their drivers to be their willing confidantes and their partners in crime.

The Indian women would make themselves so easily and readily available to them. Never mind the background, never mind the position or the grade. He is white, lives in a farmhouse, has loads of money, can get me to the US or UK and that is all that matters.

Some of the matches that Dinesh encountered were simply too bizarre to even comprehend. One of the expat women got married to her driver and they both returned to the UK where she continues to work while he manages the home. Obviously there was no ego involved here since the driver was used to doing the chores in India. However, what did change was that the driver had assumed the status of an expat in their home country. A reversal of titles with same roles.

Many years ago, Dinesh had heard about one of the expats who was a software engineer and who had married to his domestic help with three children. The techie used to live in a fancy apartment in New Friends Colony and was going through a separation in the US, The maid sensed a golden opportunity and 'helped' him through the difficult period in his life. They returned to the US as husband and wife. The software engineer had crashed.

Dinesh could imagine that this would not have been a difficult decision for the techie to make. Compared to the independent nature of most Western women that he had met or heard about and considering the fact that you need a fortune to manage a house with a babysitter, cook, domestic helper in the US on your weekly salary, the maid from India returning to the US as an expat is a package deal. She can satisfy your appetite for sex as already verified and vetted while at New Friends Colony, would ensure that your house is kept clean and dusted (that is her core competency anyway) and would cook an Indian meal every day and night (love the naan!). All this at no service cost.

Dinesh never saw or processed a termination note for a driver while working at these diplomatic missions or MNCs and the only time it happened was when the expats moved back to their home location at the end of their tenure in India to be replaced by another who would want a fresh set of clothes to start with.

It was a great evening and all were gathered around a bonfire with a motley crew of senior folks from the company where Dinesh worked after a gruelling eight hours of an intense training session. They were staying back at a three-star resort in the company of their CEO. Since people had travelled from all parts of India, all participants stayed back at the resort for the night.

"Oh, I cannot find my slipper. I have lost it somewhere," exclaimed one of the junior business executives. The CEO was quick to react and it is not often that you see a CEO on all fours trying to look for a slipper under a table on the lawn. Dinesh exchanged a smile with one of his colleagues. There was little to be said.

"I found it," he exclaimed triumphantly and handed it over to her with a glorious smile on his lips. She smiled back with a beckoning look in her eyes. The two were a pair was a well known fact to almost everyone who worked in the office.

"Thank you," she said. "I have to go back to my room now. It's almost ten and I need to sleep."

She waved to everyone and with an earnest look in her eyes, shook the hand of our CEO and disappeared towards the cottages.

The CEO's eyes followed her but the conversation continued amid our group. Suddenly the CEO had transitioned from the listening stage to the hearing stage. He seemed distracted and did not speak too much. Minutes later there was a beep on his mobile. He looked at the screen and read a message.

"I have to go now," he said trying hard to disguise the hues of joy on his face. "Goodnight!" he wished, and then walked in the direction the junior business executive had taken without waiting for a response.

*"You are responsible for ruining my career and I am going to kill you."* This message was received on a mail and was sent to Dinesh by the initial recipient: his CEO.

"What is this?" he asked looking a bit hassled.

Dinesh had barely entered the room. He could see clearly that the message had rankled him, enough to make him lose his composure. Most of the expats, and more so CEOs walk around with a sense of diplomatic immunity around them. They are almost the untouchables since they command the power, have the money and know people who know people.

That's what Delhi is mainly about. The sailing isn't smooth until you know people who know people.

"Not sure," Dinesh replied, "but not something you can choose to ignore." He looked more worried.

"I want this matter investigated and need to know who has sent this," he ordered, his face showing a mixture of anger and anxiety.

"We would need to hire a professional agency to do this. This is not something for an individual to do."

"Then do so. I want to get the fucker who sent me this."

Dinesh got up to leave the room as the CEO turned to pick up the phone and dial a number. As he dialled the first two digits, Dinesh knew that he was about to reach out to the corporate headquarters.

There would have been many who would have wanted to send him the message that he had received but a death threat seemed far too serious a development to be ignored or swept under the carpet. Dinesh's first guess was the junior business executive but he dismissed the thought. Somebody in her position, whether '69' or otherwise, would not threaten to kill the hen that would help her lay the golden egg.

Dinesh hired a professional agency who quoted a fee that almost made him think that it was cheaper to allow the sender of the mail to carry out his or her threat. However, he yielded and the investigation was on.

The operation involved the United States Embassy, Interpol, the FBI besides the local authorities in India and took almost two months to close but close it did. The message had been sent from a 'Yahoo.com' account and therefore could not be tracked in India since their servers are based out of the US. Since all incoming and outgoing messages through this server are retained for a month before being destroyed, time was of essence lest the trail went cold.

The Gurgaon cyber cell was contacted to start with, since an FIR and a request from the local law enforcement authority alone can get the required agencies across the world to act. Individual applications are not entertained for obvious reason. Interestingly, only the IG based out of Chandigarh has authority to initiate the proceedings on the case of a reported cyber crime which this truly was.

After over a month, Yahoo authorities revealed the IP address of the source which was further tracked to 'Reliance' ID. Reliance then went on to reveal the mobile phone which was used to connect to the laptop from where the mail was sent at three in the morning.

Two days later the junior business executive was terminated from service. "Wow!" thought Dinesh, "The CEO had obviously not risen to the occasion."

"Hi, I am Lancy!"

"Nice to meet you, Lancy," Dinesh said. Short, clean-shaven and with a certain niceness around him that was hard to ignore. He was representing a reputed multinational bank and they were both seated next to each other in the lobby of the Delhi District Cricket Association at Feroz Shah Kotla.

"Are you here for the corporate box?" asked Lancy.

"Yes," Dinesh replied. "Seems to be such a difficult task with being pushed around from one person to the other."

"We should be meeting the right guy who can show us the way now."

They were both waiting for Rahul. Rahul was the key resource in administration. He had a sense of clarity and knew exactly what an MNC would expect from a corporate box. Both Lancy and Dinesh were waiting to find someone who would show them the way or at least put them through to the person who could make the corporate box happen for them.

"I sure hope he can help us," Dinesh said as Lancy got up with his mobile firmly planted in his ear.

"Listen," he exclaimed looking at Dinesh, "I have my marketing head from Hong Kong coming over to talk to these officials and she is at the gate. Do you mind waiting for us while I escort her in. That way we can make a common representation."

"Sure, no problem," Dinesh said as he darted off towards the front gate.

"Hi!" Dinesh turned around to face a young guy in jeans.

"Hey!" Dinesh replied, not knowing whom he was talking to.

"I am Rahul."

Dinesh turned around again to look for Lancy but he was already at the gate at the far end and out of earshot.

"We need your help in getting a corporate box. We have been running around…"

Rahul smiled almost with a sense of déjà vu, "Let's go inside the office and I will state your case to Mr Singh. We will get this sorted out today." Dinesh knew he could trust him.

"Can we wait for a minute," Dinesh requested, "I have this friend from the bank who also has a similar request. He has just gone to fetch his marketing head who has come in from Hong Kong."

"Ok," said Rahul.

Dinesh could see two distorted figures in the distance gaining clarity as they came closer. Lancy was with a woman. He was not expecting this.

"Hello Rahul," he said interrupting his sense of confusion. "This is Susan and our marketing head."

Dinesh could see Rahul's eyes brighten up. "Hello! Let's go in," he said sounding rather excited.

After a month or so, the deal was closed. The month had seen multiple interactions with the DDCA and other officials. The meetings with the various stakeholders took them to the DDCA office, hotel Broadway, Bengali sweetshop, Defence Colony and almost every other nook and corner of the city. Susan and Dinesh had struck a rapport that also led to multiple meeting in bars and restaurants. She found everything about India 'lovely' and 'quaint' and as they met on multiple occasions, she always brought with her a small gift as a token of their growing friendship.

"I am sure that some day I will find an Indian prince to get married to," she said with an air of expectation. "Anyway, I am sure I will find my Mr Right right here in India."

They talked about everything under the sun. Every time she would visit India, they would meet. Over time, he began to look forward to meeting her. She was a wonderful person. She drew Dinesh closer, not intimately but purely as one friend would to another. She loved the adulation for the Bollywood stars, she loved the way the really fat Punjabi women would devour two or sometimes three *gulab jamuns* in one go and not care, just about everything fascinated her. For her, everything was positive, and Dinesh found everything about her positive too. She was simply in love with India.

Contrary to the popular stereotype in India, though she was an Australian, there was absolutely no trace of a racist streak in her. Dinesh often joked that for a woman who comes from the land of the convicts, she does not really look like one. "Fuck off," she used to say each time he said this to her.

After a couple of months since her last visit, the phone rang and it was Susan.

"Guess what?" she said. "I have found Mr Right finally and it had to happen in India."

When she came down to India after almost two months, Dinesh could not help but notice the change she had undergone. She had quit smoking and looked fresher and younger, full of life. Dinesh was equally excited for her because he knew how much this meant to her.

"Who is the unlucky guy?" Dinesh asked in his typical style that she had so got used to and she did not mind.

"I met him in Shalom in GK and he is the most wonderful guy I have met. He is also an Aussie and he is going to be meeting my parents next week in Sydney."

"I am so happy for you Susan," said Dinesh and could see that she could hardly contain her excitement. "I sure hope and pray that this works out for you."

Some months later she got engaged. Dinesh received a beautiful invite, but unfortunately could not make it although it was at the Lake Palace in Udaipur. Knowing Susan, it had to be so, it had to be India where she would consummate her relationship with a man she had fallen in love with. Little did Dinesh realise the marriage which consummated in his city would take a friend away from him for the most bizarre reason possible. The city had to maintain a balance. It had given Dinesh some beautiful moments and there needed to be a balancing act in play now.

Dinesh never heard from her after that. Almost a year passed and the only communication he received from her was in the form of a message wishing him on his birthday. Dinesh thought he would call her but decided against it.

Two years passed and Dinesh received a mail from her telling him that she was expecting her first child and how thrilled she was at the prospect of being a mother. Dinesh was happy for her, but found it strange that she had chosen to send out a mail rather than giving him a call. This was so unlike her. She was a woman who would announce to the world when she was happy and expect the world to share in her happiness. A mail appeared strange.

A week or so later, Dinesh decided to call her. It was 8 p.m., and for some strange reason he miscalculated the time zone difference. He wanted to congratulate her on the prospective addition to her family and essentially check out on how things were moving along.

She picked up the phone but sounded subdued.

"Hello, Susan," Dinesh said in a tone that betrayed his anxiety. "This is me!"

"Oh, hi," she responded. Dinesh could hear a lot of clinking glasses in the background so he presumed that she was in the midst of a party. "How are you?" she managed to ask.

"I am good. How are you? It's been a long time and I was wanting to..."

"Eh, listen," she interrupted. "Can we speak later. We have some people over for dinner."

"Yeah, sure. No problem," he replied as he disconnected the phone.

This was so unlike her. What had happened to her? It was almost as if he was speaking to a stranger. She sounded restrained, almost as if she did not want to take the call but did rather reluctantly. He did not want to over think, so he headed to the bar for another drink.

That night, Dinesh reached home at around one in the morning and quickly changed. As he lay down to sleep, he heard his cell phone ring. He looked at it and saw that it was 'Susan calling'.

"Hi, Susan. How a..."

"Please speak to my husband, Dinesh," she said sounding distraught. She was almost in tears and Dinesh was trying hard to understand what was happening.

"He thinks that you and I are having an affair!"... and the line went dead.

Susan and Dinesh never spoke after that. He probably lost more than he gained from this relationship. To him, she was window to the Australian world, a window which was devoid of all racial overtones, a window which gave a view of all things nice which the locals were too blind to notice, a window which told him that if you wish for something hard then you are sure to get it.

She had told him many times that she would want to settle down in India, get married to an Indian prince and live happily ever after. She always nursed the dream and had the hope that someday, it will all come true.

The city will give you wealth but will take away your right to sleep, will give you the comforts but will take away the time you have left with you to enjoy them, will give you a lot but expect a lot more in return. The city of Delhi gave Susan what she wanted: a 'Prince' that she was looking for since ages, but took away from her the right to live life the way she wanted, and turned her dream into reality, but at the same time, transformed her reality into a nightmare.

The city of Delhi takes away much more than it gives. Be it local or expats, it is universal in its application—sparing none and maintaining the balance, always. Maximum for minimum...

# Clap Clap... Hai Hai—Caught in the Middle

At long last, Dinesh got a chance to visit America for a month on an official trip. Nobody believed that he had never been to America considering the fact that he had been to almost every other part of the world. The closest that he ever got to the US was when he flew down to Trinidad. Besides that, he had been to London, Ireland, Egypt, Singapore, Malaysia, Sydney, Hong Kong, Austria, Dubai, etc., but never to the US, so he was looking forward to the trip.

Each of these trips threw at him a different perspective of life and brought into sharp focus the way most of us behave while on a trip to a foreign land. One of the worst sectors he had flown was the Delhi-Dubai-Delhi sector, not because of Emirates airlines but because of the majority of Indians (mainly males) who were hell bent on making asses of themselves en route.

"Please, can we take a picture with you," slurred one to the air-hostess. The air-hostess, who was obviously accustomed to this behaviour reluctantly obliged. The man, in his late twenties, got up excited and put his arm around the air-hostess while his friend moved back, down the aisle, and clicked from his Sony cybershot. After that, the guy shook her hand and kept thanking her till she decided she had enough and moved on with an expression of disgust on her face. Dinesh was sure that it would not be long before she would stereotype every Indian male that walked through the door and paint them all with the same brush.

"Whisky, please!" said another as the air-hostess wheeled the trolley through the aisle. He said it loud enough for the pilot to hear but the moment the spirits are in, the volume invariably goes up. It's a science that's not taken too long to perfect. She handed him a miniature bottle of Cutty Sark. "*Arre, isse kya hoga?* Give me some more." The air hostess reached into her trolley and handed him another one and the man insisted on another till such time that he had 6 miniature bottles in his hand. He opened four of them and poured them into his plastic glass, asked for some water and took a large swig. He put the remaining two bottles into his shirt pocket.

The chuckles continued as they eyed the air-hostesses on board with an obvious look of sexual frustration. As one of the air-hostessess bent down to pick up a tray, they would clamber over each other to get one quick look at her cleavage.

"Hello," said the air-hostess as she handed him a miniature bottle of whisky.

"Excuse me," Dinesh said and before he could complete she was handing him one more bottle.

"No, no," he said protesting. "I do not want any whisky. Can I have some red wine please?"

"Oh! Sorry, sir," she was taken aback as he had unconsciously broken her stereotype image of most Indian males on an economy class ticket. And suddenly Dinesh was a 'Sir', knighted yet again.

"Which wine do you prefer," she continued rather testingly.

"Merlot 2005, please."

She almost fainted.

Dinesh was looking forward to his trip because of multiple reasons. First, this was something that he was looking forward to as almost everything in India, and more so in Delhi, has a reference point to USA. Second, he was keen to understand the culture and get a first-hand view of a visitor's impression of USA. And third, he wanted to validate the myths about USA that he had grown up with.

During his childhood days, he had worn with pride a T-shirt that had been brought by one of his uncles who had visited USA. A week later, Dinesh saw a similar T-shirt being worn by their newspaper delivery boy. Of course, duplication is an art that has been perfected by us and even the original is left wanting. Eventually curiosity got the better of him and he mustered up the courage to ask the newspaper boy as to where he got the T-shirt from.

"My uncle got this for me," he replied with an air of pride.

"From where," he asked, tired of the often repeated reference to uncles.

"Oh, from his village which he visits every year for Holi." Dinesh had not known that the concept of a 'Global Village' meant getting to buy global things from your village.

"Let me see," he said, reaching out to the label sewn onto the inside of his back collar.

'Made by USA', it declared proudly.

'Made by USA', as opposed to 'Made in USA'.

It wasn't long before he was educated and indoctrinated in the essence of fine copying. Like fine dining, it hides more than it shows. 'Made by USA' meant that the product had been made by a certain Ujagar Singh Ahluwalia.

"*Hey ram,*" he cried. Later, he came to know of another brand made by USA which stood for Ulhasnagar Sindhi Association. Times have, of course, moved on. They had moved to a time where one could not buy an American souvenir that is 'Made in America'. It is 'Made in China', always and forever!

Dinesh maintained a diary with him for each day that he spent in USA often wondering why he had not done that earlier. Hindsight, he reminded himself, is always a 20:20 vision.

Each day, as he lay in his hotel room, he would take notes. As the days went by, he had painted a canvas of rich hues and each was more resplendent than the other. The more he wrote, the more he realised that it was not too different than staying in Delhi. He could be writing this on his experience with this city and not too many things would be different. The more things change the more they remain the same!

Delhi has an air of pomposity that is cultivated mostly artificially whereas USA has more farms in 'Farmville' than in reality, Delhi people live under an air of illusion, an illusion of having to show what they don't have whereas USA forces its way into an illusion of having won over the evils of terrorism through shock and awe; an illusion of being in control and deeply concerned over the rise and proliferation of nuclear weapons, but feeding it at the same time and pretending it is not being fed. The city will give and allow itself to be used but will take far more away from you in return, it is only the other way around for USA!

The child was not an illusion.

There was celebration in the air as he was told of the addition to the family. He was elated and at first could not believe his ears. Not because he had any doubts but because, like most things in his life, this too was not planned for.

He started out his life in Delhi which was not planned by him but more as an outcome of circumstance. Never planned on getting married but did more as an outcome of appropriateness. Never planned on having moved from one situation to another but happen it did. Whether it was making love to a woman he never loved and never planned, to losing a friend for the most bizarre fashion, to having risen in his own stature without having ever consciously planned it, to a certain stage in his life which was not visible to him; nothing was ever planned and therefore nothing seemed possible... but it did happen. Things happen whether we desire them to happen or not. If you do not chase your dreams they will chase you and make you a willing partner to the story that has already been pre-ordained.

Apollo hospital was the place to be. It more than took care of everything. One of his friends recommended a specific doctor with whom a relationship developed. When one has someone has actually assisted in the addition to the family and been a part of the process, that person invariably becomes a part of your family. It's not planned and it just happens.

As the time came closer, the anxiety levels had increased and so did the consumption of chocolates. One of his friends suggested that mothers to be who consume much chocolate during their pregnancy days give birth to happy babies. It did not seem like a very difficult proposition to consider and so his wife took to it happily.

"Is it possible to see an image of the child before she is due," Dinesh asked with a certain degree of trepidation. He was not sure why he asked the question because he sort of knew what the response would be. The doctors are wary of giving a response to this.

Innovative techniques, like biopsy, ultrasound, scan tests and amniocentesis, devised to detect genetic abnormalities, are highly misused by a number of families to detect the gender of the unborn child. These clinical tests are highly contributing to the rise in genocide of the unborn girl child.

Amniocentesis started in India in 1974 to detect foetal abnormalities. These tests were used to detect gender for the first time in 1979 in Amritsar, Punjab. Later the test was stopped by the Indian Council of Medical Research but it was too late. The benefits of these tests were leaked out and people started using it as an instrument for killing an innocent and unborn girl child.

Prenatal sex tests, e.g. with ultrasound, were forbidden in 1996 because they lead to selective abortion with a three-year sentence and a heavy fine, but the law applied only to government health centres and not to private clinics. Now, the job has got easier, with portable scanners taken from village to village to check whether a foetus passes its prenatal examination.

The murder of girls is a valued Indian tradition. Rajputs, Sikhs and other warrior castes preferred to marry their daughters to a husband of higher rank which meant an expensive dowry, or the rapid disposal of the unwanted child at birth. The British became concerned when they saw the results of the first census of 1871. In some villages, the commissioners reported, not a single female child was to be found. The authorities brought in the Female Infanticide Act, which set heavy penalties on child murder, and policemen were stationed in such places but, twenty years later, some provinces still had twice as many boys as girls. For a time, the habit began to fade, but now things have changed for the worse. Dowries often take half of a poor family's disposable wealth and the death of unwanted children has become more, not less, common with India's new affluence.

*Dai*s, traditional birth attendants, often kill the child, for a fee of around a hundred and fifty rupees. They can, they claim, assess a baby's gender even before birth, and stand ready to do their duty. In some places, each admits to a murder a week. The relatives may do the job themselves by forcing the mother to place tobacco under her child's tongue. If she refuses, she is herself killed or thrown out of the house.

Now the incidence of child murder is among the highest in India. In one recent year, five hundred and seventy of the six hundred girls born were dead within days. So scandalous were the figures that the law became involved. For the first time in India, somebody was found guilty of child murder and went to prison. She was a woman. But who was responsible? No man was charged with any crime.

"Yes, sure," the doctor replied as she pulled the drawer and searched from a pile of visiting cards. "Here," she said as she triumphantly pulled out the card she was looking for. Dinesh could not believe his ears. "Call him and give him my reference. He will be able to help you. He has one of the few 3D ultrascopy machines in the country."

Dinesh took the card and noted the number. Later they thanked the doctor and made their way to Defence Colony for the 3D test. Luckily, the centre was open and had a sizeable number of expectant mothers waiting outside. Soon, their number was announced and they made their way in.

After the initial discussions, the doctor proceeded to apply a certain gel on the stomach and for the first time Dinesh saw images of their child to be. The feeling was unparalleled and he almost wanted to reach out and hug the image in front of him. There it was within the safe confines of the stomach walls with eyes closed and fingers clenched. He did not have anything to say. Is that how his father would have reacted when he first held Dinesh? The fleeting thought passed by Dinesh's mind leaving him at war with himself.

As they were given the CD of the 3D ultrasound, Dinesh braved a question with full knowledge of the answer. The question was with a genuine desire to know and to validate, so he could be mentally prepared. They were building a new house so he wanted it to be ready on time.

"How many more months to go?" he asked barely able to hide his anxiety.

The doctor smiled at him. "Anxious, aren't you? Say, three or four months from now. Heading towards a normal delivery. The progress is good and the child is healthy." Dinesh smiled back and pleased with the assurance that the baby would be out in nine months in keeping with the general trend. He was not even sure about why he had asked that.

He passed the reception and headed towards the cashier. As he stood awaiting his turn, he could hear another couple in the open doorway consulting with another doctor who seemed rather exasperated and keen to see them go.

"Should I paint the child's room blue or should I have it painted pink?" the man asked in a not so subtle attempt to know whether the soon to be born child was a boy or a girl. The wife looked askance at the doctor with her dupatta spread across her rather enlarged belly in a psychological effort to hide the obvious.

The doctor looked at him pained and said, "Paint it white so you can always change the colour whenever you wish to." He managed a smile and asked the attendant to usher in the next patient. Dinesh looked at his wife who was looking heavenward and smiled to himself as they made their way out silently…

As they left the gate, Dinesh could hear a couple, who were now near their scooter talking animatedly among themselves. "Should we ask him what the sex of the child is?" the man said.

"What difference does it make," the woman replied, "as long as the child is born healthy?"

"Yes, I know," he continued, "but if we are paying him so much money we must get more information than just a test result of the child's health."

Maximum for minimum...

They were blessed with a baby girl four months later and their joy knew no bounds. Even before their parents arrived, the eunuchs were at the door of their house. With their typical clapping style, they gathered around their front door and sang out in unison. One of them asked Dinesh to create space for them to dance. In asking him, the eunuch placed his hand on his penis and gently asked him to move aside. Dinesh did not know what to do. The eunuchs are notorious not just in Delhi but almost in all parts of the country. They are more visible in Mumbai as they gather around most traffic signals asking for alms from motorists who wait for the traffic light to turn green. Most of them have no choice but to pay. The car drivers have the option to roll up their windows but the two-wheelers are screwed.

The term eunuch–*hijra*–has been defined in the dictionary as 'a man who has been castrated, esp. (formerly) for some office such as a guard in a harem'. *Hijra*s have a history of more than 3000 years and the history of the Mughal Empire is replete with stories of the eunuchs and the significant role they used to play during those times either as guards or as part of the kings harem. The term *hijra* or even *kinnar* (as sometimes referred to) is often translated as 'eunuch'. A typical *hijra* is raised as a man and undergoes a fairly elaborate ritual which leads to the removal of the genitals to become a *hijra*.

The eunuchs were referred to as the *khoja*s during the time of the Mughal Empire. A Mughal king, for the most part, could not do without a harem (no pun intended) and in the same vein a harem was inconceivable without *khoja*s. These were the guards to the king's harems who were castrated to ensure that no cohabitation between royal wives and guards took place. This led to the creation of the 'third sex'—the castrated eunuchs. They guarded the gates of the palace, checked and regulated access and served the inmates even while keeping surveillance over them. The eunuchs also used to guard the secrets of their mistresses. The women sometimes even arranged through the eunuchs to invite men into the harem. In exchange for such delicate and risky services the eunuchs could get from them whatever they needed, for they could blackmail their women clients. Dinesh did not find much difference between them and the drivers at the diplomatic missions and MNCs. It is such errands of secrecy that sometimes made the eunuchs powerful, arrogant and even invincible, much like the drivers in the expat populated localities in Delhi.

The practice of converting men into *khoja*s was common in Bengal. During the castration process, which was often conducted with unsterlised surgical equipment, many died since there was no anaesthesia that was administered prior to the so-called surgical exercise. Those who survived found their way to royal households at that time and now find themselves in *kotha*s soliciting customers, at traffic signals begging for alms, in a group at a wedding or at the time of child-birth where they would embarrass the parents of the newly born child into submission and payment. The surgical exercise is referred to as *nirbaan* meaning *mukti* because the act suggests a transition of the person from one life to another—a third life. Indian legal statutes do not permit such forced castration of males and therefore, there is secrecy around the act of *nirbaan*. It is always conducted between three and four before the crack of dawn, while it is still dark, and no one else but the mid-wife and her assistant is present for this ceremonial ritual. The method adopted for the surgery is crude, unscientific, threatening to the health of the patient and done in the most unhygienic conditions. The genitals of a normally born male baby are slashed off with a knife dipped in boiling oil. After dressing the wound, a nail with a string attached is tied to the waist and pushed through into the stump, which would, with tribal medication and time, begin to look like a female crotch. There are other methods too and the severity of this operation becomes more intense in the case of abducted boys or men who are forcibly castrated in a similar manner with the juice of the datura seeds working as the anaesthetic. It works well until the effects of the seeds wear off and the victim has to endure days and even weeks in pain before the pain subsides. Not to mention the effects of the trauma that he would still need to overcome.

Castrated or not, eunuchs are sexually active. As they cannot form intimate relations within the limits of either acceptable or aberrant behaviour due to lack of takers, they take to prostitution. Gully no. 1 of Shuklaji Street, a notorious red-light area of Mumbai, is an almost only eunuch preserve.

According to estimates, only one in a lakh is born a eunuch. What the statistics don't reveal is how kids and youths are kidnapped for sex work. Most of them practice bizarre rituals to win from God their one great wish: to be born as man or woman in their next life. The story goes that after a eunuch dies,the others of the group give the dead body 27 beatings with their slippers so the person is never again born a eunuch.

*"Arre seth, nikalo paise,"* said a gruff voice. Dinesh looked around and saw the face of a woman and man all rolled into

one with a garishly paint on the face and pouting at him in a sexually suggestive manner.

He reached out into his wallet. *"Ikkees hazaar,"* the eunuch cried out before he had a chance to even offer any money.

*"Panch,"* Dinesh repeated.

"The rates are fixed, *seth. Ikkyawan hazaar* for the first male child and *ikkees hazaar* for a girl child."

"That's too much," he said.

One of the *hijra*s advanced towards him. She had her hands holding the bottom of the saree that she was wearing and about to hoist it up. The other *hijra* held her back.

"Seth, we will take this much only," the leader of the pack exclaimed as she and her group clapped loudly in their characteristic style.

"I don't have so much," Dinesh said rather truthfully. He began to feel weary. These eunuchs are much like the diplomats in the country. They enjoy the immunity of law. Even if they can be arrested for indecent exposure and disturbing the peace, the police are a reluctant lot when it comes to exercising the rule of the law. They just assume the role of innocent bystanders. It is hard to tell then who the real eunuch is.

After much back and forth, they settled for ₹5,000. They took it reluctantly but did say that they were taking the reduced sum because it was a girl child. They moved on and Dinesh shut the door behind them.

They are a dying community and he could well see that the community was well on the verge of extinction much like the Parsis. With no continuum in sight, these eunuchs had now begun to resort to kidnapping children and forcing them to become eunuchs by castrating them against their will. Dinesh felt sorry for those who were forced into this but there was only that much that one could do.

# Playschool for Adults

The Ganguli Commission succeeded in screwing up any sense that existed in the school admission process before it was set up. Countless affidavits of the Ashok Ganguly committee report, which tried to regulate preprimary admissions in the region, are pending in courts. The casualty to this has been the parent whose only objective is to get his child or children to a good, decent and reputed school. Nobody, including the authorities have any clue about how the schools will go about conducting the admissions. While guidelines from the directorate of education do exist, these exist only on unread pieces of paper and anyway schools have been granted rights to interpret and implement the points system to what best suits their purpose.

The points system that private schools must follow is a cracker. Previously, interviews with the children were the norm. And many parents and playschools feel the old system was better as the onus to get their wards in the best schools has now shifted to the parents. There are points given to the neighbourhood criterion (20 if the child lives within a radius of three kilometres), add some points if you have been blessed with a girl child (party time finally!) and another five points allotted to any child with special needs. If the child seeking admission has a sibling in the same school, he or she gets 20 points. Another five points each for a father and mother who happen to be alumni. And ten points if the father is a postgraduate—double that if the mother is also one. You are a goner if you are illiterate. So in one merciless stroke, the Ganguly Commission has succeeded in erasing any hope that an illiterate parent would have had in wanting to secure the best of education for his or her child. These children in a misplaced sense of deductive reasoning would be best served to follow the examples of Mr Abdul Kalam who got it alright by gaining his pearls of wisdom from under a lamp post. Since he was adopted too, he would have found it easier to secure admission and because he is from the minority community, his points would have stacked up high.

Even if you manage to scale past the formidable walls of the point based system, you still need to overcome the interviews conducted on the parents by the school administration. A Delhi High Court order not only banned interviews with the children but has also asked the schools to avoid keeping children in any formal or informal setting. This is to ascertain the child's background. The success or failure of the interaction with parents will determine the child's future.

Parents are now scrambling to get their children enrolled into the best playschools, which offer workshops and programmes for parents as well. Delhi is peppered with such playschools with some being run in the back lawns of palatial houses. A kid who has just managed to achieve a great milestone by having learnt to walk is now subjected to all forms of exercises to achieving excellence in every field possible. Being mediocre is not a choice. Dinesh reminisced about his days as a child which were devoid of any complication. It was as simple as getting admission to school by simply applying, studying, coming back home, playing with friends, studying a bit, watching TV and going to sleep. He couldn't help but draw an uncomfortable comparison to the present days. There are summer workshops which teach children how to make pottery, paint glass, horse-riding, lawn tennis and all this when you are six. There was one such playschool in Gurgaon which taught children such craft at the age of five. Adjoining this playschool is the DLF Golf and Country club. Dinesh found the switch in roles almost amusing. This meant the children could go about learning craft at such a young age while the grown-ups played sport next door. At an age, where the child needed to recognise the beauties of nature and absorb the resplendent hues around, they were caged in a room to learn craft.

The parents too waste no time in praising the virtues of their child in front of all their guests. It has now become a status symbol to do so.

"*Arre*, my daughter isn't home yet as she had to go for her music classes. After that she needs to attend the Shiamak Davar's dance classes and finally, the computer classes. She is a bright child and she is picking up fast," said one parent obviously proud of his daughters 24x7 work schedule.

Dinesh nodded, not knowing whether to be appreciative of the initiative or just offended at the blatant exploitation of a fragile mind. Playschools before real school and more school after real school. Where does it all end? He had no fucking idea! Amid all this, childhood does not even get a chance to rear its head.

Dinesh had finally cracked the 'School Vinci Code'. The sure-fire way to achieve an admission for the child without any sense of doubt or anxiety.

Base your operative radius around the school you passed out from. Have a girl child preferably disabled or having special needs out of a mixed marriage (now separated, preferably widowed), from a minority community. Ensure that you are staying around Prithviraj Road, Vasant Vihar or Jor Bagh (if you are from the elitist school around this area). Brush up on your interviewing skills and bingo, your child is through! Your life may suck having to contend with the complications that you weaved around yourself to get your child into a school of your preference but as they say, 'Nothing ventured, nothing gained.' *Sab chalta hai!*

"I have put my son at Palovia playschool," said Maya. "It is a sure way of ensuring that I manage to get my child admitted to the Mount Mary's Public School," she had worked it all out in her mind.

"And what is the logic behind that," asked Dinesh's wife rather inquisitively but also with a whisper of amusement.

"Ah well, they have a tie-up with this school!" she exclaimed with an air of someone who had mastered the admission system. The gullibility of a grown up was appalling. More than the child, it was she who needed to have gone into a playschool when she was a child. She may have learnt more than she knows now.

Dinesh almost choked on his coffee. In all his years in a corporate set-up, he had heard of mergers and acquisitions, joint venture but this was one of a kind. A tie-up between a playschool and one of the most prestigious and reputed schools in Delhi and Gurgaon.

The school admission exercise has created an acute strategic and competitive spirit within the psyche of most parents. Secrecy governs the conduct of all. Information is not readily shared lest it dilute the chances of their child's admission to the particular school. The lesser the number of people who know about it the better the chances. With so few schools worth running for, the concern is understandable.

"So where are you trying for?" Dinesh asked his friend Bharat whose daughter was about the same age as his.

"Oh, all over," he replied. That was the most definitive answer he could elicit from him. The school admission exercise had made cut-throats out of all of them. It had inadvertently prepared the child, at an early stage, for the future. Cut-throat competition. That is one of the ways to survive in this city that takes away so much if you do not watch out.

"I have heard that the DBS school is a good choice and it is CBSE based."

"I do not want my child to go there. It is not happening. I want to get my daughter into Mount Mary's Public School and I do not care if it is ICSE based." Dinesh had to hand it to Maya. So damn focused!

"Do you know there is a 5 per cent deduction from the overall percentage in case an ICSE pass out applies for a competitive examination compared to a CBSE pass out?" Dinesh said.

"I know," replied Bharat. "But the ICSE board is still a superior board. Do not forget that we are ICSE pass outs too."

"I do not deny that but do not forget that times were different then and the competition far less severe," Dinesh reminded him. "During our time, we could walk away with a 60 per cent in the board exams and still expect to get into a decent college. In today's time, even 95 per cent seems less. Do you want your kid to end up in Dayal Singh College?"

"I would still want my child to get into the Mount Mary's Public School," he reiterated as he took a sip from the whisky that was purchased from the army canteen at a subsidised rate.

"Ok, but considering the difficulty in getting admission to schools nowadays, perhaps we should try to get our child to a number two school as well so we do not put all the eggs in one basket. In case the first is not available, we do not want our child to lose a year because we did not work on plan B."

"Yeah, maybe," he replied rather listlessly.

257

A few days later, Dinesh called up Bharat to tell him that he had secured admission for his daughter at DBS.

"Maybe you should apply here too as a back-up," he suggested not sure that whether Bharat was registering anything at all.

A few days later, Bharat told him that he too had secured admission for his daughter at the DBS. He congratulated him and they even spoke about how schoolmates would continue to enjoy the school bondage through their siblings. Somehow, Dinesh failed to discern on why his enthusiasm was not mirrored in the reaction that Bharat exhibited.

Neither of them spoke about Mount Mary's Public School.

Dinesh had applied to Mount Mary's Public School too but did not think that he would be able to get his daughter into the school for multiple reasons. First, the number of seats available was woefully inadequate to accommodate the huge demand. There were only 150 seats against over 4,000 applications that were given away. Second, the Ganguli Commission had ensured the sword of doubt and interpretation remained in the mind until well past the admission date.

"Have you got the interview letter yet?" Dinesh asked.

"From Mount Mary's school, no," he replied. "But let's see. I am sure I am going to lose out on the points system since I am not staying within the radius specified to get those additional points. But I have devised a way."

"What do you mean?" Dinesh asked.

There was a pause as he wrestled in his mind as to whether he should reveal the modus operandi or not. He finally decided that he could because Dinesh had the advantage of proximity already as compared to his, so revealing his plan would not hinder much progress. "I had submitted the rental lease documents of my friend's house as my own so that I get the proximity benefit. He stays just next to the school."

"But," Dinesh said, "the stamp papers are going to be checked and they have to be older than a year."

"*Yaar*, this is Delhi. We can get anything done here. I went to the courts and paid ₹1,000 for a ₹50 stamp paper that was dated back by a year. It works so professionally that the clerks at the court actually leave spaces in the register so that future sales can be recorded on a back date."

"Wow," Dinesh said. He marvelled at the ingenuity in corruption. All was so well thought through. "All the best!"

Five minutes is all you get to make it or break it. That is the duration of the interview. Dinesh came out of the interview room elated and overjoyed. They had answered the questions put to them but most importantly, their daughter had answered the posers put to her in a manner that would keep her out of the exclusion zone, for sure. "There is no way that she is not going to be admitted!" he exclaimed proudly to his wife as they made their way out after the interview. "I will jump out of the seventeenth floor of our apartment if she does not get the admission notice." His wife nodded and smiled. She was still sceptical.

As they stepped out, he saw Bharat and his wife dressed as if they were going to a wedding reception rather than an interview for their child's admission. The interaction was brief and limited and they were soon ushered into the interview room while Dinesh made his way back home. He even treated the family to a good meal at a fancy restaurant since he was sure that their daughter had made it in the first round. This was a time for celebration. Almost like Dinesh had received a fancy job offer.

Shortly after he reached home, he called up Bharat to enquire about his experience.

"Not too well," he replied. "They did not ask too many questions and our daughter preferred to remain quiet."

259

"I am sure it will work out," Dinesh said, a bit disappointed in his friends disappointment.

It was a good two weeks later that he got the letter confirming their daughter's admission to Mount Mary's Public School. "But of course," he told his wife, "this was to be." He was also relieved that he did not have to jump off the seventeenth floor any more.

He had not heard from Bharat. Considering the fact that he was hell-bent on getting his daughter to this school, the silence was almost deafening.

A month later, Dinesh got a call from Bharat's wife. "Hi Dinesh! *Achcha* listen, have you guys not confirmed your daughter's admission at DBS?" she shouted out amidst the din around her mobile phone.

"Why do you ask?" Dinesh enquired, surprised at the sudden burst of inquisitiveness.

"No, I had gone to get the refund from DBS for our daughter and did not see your daughter's name there in the confirmed list. I presume all is ok."

"Yeah, all is fine!" Dinesh replied, not sure where this conversation was headed. "But why have you taken the refund from DBS?"

"Oh, our daughter has managed to get into Mount Mary's Public School," she stated triumphantly almost as if she wanted him to ask. Never in those intervening months had the family ever given the impression of what they were up to for the school admission and now this surprise. Obviously, the whole approach was shrouded in secrecy.

"Oh, congratulations," Dinesh blurted out, "but I thought they had not accepted the application."

"I have been hounding them daily without any respite. I also brought up the fact that my father had served in the Indo-

Pak war in 1961 and was a decorated army staff member. He even accompanied me to meet with the principal and finally the efforts had borne fruit."

All this, without even a mention in the past. Dinesh remained silent and let her continue with her list of potential questions.

"What happened to your daughter?" she finally asked. The call was obviously to relay her good news and receive, what she assumed, their bad news.

"Oh, we took the refund from DBS," Dinesh replied.

"Why did you do that? Does that mean that she is without a school?" Dinesh sensed a tinge of jubilation in her voice.

"No, she has secured admission to the Mount Mary's Public School in the first attempt," he replied.

There was a long silence before Dinesh heard the phone disconnect.

# Past Perfect, Present Tense and Future Continuous

Life moved on and afforded Dinesh enough opportunity to carefully evaluate and understand what the city meant to him and what he meant to the city in turn.

Having reached thus far, with one child and a mega job under his belt, the experiences had left him much confused and perplexed. Confused and perplexed as to where he was heading, without a direction. Living this life of mere existence in this city, a city to die for.

"Let's go for a movie tonight," exclaimed his wife as she scanned the Sunday edition of the newspaper.

"Which one?" Dinesh said rather disinterested.

"*Chandni Chowk to China* is the only option we have," she said.

The range was telling and it somehow captured the thoughts that were being nursed in his mind at that point in time. From a small government locality in Netaji Nagar to the well-off wannabes in East of Kailash, from the refugees in Malviya Nagar to the well heeled folks in Vasant Vihar, he had seen much, absorbed much more, unlearnt a lot and settled down. The movie with its telling title seemed to be the right thing to watch.

At home in DLF, he was rested but impatient. DLF which is now referred to as Greater Delhi, is but a microcosm of the real Delhi. The rude demeanor which had very much become a part of daily existence had managed to rub its effects on him, making him one of their own. The comforts were all in place. Multiple apartments in expensive areas, three cars each one more expensive than the other, were all artifacts of his pseudo positioning in society. The bike lay in a corner as a symbolism of his simplicity that he had left far behind.

The movie was lousy and they were walking towards the car parked in the basement of the shopping malls which was overflowing with cars of all shapes and sizes, one more fancy than the other. The cars in Delhi serve far more purposes than just taking you from point A to point B. A car is a social compartment in life—you sms when you are driving, you eat when you are driving, you drink while you are parked especially as a mobile liquor vend during marriage receptions, sometimes you want to teach your five-year-old son to drive and so place him on your lap while you are driving, you smooch, read, chat and make love, hold clandestine meetings with your mistress and much, much more. These cars are very important to ensure that you carry on with your existence in a sociable manner. It is practically a room outside your home.

You like to retain the plastic covers on the car seats for well beyond months. It serves as a constant reminder of two things. Firstly, it reminds you that your car is new and secondly it reminds you that your bank balance is going to dip significantly in the following months on account of the EMI you have committed to on account of the car loan you have taken. Of course it breaks your back to pay the EMI every month but you have won the battle with your neighbour who thought, until then, that they had the bigger car. It does not matter if your back gets broken in the process.

They drove out of the basement and joined the NH 8 road. As they drove, Dinesh noticed a eunuch on the side of the road soliciting a potential customer. The man was leaning out of the car while three of his friends inside were having a hearty laugh with bottles of beer in their hands. He was instantly reminded of someone he had promised never to forget.

He drove in absolute distraction thereafter.

It was 10 p.m. The family had gone to sleep and Dinesh was flipping channels. His thoughts went back to the other child in his life, Vandana from G.B. Road. He had no clue as to where the thought came from but it came in a flash. It happens most of the time when an unconnected, orphaned thought flashes through your mind and you are left searching for its origins. Almost five years had passed and it seemed like yesterday. He could still recall her face. He instinctively called up Manoj. The phone kept ringing for a while before it was picked up. Dinesh did not wait for the greeting.

"*Arre yaar*, remember Vandana?"

"Vandana who?" Manoj asked in a drowsy tone.

"The same girl whom we met at G.B. Road around five years back or so," Dinesh replied hoping that he would recollect.

"Yes, what about her? Don't tell me you are missing her *gaandu*. She will be busy now," he said and let out a loud laugh. "I need to go back to sleep. Let's talk tomorrow."

"No," Dinesh replied in a straight tone. He was not in the least bit amused. "I want to meet her one more time. Will you come with me?"

"Are you bloody crazy? *Chutiya ho gaya hai kya?* We swore that we will never go to that place again."

"I know, but I just want to see how she is doing. I owe it to her. I cannot afford to forget her yet again like her customers do. Call it what you will but I want to. Don't ask questions. If you do not want to come then I will do it on my own. I need closure."

Manoj understood and was quiet for a while. Dinesh knew that this was not easy for him. He was out with another woman himself and much as he despised his company, he was clearly too scared to make this mission on his own.

"When do you want to go?" he asked.

"Can we go tonight, Manoj?" Dinesh asked not sure if he would agree.

"Not a good idea to go there at night. She will be busy and…" he stopped, conscious that he had said something that Dinesh would not necessarily have liked to hear. "I mean, let's go tomorrow morning, same time as we did last time."

"Thanks Manoj," Dinesh replied as he disconnected the line.

"Who were you speaking with?" it was Dinesh's wife.

"Oh, that was Manoj. I thought you had gone to sleep."

"No, I could not sleep. The power keeps going off and the ACs do not work. It's so bloody hot… anyway, what was Manoj saying?" she asked as she sat on the sofa tying her hair into a bun behind her head.

"I was planning to go out with him tomorrow morning," Dinesh was not sure how he should broach the topic with her. Should he just say it as it is and expect her to understand or lie and live in permanent guilt of having lived an untrue life with someone that he had committed his life to.

The predictable question came a second later. "Where are you guys planning to go?"

"There is something I need to tell you," Dinesh replied as he continued to tell her about his first trip to G.B. Road with Nisha. He deliberately omitted to tell her about how he had felt about Nisha at that point in time. It did not seem important but he did tell her in great detail about how he had been to a girl-child and her world; a girl named Vandana in a world where innocence and depravity coexisted, where Amar Chitra Kathas and Barbies were regularly attacked by pornographic pictures stuck on walls and stained bedsheets, with a used condom that was flushed down the toilet being the only escape from torture.

There was no response. Just silence. Deafening silence. "Why did you not tell me this until now?"

There was no response in Dinesh's mind. How could he bring himself to telling his wife that he had been to G.B. Road and its many *kothas*, that he was so deeply moved by a girl-child who was a sex worker that he had promised to return and help her, only to forget and be reminded many years later. It sounded incredulous. "I was not sure you would understand."

"But I do understand, Dinesh," his wife replied, her eyes welling up with tears. "What I do not understand is why you kept this from me and if there are other things that you still need to tell me." Dinesh winced but shook it off. "Is there anything else that you need to tell me?"

"No," Dinesh lied, "this is the one truth that I am proud of." The tear ducts opened in each other and they hugged.

"Can I come too?" she asked.

"No," he replied, "It's a different place, not suitable for..."

"But ok for a girl-child," she interrupted.

Dinesh did not have an answer to that, but knew that it was the mention of a girl-child which had saved the day. His wife understood the matter as a woman, but he was not sure if she understood the matter as a wife. Dinesh could tell his wife was disappointed, and he was sorry.

"Good night," she said as she got up. Dinesh looked at the watch. It was nearing 3 a.m. "Sleep now, you have a busy day ahead."

Dinesh wasn't sure as to how he should construe what she had just said. He let it pass, got up and followed her into the bedroom.

For some strange reason Dinesh could not sleep a wink that night. He was excited that he had finally put thought into action and come clean. He was happy that he had been truthful to himself and his wife at least on this point. It felt like a great load had been lifted from his head. He promised himself once again that he will give all it takes to give his wife her sense of balance from the city that has always taken away more that what was taken from it. This time he would not let the city of Delhi win.

He had not bothered to validate his thoughts with hers. What was she feeling? Did she want to be in the world that belonged to Dinesh? What about her own world? The world that was her own and what she had come to accept. Dinesh was being selfish in wanting her to be part of his world. What if his world did not matter to her any more? There was a gap he had to bridge.

The morning was bright, made brighter by his intent. His wife had come to terms with the conversation they had the night and the morning before. She waved as he got into the car. That was a good sign.

Dinesh landed up at Wimpy in Connaught Place and as usual Manoj arrived an hour late. Each time he would call him during the hour, and the standard response would be that he is just five minutes away from the agreed place. That's always the case with almost all the vendors, clients, traders. Always late and always five minutes away when you call. '*Bus* sir, *paanch minute mein pahunch raha hoon.*' Another option is to rely on the misfortune that almost happens with every latecomer. The car had a flat, the traffic jam, got challaned by the cop, etc. It happens as a standard norm in the city.

"Sorry *yaar*, something came up," Manoj said as he leaned across the driver's seat and opened the passenger side door for Dinesh. By now he had heard this so many times that Dinesh did not even bother to respond. Manoj sensed his annoyance and simply smiled. The closer they reached their destination, the more his annoyance dissipated. For some strange reason, Dinesh was beginning to realise the futility of this trip. It had been five long years without any contact but somewhere deep within the recesses of his mind, he nursed hope ... hoping against hope that the blue-eyed girl with the jet-black hair would still be nursing her hopes of freedom, of life rather than existence. Dinesh was also disappointed and upset with himself. How could he have forgotten somebody so deeply etched in his mind so easily? He wanted to help her in those minutes that he had met her and had so easily forgotten her for over five years. He had to get closure, he had to help out in any way he could. This time he promised that he would not forget.

They took a cycle-rickshaw and soon enough they were there, right in front of the hardware shops. It was déjà vu. Nothing had changed and everything around him looked similar like it used to be, five years back. Dinesh looked for a familiar corridor or shop and the stairway that had led him to Vandana the first time he had met her.

"Come this way," said Manoj interrupting his state of thought. He was from the area and therefore had a photographic imprint of the place. Dinesh followed him and within minutes were in front of a familiar staircase flanked on both sides by hardware shops. The shop owner looked familiar but he wasn't sure and anyway, they all looked similar. He looked around hoping to meet the pimp that would make the whole endeavour so much simpler. Manoj read his thoughts.

"*Woh nahin milega.* You will not find him. There are thousands of those and they keep moving around. We will have to go up," he suddenly seemed emboldened, almost understanding his purpose as his own. Dinesh's view about him was also changing with every passing moment.

They made their way up and were stopped by a burly, dark person who looked like a pimp. He looked ugly and empty of any feelings, an insensitive *bhadua*.

"Where do you want to go?" he asked rather suspiciously and aggressively.

"We want to see Vandana," Dinesh said and bit his tongue almost immediately. Manoj was glaring at him and thought it best to quickly intervene. "We had come here some time back and had a great time with this girl named Vandana. We want her again for the whole day now," he was speaking their language and the burly man seemed more at ease now.

"*Kaun* Vandana? Are you cops? There is no Vandana here. Now go away," he said, suddenly guarded and angry.

"Sir*jee*, we are not cops," Manoj continued.

"*Abe, maadarchod.* Get lost from here or else I will have that rod shoved up your backside," he said pointing to a rod resting on the beetel juice stained wall.

Manoj was relentless and continued, "We are from America and had come to India five years back. We had come here then and paid a good price for a small girl called Vandana. She was young then, I think around eleven or twelve years old but we enjoyed ourselves. We now want to have her again since my friend here enjoys the experience with her."

Manoj laughed out loud and back-slapped the pimp. He was now being one of them. It helped him and Dinesh come under the pimp's circle of trust.

"Fuck off," said the man angrily. "*Behenchod*, do I look like a caretaker of some hostel to you. There are thousands like her who come and go and you expect me to keep count. Go to hell and talk to me if you want anyone else. We have some fresh stock now. Young and equally good. One of them is a virgin. We can fix a good price for both of you."

Dinesh almost hit the guy but Manoj looked at him and suggested that he lay off while he conducted the session. "Sir*jee*, we were just enquiring. We do not mind another but that one was great. Money is not a constraint."

"When did you last see her?" he asked suddenly interested since the mention of money had now been made.

"A week or so back," Manoj lied.

The pimp extended his hand and motioned to Manoj "*Hazaar rupiye rakh* and I will give you the information you need." Manoj dug into his pocket and pulled out two ₹500 notes. The pimp pocketed it quickly, each time conscious there was no one else looking.

"Do you think we are fools here? How could you have seen her a week back when she left us years back? I remember her because she was different. Her eyes were different. She was sold to a *seth* some years back. I made a good commission on that deal. Now get lost or you will not go back on your feet," he said as he advanced menacingly.

"Sorry *bhai sa'ab*, we are leaving," said Manoj and he pulled Dinesh down the stairs. "Now what do we do?" Dinesh asked him on the way down. "Get out of here, that's what."

"Listen," Manoj continued, "There is no point. It's like looking for a needle in a ugly haystack. We are bound to be mistaken for cops and would probably get beaten up here. Let's forget about her."

"The *paan-wallah*," Dinesh shouted in glee.

"What *paan-wallah*?" asked Manoj rather confused.

"Remember the *paan-wallah* we had spoken to and who knew her well? Maybe he will be able to help," Dinesh said as they walked in the direction they had taken after their last encounter five years back.

Old Delhi is a place where time seems to have stood still. Inspite of much development in infrastructure all round, the real Delhi still retains the vestiges of the bygone era. The charm is still saved in spite of the demons of modernisation looming large over it.

"*Kya lenge saab?*" said the *paan-wallah*. Dinesh recognised him immediately. He was the same guy with the twirly moustache, slightly pockmarked face and a pleasant air. He had more grays which was expected but his fingers were just as swift as he applied *kaththa* over the betel leaf while a customer waited.

"Do you remember us *dost?*" Dinesh asked rather stupidly. He handed over the *paan* to the customer and looked down at them. He was straining hard but his memory was failing him. He was one for them but they were part of a million for him.

"You guys look familiar," he said trying hard to focus on their faces. His face changed expressions as he looked at Dinesh and then at Manoj. "You look familiar, but I cannot remember. I am sorry."

"Vandana," Dinesh said.

He froze and all was still. Manoj looked at Dinesh and then at him. His hand stopped moving across the betel leaves

271

and Dinesh could sense his brain receptors trying hard to process the information that had just been passed on to him.

"Oh, my god!" he exclaimed after a pause that lasted forever. "Are you the same guys who came here some years ago? I remember you now. It is all coming back. Nobody ever enquires about anyone here and nobody cares but, yes, you had enquired about Vandana. I remember now, yes it's all coming back. How is she? Have you met with her?"

Dinesh was delighted and disappointed. Finally a breakthrough but coated with questions that betrayed the eventual result of their search. Manoj was smiling.

"We have not met her since the last time we met you," Dinesh said and the *paan-wallah*'s face fell. "Can you tell us where she is?"

The *paan-wallah* looked around him furtively and continued, "She left shortly after you guys left. That was a long time ago. Haven't heard from her since then."

"Left?" Dinesh repeated, "But I thought that was not an option here."

"She was sold to someone for a good sum," he continued. "I have, with time, forgotten she existed. It helps numb the pain of having lost someone; I was beginning to get emotionally attached to her as a father. I should have known that you do not get emotionally attached to anyone in a place like this."

"You would not know where she went, would you?" Manoj asked with a misplaced sense of optimism.

Some other customers had come in by the *paan* shop. He paused to serve them and continued after they left, "Before she was being taken away, the man who had probably bought her stopped here for a *paan*. You see, it helps to be the only *paan* shop for a mile around." Neither Manoj nor Dinesh reacted.

"She had handed over a chit to me which had an address that she had scribbled. She must have overheard the conversation between the man and the *malkeen*. The *malkeen* would have asked for the man's address just to ensure that he is not a cop or a decoy or any of these stupid reporters doing a sting. The deal would have settled after she had verified the details. That's how it works here. The price must have been good."

"And?" Dinesh asked barely able to hide his impatience.

"I had kept the slip carefully and noted it somewhere hoping to visit her sometime. But with each passing month, my hopes of ever visiting her also got progressively remote," he said as he smiled at his own stupid hope of being able to meet her again at the address that was handed over to him.

"I guess that makes the two of us," Dinesh thought. He looked at an old diary and then looked at another. The pages moved quickly and with each movement, a part of hope vanished. "Sorry *saab*, I do not have it with me now. It is been a long time and I would never have thought that you would be coming back for her. I was hoping you would, but you know…"

"Oh shit," Dinesh said again. "Hope to despair, all in such a brief moment. They come in a package deal."

"Let's go," said Manoj. Dinesh looked in his direction and saw that was looking beyond him. He turned and saw that the ugly burly man had now come into the corridor for a smoke. It would not be long before he saw them and begin to wonder what they were doing hanging around a *paan-wallah* for so long.

Dinesh quickly pulled out a ₹100 note and gave it to the *paan-wallah*. "Thank you. I am sorry I took so long but I always thought of her and wanted to help her. It is so easy to forget everything inspite of the best efforts," he said and walked away with Manoj.

They found a cycle-rickshaw after a brief walk and got into it. The rickshaw-*wallah* got down and helped himself to a glass of water from a tap nearby. As he wiped the beads of sweat from his forehead with his vest, Dinesh felt a tap on his shoulder.

He turned around and saw that it was the *paan-wallah*. He had a jubilant expression on his face and he was beaming from ear to ear. Before he could even acknowledge him, he thrust out his hand onto his. "Address *mil gaya saahib*. I had to find it. *Yeh lo*," he said as he handed over a piece of paper with an address written across it.

Dinesh looked at him in disbelief and saw that he was just as overjoyed as he was. Dinesh reached out into his pocket. "No sir*jee*. I will not take it. Just let me know how my girl is, if you find her. God knows if she is even ali…" he did not complete the sentence as he quickly turned and walked briskly back to his kiosk.

Manoj asked the rickshaw-*wallah* to move and he made his first strong effort to get the wheels moving before breaking into a regular rhythm with ease. As the rickshaw-*wallah* pedalled away, Dinesh looked at Manoj who was in confusion. Dinesh turned his head back and met the *paan-wallah*'s eye. He thought he saw him wipe his face before moving back to his kiosk.

Dinesh looked at the slip of paper he had been handed over. It had an '*OM*' at the top of the sheet and below it was a scribble, an ugly scrawl which read.

*B 16/22, Khirki Extension*

*Malviya Nagar ke pass*

At the Chawri Bazaar crossing, they got down and moved into his car. It had been an eventful trip. He did not want to lose any more time. He had already lost five years and he wanted Manoj to support him in this journey but was conscious that he was asking for too much from him. Manoj was looking at him askance and before Dinesh could even speak, he punched him lightly on his face and said.

"You do not have to say anything," he said. "Let's go to Khirki Extension."

# An Extension of Hope & Refuge

Millions of fruit stalls and 'juice corners' had sprung up all around and mobile water carriers selling 'refrigerated cold water' for 50 paise had diversified their trade to include *nimbu paani* as well. We are not so much of a juice drinking nation conditioned as we are to drinking *nimbu paani, jal jeera, shikanji, aam panna* and *chhaas*. Yet the *'kiraane ki dukaan'* and departmental stores are full of the choicest range of fruit juices from all over the world.

As they made their way through the pot-holed roads, Dinesh's mind was on a roller-coaster ride. Manoj did try to keep the conversation flowing but Dinesh was not sure if he was listening to him. There was a sense of excitement coupled with a certain degree of anxiety and desperation. It's been five years … and five years is a long time in the life of any individual.

*"Kya lagta hai*?" Dinesh asked Manoj suddenly. "Will I find her?"

"Listen dude," Manoj began. "Firstly, I have yet to figure out this closure bullshit. Secondly, I cannot understand what you are trying to achieve by chasing a girl you had met five years back as a chance meeting in a place where we had sworn never to go again. Why you are putting yourself through all this? Finding her is not important. There are a million Vandana's around in this city in different social set-ups."

"Manoj," Dinesh interrupted. "I want to see how life has changed for her. She was just 12 when we met her and we clearly had no understanding how we could possibly help her. What she had to say choked me mentally and I cannot understand how someone so young could have seen so much of life so soon. So soon that time decided to add years to her face and take away many years from her innocence each successive night and day. How could we just see all that and turn away. I want to assure myself that she is alright and then I will have closure. She is out of G.B. Road so it's a start but I am not sure…"

*"Dekh ke chala behenchod,"* shouted one of the pedestrians as Dinesh swerved past him after having jumped a traffic signal.

"Ok. When, or rather if you do find her then what is it that you plan to do?" asked Manoj. That was a good question. A question that Dinesh did not have an answer to.

"I don't know," he replied. "I just have to see her."

*"Theek hai* boss, not sure if I still understand but *theek hai,"* he said in a resigned tone.

"This is a fucked up place man," said Manoj as Dinesh steadied the car through the narrow by lanes of Khirki Extension. "This place is so screwed up, I am surprised that it has an extension."

Dinesh did not react. His mind was preoccupied.

"B 16/22, Khirki Extension *kahaan padega bhai saab?"* Manoj shouted out as Dinesh braked the car next to a man with a white cap. He thought a little and suggested a direction. No matter which part of Delhi you are in, no one will ever say that he does not know the route to a place. Everybody knows everything. Everyone will have a view or will suggest a view. It does not matter whether he is convinced it to be right or wrong. "Go straight and after two speed breakers take the first left. You will have to park the car there as I do not think you can take your car into the B lane, but you can try."

The directions were specific so they decided to follow the route suggested. They turned left and instantly knew that we had to park the car by the side. The alley funnelled up as it progressed and a rusted signboard said B-block. They got off the car and walked their way past B-14 and soon enough, they had before them a faded signpost that pointed right and read B-16. Dinesh's heart was pacing faster and he did not know why he was beginning to act like a teenager in love. It was an attachment, a bonding that had intensified and he was going to have closure soon.

The nameplate outside proudly announced:

'Abdul Raashid
B-16/22, Khirki Extn.'

He walked up to the door and knocked. An elderly gentleman opened the door and greeted them.

"*Salaam walekum,*" Dinesh said as he respectfully raised his hand in salutation.

"*Walekum asalaam,*" replied the elderly gentleman and tried to recognise the visitor. "*Aapki tareef?*"

"I wanted to talk to you for a few minutes. It is on a serious matter," Dinesh said. He looked us up and dressed as we were, wasted no time in ushering us in.

"How can I help you?" he asked as he was quickly joined by another girl who seemed 20 and incredibly beautiful.

"I will come straight to the point, *chacha*. We are looking for a girl who was taken away from G.B. Road around five years ago. She was called Vandana. We were told that she was being taken to this address."

The silence in the room was deafening. The room felt colder and Abdul Raashid became motionless. Everything around him froze. The girl sitting next to him let out a gasp and walked out of the room. It was almost like Dinesh had dropped a bomb. Everything still and almost dead. He looked at Manoj. He wasn't moving either.

"*Chacha*, are you ok?" he asked.

"Who are you?" Abdul asked finally after what seemed like eternity.

"We are her brothers," Dinesh lied. "We had come to Delhi many years ago and she had disappeared. We even filed an FIR at the police station."

"Who gave you the address to this place?" Manoj could see that he was beginning to lose his temper and composure in turn. The image of the well meaning *paan-wallah* flashed before his eyes.

"We found out," replied Manoj taking on the role of the aggressor. "And we know she came here."

That approach worked as the old man settled down and appeared less agitated. "I had told them not to reveal the address and they had given me their word. *Saali kameeni*, did not keep her word," he responded. "She does not stay here any more. She ran away within a week of coming here with some boy in the neighbourhood. *Saali ki jaat hi aisi thi.*"

"When was this?" Dinesh asked.

"Around five years ago. I had bought her from the *kotha* in G.B. Road as I did not want her to lead that life. She was so young. I paid a big sum and had her released, hoping that I would provide her with education and a home here. She would have been company to my daughter Nilofer but that *kutiya* did not appreciate it. She ran away a week later with a boy from the neighbourhood."

"Ran away within a week with a boy?" Dinesh repeated to himself. "That does not sound like Vandana."

"I am sorry but I cannot help you any more. I need to go out now so if you have finished, can you also leave?"

They nodded their heads and got up. This was a dead-end. Clearly no purpose would have been served by staying there and interrogating an old man who clearly had nothing more to say to them.

They apologised for the inconvenience and walked out as the door slammed behind them. This was it! End of the road.

Manoj put his arm around his neck and muttered in his ear, "It's ok, man. At least you tried. God bless her wherever she may be."

Dinesh did not answer and continued walking towards the car. They turned left and the car stood 50 metres ahead of them. He was disappointed at this but had nobody to blame. Too much time had been spent. Would Vandana have been waiting for him? He was not sure if he would ever find an answer to that. Surprisingly, it was beginning to hurt him less now.

As they reached the car, both Manoj and Dinesh parted their ways to take their respective sides in the car. As Dinesh reached the driver's side of the door, he looked up and saw that Manoj had opened his door but was not getting into the car. He was looking past him at somebody or something behind him. It was only then that he felt the presence of someone behind him. Dinesh turned instinctively.

It was Nilofer!

It had been a crazy day! Hope to despair to hope again and finally the end of the road. All in a single day. The interaction with Abdul was brief and Dinesh was not sure if they had heard all the details. It did not matter. The end point was that she had left without a trace. As far as Dinesh was concerned, that much summed it up for him, until this moment when he had Nilofer, Abdul's daughter, standing in front of him.

*"Adaab bhai jaan,"* she said. Dinesh recognised her instantly and muttered out, *"Adaab."* Dinesh did not know what else to say or do. He looked at Manoj and back at her. Why had she risked so much to meet him in the open? She had obviously managed to sneak out of the back door or something but why did she want to do that?

"I heard your conversation with my father. I know where Vandana is."

Dinesh could not believe what he was hearing. "Where is she?" he asked, stunned at the possibility of being able to meet Vandana.

"Let's sit in the car. I do not want *abba* to come looking for me and find me here talking to you," she said as she helped herself into the rear seat of the car. "It is true that Vandana came in here around five years ago and it is also true that she ran away with a boy who used to work around this area," she fell silent as she struggled to fight off the tears that were welling inside her. "I was like an elder sister to her but that was not why my father had brought her. My father buys these minor girls to sell them to older men for marriage or to export them to Middle East countries. That is his profession. I am ashamed to be called his daughter."

Dinesh could tell that she was clearly ashamed of what she was saying. She was choking with every sentence but she continued, "She was with us for a month or two and we bonded well. She was well taken care of and with time she started looking normal!" Nilofer paused yet again to ensure that we understood.

Dinesh nodded.

"She ran away to escape her sale. She was like a commodity. She had told me that she had been sold in Sonagachi in Kolkata to somebody in G.B. Road for a pittance. She was bought by my father and then the plan was to sell her again. With each sale she became bolder but was at peace with her inner self, her own world empty of any muck and depravity. There were two worlds that existed for her. Her world as she lived it without the outer world being a part and the other world she lived to survive and exist. Both the worlds ran concurrently and she was happy with that. It has now been almost four years since she left and I have not heard from her since then," Nilofer paused as she wrestled with what she wanted to say next. "Please do not chase her or try to look for her. What will you achieve or what are you trying to achieve? Are you trying to bring her into your world? She does not want to be a part of your world. She is content in the two worlds that she has woven around her. One gives her peace and strength while the other is her means to survive in this city. Be it the man who sold her, many men who ravished her day after day and night after night, be it the boy with whom she ran away, it is the way her destiny is chartered. Do not try to alter her world because of what you think is an ideal world. To her, such a world does not exist," Nilofer stopped, partly surprised at her own aggressiveness.

Dinesh was silent and did not say a word. He looked with an air of understanding and nodded an affirmation to her request. He was not going to look for her. It made great sense.

*"Khuda hafiz, shabba khair,"* she said and got out of the car quickly. She walked briskly and broke into a run as she headed for her house. She looked back one final time and waved before disappearing round the corner.

Vandana and the journey was adorned with all possible roles that she had been born with or been forced to adopt for her own survival. From an orphan, to a minor prostitute, to being a daughter to the *paan-wallah*, to a sister to Nilofer and finally what seemed like to being a wife to a boy in the neighbourhood.

"Let's head back home now," said Manoj looking rather tired and not wanting to engage in any further discussion on this topic.

"Yes, let's head back home and live our life in the world that we are used to."

"Yes, but we do need to eat first. It's well past lunchtime."

Both of them smiled and headed towards Sant Nagar to taste the delicious mutton korma from 'Saleem's *Dhaba*'. World famous in Sant Nagar!

# *Dhaba* and *Khana*...

"Saleem *ke dhaabe mein khana kha lete hain*," said Manoj. Dinesh smiled possibly for the first time that day. They had achieved closure by leaving it as it is. There is a closure in everything if you let it run its course.

"Nothing is good and nothing is bad. Only our thinking makes it so," muttered Dinesh

"Oh, absolutely," agreed Manoj.

"There it is," said Manoj pointing to a large green signage mounted on top of a bamboo structure. It was located right next to the main road and so there was no problem in finding it. Nestled between a zillion automobile repair shops was a large signage which said 'Saleem *Dhaba*'.

"*Dhaba band hai sahib,*" said a boy in his early twenties as he collected the last of the glasses from the table.

"*Roti aur daal toh milegi.* We will give you a good tip," Dinesh said as they sat on one of the many plastic chairs. He looked around and could see just one table occupied with 5 boys munching on their julienned onions, *roti* and *sabzi*.

He smiled and placed a laminated sheet of paper in front of them, "Please speed up with the order, sir*jee*. The *sahib* will be here any minute and he will think that I am being extra hospitable because of the extra money. He does not trust anyone, *saala.*" There was some bitterness in his tone.

"What's your name?"

"Chandu … but everybody here calls me by my shorter name chhotu…" Dinesh and Manoj burst out laughing.

"How long have you been working here?" Dinesh asked. Manoj was beginning to get irritated with the questions. Dinesh could see that he was hungry.

"Ten years, *sahib*. Tell me, what will you like to eat?"

"Ok, listen," it was Manoj. "Get us some *roti* and *kaali daal* fry. Get us four *roti*s now and we will decide later. That can be done, right?"

"*Roti* and *daal* can be managed, *saab*," he said and scampered off towards the kitchen.

After what seemed like eternity, Dinesh saw chhotu emerging from the kitchen with two plates and a bowl of *kaali daal* fry. He placed it in front of them and scampered off returning soon after with 4 piping hot *tandoori roti*s. He placed them on the table and scurried off as Manoj got up to wash his hands at the nearby wash area.

The *roti* tasted heavenly as did the *kaali daal* fry. Dinesh was reminded of his father, his moral compass who always used to relish the simplest things in life. Going by a bus to wherever he wanted, happy in the Delhi summers or the chilly winters, he was committed to his work and his sense of extravagance that never spilt beyond a Chinese meal from the mobile vans parked around most shopping areas. He had preserved himself in this city for a long time. As he had aged, his immune system had given way. He had to, therefore, leave the city to live.

Dinesh would have liked to be like him but the fabric of the city did not allow him to consider that as a means of survival. Dinesh had kept that as part of his inner world just as Vandana had and suddenly Dinesh was now more aware of what Nilofer had meant to convey to him. He too, had the two

worlds within him. One was a world inhabited by the things
and people who were the purest to him, whom he knew would
always mean well, would stand by him, guide him, advise
him and be the source of immense joy. His family, his parents
especially his father, his daughter, his home, his job. He would
never share that with anybody. These were the non-polluted
factors in his life. The other world was the world he had to
live with to survive, lacking of any sensitivity, ruthless, cut-
throat, selfish. This outer world had, thankfully, allowed him
one concession. He did not need to become all that to survive.
He would simply have to pass through them without having to
make any tries to change it. Things will fall in place. Vandana
lived the same two worlds as does everybody who.

"What are you thinking, *gaandu?*" said Manoj interrupting
his chain of thoughts."Forget her *yaar!*"

Dinesh smiled as he tore the *roti* in half, "No, I have
forgotten about her. I have realised the experiences in life are
meant to be experienced and not to alter or make changes to."

"Absolutely."

"Anything else, *saab?*" it was chhotu.

Before anyone could respond, a car suddenly screeched to
a halt in front of the *dhaba* and a man stepped out. "That is
Saleem," chhotu whispered in fear and the degree of trepidation
was writ large on his face. "Ok *saab*, please do not say anything
to him. He will kill me if he finds out that I have been serving
you well past the time."

"Don't worry and thanks for all your help," Dinesh said
as he slipped in a fifty rupee note onto the small tray being
held by him.

Chhotu quickly gathered the plates with the food still in it,
as they had hardly eaten, and walked back to the kitchen. The
boys on the other table had finished and were also heading out.

Dinesh waited for the bill and as chhotu returned. Chhotu's gaze was fixated on Saleem as he kicked the bumper of the car and examined a dent on the side of the door. He had, obviously, brushed his car on his way to his *dhaba*.

Dinesh paid the bill and did not bother for the change nor did he bother to look back at him as he exited the *dhaba*. The other boys had already left.

As they passed the exit, they passed Saleem. He appeared to be an old man. He did not look up and neither did they. *"Abe chhotu, paani la,"* he shouted across as he walked into the main seating area in the *dhaba*.

It was past 5 p.m. and Manoj said, "Time to go boss. I have a life too. If I continue to be your accomplice in your Indiana Jones exploits then I have had it." They both laughed. Dinesh did not forget to thank Manoj for all his help. Somewhere along the line, he suddenly shared his sense of purpose and considered this search as something he wanted to close as well…

"Thanks buddy, I could not have done it without you."

"Wish you could have," he said and laughed out loud as he revved up his car and was gone in a flash.

Dinesh got into his car and headed home as well. It had been a long day and he was glad it was over. The closure, unknown to Dinesh, was yet to come.

*'Mrs & Mr Surinder Kapoor cordially invite you…'*

The maroon wedding card, with some curvy lines decorated in gold depicting lord Ganesha was an impressive one. It came with a small cloth bag filled with almonds and pistachios. Dinesh looked for the mention of dinner on the card, since he wanted to be sure lest the small bag with its almonds and pistachios be passed off as the symbolism of having fed the

287

receiver. Not only was there dinner but cocktails as well. "Well," he thought, "the wedding reception is in Punjabi Bagh so it would be a grand affair."

The woman used to work in his office and had considered it appropriate to invite the top management team in the company for the wedding reception. Dinesh was not surprised that she was in the 'Sales and Marketing division'.

"You must come," she had insisted. "Of course, I will be there," Dinesh had confirmed his attendance. He was surprised that she was to be wedded to a guy named Kapil. The whole office was rife with rumours of her being involved with her head of Sales and Marketing. There are two worlds in everyone's life and she was no different. Both, the personal life and the professional one, could coexist.

The marriage was a grand affair with majestic entertainment elements. The richer sect of the society add flamboyance and ostentation to the party, by hiring music and dance performers from all over the world, and this was no different. Shah Rukh Khan was supposed to come. He would probably charge more than the wedding itself, thought Dinesh.

The theme of the party seemed to be romance as the ambience at the venue was softened with dim lights. The entire hall was decorated with scented candles which added a sophisticated look to the wedding hall, yet saving the romantic feel of the place. There were some Martini bowls with floating candles in them. The soft and soothing music which was being played in the background only added to its aura. The centrepiece which is almost like the show-stopper in any fashion show was a giant swan made with ice and surrounded with flowers such as the white calla lilies, hydrangea and snowball mums. Dinesh did not know of anyone as most of the invitees from the office had chosen to stay away. He felt alone, much like the ice swan.

"Dinesh *saab*! How are you?" it was the bride's father who had been pointed out in his direction by the daughter. "I am Aarti's father."

"Oh, hello Kapoor *saab*. Congratulations on this big event. You must be the more stressed out person here today."

"*Arre*, it's alright. After all she is only one daughter that I have. I want to make sure it all goes well and the journey hereon is comfortable for her."

A decorated 5 series BMW parked outside exemplified what Mr Kapoor was saying.

"Sure, of course. Please let me not hold you. I am sure you have pressing things to take care of."

"Yes, yes," he replied as his mobile began to ring. "Please make sure that you eat and go. Please have some drinks. Excuse me!" so saying, he walked briskly towards the food counters.

Dinesh helped himself to some Black Label and could hear a couple of middle-aged people next to him in an animated conversation. "C'mon *yaar*, have another drink."

"No, I am done. I need to drive back home."

"Oh *yaar*! Don't be silly. My driver will drop you. You are not having to pay for it yaar. *Chal lagale ek aur.*"

Anything free is a sure best-seller. Buy one get one free. Holiday packages with free breakfast, free insurance, etc. It does not matter whether the free item is going to be put to any use at all or not. Dinesh was reminded of a friend who got a free mariners compass with an Atlas that he had bought for his son. He bought the expensive Atlas primarily because of the free item little knowing that it would be the last thing that he would use.

Dinesh walked past a table and stopped as he tried to catch a glimpse of the married couple placed on two throne-like chairs on a raised platform. Next to him was a table that had a couple of aunties seated with a pile of food in front of them.

"Party is alright but the boy is a bit dark, isn't he?" Dinesh turned trying his best to seem discreet. It was one of the aunties as she tore the naan and took a generous helping of the chicken dish.

"Yes, he is a bit *saanwla*. My son is so fair that I cannot tell you. Wonder why the bride agreed to this match. At least the groom could have been fairer."

"Must be the money, Mrs Gupta. They are loaded. They are giving a BMW to the groom. He stays in Jor Bagh and is the only son, so everything dark becomes bright," they both burst out laughing.

Dinesh smiled at the hypocrisy of it all. Being invited to a party, making pretence of being well-wishers and then showing the true colours after the meal and the drink had been consumed. Mrs Gupta and the other woman were soon joined by another.

"What does the boy do?"

"He is a software engineer," spoke the woman without a name. "He works in a call centre."

"*Achcha, chalo theek hai*. At least he is employed."

Dinesh wondered whether they were from the groom's side or the bride's side. They seemed to be far from the bride's family and Dinesh was much certain that they were not relatives, just some invitees from a long-lost connection.

"What employed? That is not the criterion, Mrs Chopra." Ah, finally the second name. "The boy stays in Jor Bagh and is the only son. Employed or not employed hardly makes a difference. He is simply biding his time before he moves into his father's export business., I had proposed a far better match for the boy. The woman who was known to me was tall, fairer and educated. She had just completed her B.A. and was doing a fashion designing course from NIFT. That would have been a great match. But they chose this woman."

The videographer zoomed in on them with the assistant holding aloft a powerful light source. Mrs Gupta immediately reached out for her napkin as she then proceeded to touch the corners of her mouth in elegance. The other aunties followed suit. The conversation was replaced with smiles and good cheer. The videographer zoomed in on the food, panned the aunties and then left.

"These guys do not even let us eat in peace. It is good that I got my gold *fashiaal* done today morning. Spent ₹5,000 but I think it was worth it. I asked them to include the saree draping free. Anyway, let us go to the desserts section now and see what all is available."

They all agreed and got up to get their favourite desserts. Dinesh quickly turned away.

He was smiling at each passing step. The tenor of the conversation jarred with the general mood of happiness and good cheer. Where was the talk of love, wishing the couple well in life and all that? What more could the parents do? It would perhaps have been a far better idea to donate the money spent on all these ostentatious display of wealth into a fixed deposit account for the daughter. Dinesh was reminded of his middle-class way of thinking. He quickly aborted the thought.

He made his way onto the dias and wished the couple. The woman was looking beautiful and the boy seemed happy. He handed over an envelope, which had ₹1,001 in it, to the bride and wished them well. She seemed happy that he had come. The videographers and the photographers insisted on the pictures for which Dinesh posed. He then got down and proceeded to walk towards his car. It had been late and there was office to attend the next day.

As he headed towards the car, he saw Mrs Gupta getting some *paan* packed to take home as some others grabbed the *churan* and *anardana goli*.

The drivers were huddled together in one corner chatting about their masters and eyeing each guest as he walked out of the *mandap*. Dinesh thought he saw a familiar face in the group. It was Qaazid. He looked relaxed and had put on some more weight. As his eyes met Dinesh's, he raised his hand as a mark of greeting and Dinesh responded. Life had moved on and he had survived.

The Santro, parked at a distance blaring loud music with a group of four people gathered around had its hatchback open and Dinesh knew what was happening. These portable liquor vends were all too popular in the city.

Maximum for minimum...

# Jana Gana Mana...

Many years passed and Dinesh continued with his existence with generous sprinkling of fun, monetary gains, hard work and so on. His latest buy was a 46 inch LED TV and he was proud as the technicians went about installing it in his room, which he, for lack of an original expression, preferred to refer to as the TV room. He had toyed with the idea of a 3D TV as well but quickly banished the thought as he could not bring himself to visualising a scenario in which the entire family would be seated in front of the TV set with dark glasses on, in the middle of the night. It would have looked rather strange, something from another planet.

"This is so shocking," exclaimed his wife as she was going through a newspaper article on a Sunday morning. She was referring to an article on the most fashionable issue in most villages in the North of India, 'Honour Killings'. Dinesh had read through so many that it had failed to evoke a reaction any more. Honour killings and punishments have been documented over centuries among a wide variety of ethnic and religious groups throughout the world. It had now gained prominence in India, especially North India. Dinesh had spent far too many years in this city to be disturbed or affected by the incident which was being narrated by his wife.

"Happens all the time nowadays," opined Dinesh, without getting moved or affected by the newspaper article.

"How can anyone end love in such a gory manner? How can anyone bring themselves to doing this and expect to get away. The law is an ass."

To be young and in love has proved fatal for many young girls and boys in parts of northern India as the intolerant and bigoted society refuses to accept any violation of its rigid code of decorum, especially when it comes to women. Two teenage girls were shot dead by their cousin in Noida for daring to run away to meet their boyfriends. These were the latest victims of honour killings, a euphemism for doing away with anyone seen as spoiling the family's reputation. These are socially sanctioned by caste panchayats and carried out by mobs with the connivance of family members.

"How can anyone possibly catch the perpetrators?" asked Dinesh. "The murders come under the general categories of homicide or manslaughter. When a mob carries out such attacks, it becomes difficult to pinpoint a culprit. Collecting evidence becomes tricky and eyewitnesses are never forthcoming."

The wife did not reply and Dinesh could tell that she was affected. She finished reading the first page and turned to page 12 to continue reading the article. Dinesh helped himself to some crisps which he noticed were priced at ₹20 for a 40 gram pack, meaning he paid ₹400 for a kilogram of potato. Dinesh felt rich and stupid.

"Now look at these two who have been murdered," the wife continued. "What have they done to deserve such a fate? Hacked so brutally just because they had run away from home in love and dreamt the impossible dream of starting a new life, yet to be lived. They look like a good couple."

"Show me," said Dinesh with a certain voyeuristic inclination that he could not contain. He was a Delhiite after all. A place where what the neighbours cook for dinner held infinitely more appeal than the paranthas cooked at home.

He surveyed the two pictures that were placed side-by-side alongside a blurred picture of two bodies lying by the tube well. The two pictures threw him back in horror. The caption at the bottom read, 'Gopal and Vandana'. She was the same one. Although, the photograph was a dated one, it did not fool Dinesh. Dinesh had sought closure but not in this fashion!

The article stated the two had married after running away from home and had been living in the outskirts of the city for many years. After a while, the boy's parents had declared truce and asked them to come back home. "All is forgiven," they had said. The boy had believed the story and come back home with his wife Vandana. The deception was complete as the family beat the couple mercilessly as soon as they arrived and bludgeoned them to death before dumping the body by the farms near the tube well.

"Is she..." his wife started suddenly drawing a connection between the name and the mission that Dinesh had set out to close many years back...

"Yes," replied Dinesh not waiting for her to finish.

"Oh god," she said as she slumped into the chair next to her.

The contradiction in the life so ended was hard to ignore. Gopal and Vandana, seemingly murdered by the boy's family, as the article read, were victims of the latest trend in honour killings. Vandana's family had experienced no loss of honour in selling her to a pimp in G.B. Road but the society sensed a loss in honour in her attempt to start a new life. To Dinesh, this was an epitome of contradiction much like the city he was living in. Nothing is what it seemed, it was all over and all pervasive.

◈

Time, the great healer!

"*Yaar*, want to watch the Republic Day parade. I have free passes to the event," it was Girish who was connecting after a long time.

"I would love to," replied Dinesh in an excited tone. He had always nursed the desire to watch the parade live. Watching the parades on television was far from the real thing. He wanted to share in the spirit of the day when the Constitution of India came into force and India became a Sovereign, Democratic and Republic state. On this day India finally enjoyed the freedom of spirit, rule of law and fundamental principle of governance. Dinesh wanted to experience the patriotic fervour of the Indian people on this day live, and wanted to understand what brought the whole country together even in her embedded diversity.

"That's great," replied Girish. "I will pick you up in the morning and then we can head for Shantipath together."

"What time?" Dinesh asked aware of what the answer might be.

"Say, 3 a.m.," replied Girish almost simultaneously breaking into a laugh. "With all the security in place, we will have to arrive early if we need to ensure that we get the right seats."

Girish was right but getting up early on a wintry morning was certain death for Dinesh. Sure enough, he enjoyed the winter months in Delhi. The nip in the air, the *elaichi-chai* consumed inside the quilt while watching your favourite TV programme, no power cuts to worry about, the delightful early morning fog which ensured that air travellers spent more time on the ground than airborne—incredibly beautiful and enjoyable.

"Let us meet up at 6 a.m.," said Girish, interrupting his chain of thought.

"Ok," Dinesh replied. He would manage to wake up at 6 a.m. "It's all for the country," he said out loud.

Dinesh woke up early that day. He knew from experience that Girish was a punctual man. He made his way to the bathroom and he could hear the familiar sounds of some early risers gargling, coughing, spitting as they went about their early morning ablutions. Everything had to be loud to be effective. Loud music, loud talk, loud clearing of the throat, loud dressing. The louder the better.

Girish arrived sharp at 6 a.m. and Dinesh was ready for him. They were both on their way almost immediately.

Some of the sights and sounds were new to Dinesh as he had never seen the city so early in the morning. It seemed and looked better. No crowd, a mild onset of fog, no traffic and therefore no blaring of horns to upset an otherwise calm person. Everything looked so serene.

"Look at those labourers," Girish said pointing to the side of the road next to a construction site.

Dinesh looked in that direction and thought that he saw two labourers on fire before he quickly realised that it was the mist rolling up from their bodies as they went about having their bath. As the water pumped out of the handpump, they poured it on themselves oblivious to the winter chill.

"*Yaar! Meri to gaand phat jaati hai* when I look at them."

"That explains the way you look," Dinesh joked. With a friendship that spanned over a decade, each one was comfortable with the other and did not need to explain anything.

After parking their car in another city, thanks to the most stringent security cover around the venue, Girish and Dinesh walked the long distance to their seating area. "I can imagine what the Dandi March would have felt like," Dinesh said. They sat on the green planks of wood that was wet with the

297

early morning fog. *"Phat bhi gayee aur geeli bhi ho gayee,"* Girish said shivering with each passing gust of wind.

The President arrived followed by a retinue of ministers and not much later, the parade had kicked off. The grand parade is held from the Rajghat along the Vijaypath. The different regiments of the Indian Army, the Navy and the Air force march past in all their finery and official decorations and even the horses of the cavalry are attractively caparisoned to suit the occasion. The crème of N.C.C. cadets, selected from all over the country consider it an honour to participate in this event, as do the school children from various schools in the capital.

Dinesh thought of his father and for a brief second he imagined him sitting next to him. He, Dinesh knew, would have been proud having his son sit next to him watching the parade, a matter of honour, a part of his inner world. In spite of all the shortcomings and issues of the city, this display of strength and honour made everybody feel proud. It was pure and sacred, much like his inner world which consisted of all things dear and unpolluted, in his mind. Dinesh, in turn was proud to be part of his inner world.

The parade was followed by a pageant of spectacular displays from the different states of the country. These moving exhibits depicted scenes of activities of people in those states and the music and songs of that particular state accompanied each display. Each display brought out the diversity and richness of the culture of India and the whole show lent a festive air to the occasion.

Beating The Retreat officially denotes the end of Republic Day festivities and is conducted on the evening of January 29, the third day after the Republic Day. The ceremony starts by the massed bands of the three services marching in unison, playing popular marching tunes. The drummers also give a solo performance known as the Drummer's Call followed by *Abide With Me* (which is also said to be Gandhiji's favourite). The chimes made by the tubular bells, placed at a distance, create a mesmerising ambience.

This is followed by the bugle call for Retreat. At exactly 6 pm, the buglers sound the retreat and the National Flag is lowered, and the National Anthem is sung, bringing the Republic Day celebrations to a formal end.

This was such an appropriate end so aptly titled as 'Beating The Retreat'. It applied so well to his own life so lived. Having resented the suffocating life with its restrictive ways in the Hindu undivided family that he had been brought up in, Dinesh always sought independence, a chance to become his own republic. However after having achieved it, he had sought retreat into his own inner world. A world partly inhabited by the own he had chosen to desert. He had in his own little world, his family, his daughter, his father who represented a world untouched by the polluting influences of the society he had lived with. The world was devoid of any ugliness, any obscenity, any complication or contradiction. That was a world he was not willing to or had to share with anyone.

As he stopped at a traffic light that had signalled red, a car behind him blared its horn with full gusto. The person at the wheel continued to honk. After what seemed like a few seconds, he turned his car with the limits the steering wheel would allow and inched past the rear side of his car to draw up alongside Dinesh.

"*Bhonsadike*, horn *nahin sunayi deta*. Are you deaf?" he hollered above the deafening din of his 1,000 PMPO music system. Before Dinesh could respond, he had jumped the red traffic signal and sped away.

As Dinesh had started his life in Netaji Nagar, worked through East of Kailash, started a new journey as a married man in Malviya Nagar before finally roosting in DLF, he had learnt a lot and unlearnt much more. The journey, with its own bouquet of experiences, each one rich and equally impactful, was looking forward to a new dawn and a new horizon. Each passing day had thrown surprises at him and reminded him that he would have to give much more than he had taken away from the city.

The city had ensured equilibrium. Everyone, in their life so lived, had taken so much away from the city as evidence of their primordial traits—more for less. Little did each one realise the city had taken back from them too, only much more. It had taken away from each one their sense of values, their ability to consider all as equal and devoid of any superficiality, the ability to be polite to one another, the ability to respect law and not break into laughter at the sight of an old beggar trying to wade his way through the bustling, noisy traffic only to surrender his earnings to the *seth* who ran the begging mafia, the ability to understand that a small girl could get her warmth from a headlight and that an urchin selling peanuts in the bristling summer heat would still want to surround his world with colours from comic books. That a girl would live two worlds and her real world would be taken away from her under the garb of honour, and that over time one would be robbed of one's sensitivity or the ability to be affected by such.

The inner world Dinesh lived with balanced by the outer world he lived in, it is a city that had allowed him to survive with its fair share of collateral.

A city to die for.

# Acknowledgements

I express my most sincere appreciation to the entire team at *Om Books International* for having transformed my dream into reality. First and foremost, a big thank you to Ajay Mago for his support in elevating me to the status of an author for which I will remain eternally grateful, and to Nitin Abbey for his incredible effort and hard work right down to the last minute and in helping bring this book to its current state with a passion and commitment that matched mine. I owe you!

To Mayank Austen Soofi for sharing his insights and experiences, to Jalees Andrabi at *The National* (Abu Dhabi) for supporting me with his research on the beggar mafia.

To all my friends who find a mention in this book. Some names have been changed but they know who they are. Your presence has only made my experience richer.

To my family for putting up with my eccentricities and tolerating me during the creation of this book. To my daughter Carissa who makes it all worthwhile with her interest and who wants the first copy. She will have to make do with an edited copy suitable for children!

To all I have not named, I am grateful for your support. Your inputs, views and suggestions have helped shape this book.

And then to this wonderful city of Delhi and its people; without you there would have been no book.

A big thank you!